Karma's a Bitch

"And this year's homecoming queen is Angel Ives."

Miss Hott sticks the combs on the ends of the tiara deep into Angel's scalp, making her wince; either that or standing so close to Rand is actually causing her physical pain.

"Okay, congratulations to our royal couple. Tonight is the bonfire, so everyone dress warmly." The final bell cuts off Miss Hott, and the entire student body erupts into screams and rushes out the door.

Angel spins on her heels and rushes toward me. She gets right into my face and starts yelling at me. "I'm going to destroy you." She's so close I can feel her spit landing on my perfectly applied MAC makeup.

"Say it, don't spray it, psycho." I hop back, hoping to avoid any more of her germ-filled spit spray. She turns and runs into the sea of students piling out of the gym.

"Angel, my ass. More like Demon Spawn."

Revenge of the Homecoming Queen

Stephanie Hale

BERKLEY JAM, NEW YORK

THE BERKLEY PUBLISHING GROUP
Published by the Penguin Group
Penguin Group (USA) Inc.
375 Hudson Street, New York, New York 10014, USA
Penguin Group (Canada), 90 Eglinton Avenue East, Suite 700, Toronto, Ontario M4P 2Y3, Canada
(a division of Pearson Penguin Canada Inc.)
Penguin Books Ltd., 80 Strand, London WC2R 0RL, England
Penguin Group Ireland, 25 St. Stephen's Green, Dublin 2, Ireland (a division of Penguin Books Ltd.)
Penguin Group (Australia), 250 Camberwell Road, Camberwell, Victoria 3124, Australia
(a division of Pearson Australia Group Pty. Ltd.)
Penguin Books India Pvt. Ltd., 11 Community Centre, Panchsheel Park, New Delhi—110 017, India
Penguin Group (NZ), 67 Apollo Drive, Rosedale, North Shore 0745, Auckland, New Zealand
(a division of Pearson New Zealand Ltd.)
Penguin Books (South Africa) (Pty.) Ltd., 24 Sturdee Avenue, Rosebank, Johannesburg 2196,
South Africa

Penguin Books Ltd., Registered Offices: 80 Strand, London WC2R 0RL, England

This book is an original publication of The Berkley Publishing Group.

Copyright © 2007 by Stephanie Hale.
Cover photography: *Young Woman* copyright © by Gabrielle Revere/Stone/Getty Images; *Frog*
copyright © by GK & Vikki Hart/Iconica/Getty Images.
Cover design by Monica Benalcazar.

PRINTING HISTORY
Berkley JAM trade paperback edition/July 2007

Library of Congress Cataloging-in-Publication Data

Hale, Stephanie.
    Revenge of the homecoming queen / Stephanie Hale.—Berkley Jam trade paperback ed.
        p. cm.
    Summary: When beautiful, popular, and seemingly perfect high school senior Aspen Brooks loses
out to her rival for homecoming queen, it is only the beginning of a series of strange events including
thefts, kidnappings, and Aspen falling for the dorky but endearing Rand Bachrach.

    ISBN-13: 978-0-425-21615-6
[1. Beauty, Personal—Fiction. 2. Popularity—Fiction. 3. High schools—Fiction. 4. Schools—Fiction.
5. Mystery and detective stories.] I. Title.
    PZ7. H138244
    [Fic]—dc22

                                    2007007998

PRINTED IN THE UNITED STATES OF AMERICA

10 9 8 7 6 5 4 3 2 1

For my king and our two tiny princes,
who always make me feel like a queen.

Acknowledgments

So many people have contributed to this dream of mine that I barely know where to begin. The first person that comes to mind is my fabulous agent, Jenny Bent. Thank you for seeing the potential in my novel and for giving me a chance. A girl couldn't ask for a better agent or friend. Special thanks also to Victoria Horn and Holly Root for being Jenny's second and (ahem) third set of eyes.

Huge thanks to my fantastic editor, Cindy Hwang, and her assistant, Leis Pederson, who loved Aspen and her story and brought my dream to life. Everyone at Berkley has created an amazing home for my novel and I will be forever grateful.

Thank you to all of my family and friends who never doubted my dream would someday turn into a reality. I'm a lucky girl to have so much love surrounding me.

My writing life changed forever when I met two incredible women, Carmen M. Rodriguez and Bethany Griffin. Thank you both for helping me become a better writer and for being such good friends. Sharing this journey with both of you has made it even more special. BTW, I totally expect my name to be on your acknowledgments pages!

I have always believed in saving the best for last so my final thank-you goes out to my adoring husband, Warren, and our adorable little boys, Carson and Boston. I don't know what I ever did to deserve the three of you, but I am honored to be your wife and mommy.

One

This is such a movie moment. This is the part where the fabulous heroine's dream finally comes true. I, of course, am the fabulous heroine. My dream of becoming homecoming queen is just moments away. I can almost feel the weight of the tiara on my head. Eww . . . I hope it doesn't mess up my hair because I'm having a stellar hair day.

"Aspen Brooks? Is she here today?" Miss Hott, my high school principal, asks, announcing my name for the second time. My best friend, Tobi, gives me a shove, knocking me out of my daydream. I can't believe this day is finally here. I carefully start to weave my way down the student-covered bleachers. I am concentrating very hard on making it down to the gym floor in one piece. My new high-heeled brown leather boots look awesome with my wide-leg jeans, but they are not the best combo for trying to climb bleachers. The last thing I need to do is go tumbling face-first onto the sweat-covered gym floor. I can only imagine the millions of germs breeding on that floor, not to mention the horrible effects it could have on previously mentioned adorable boots. Besides, this is not the sort of stunt that a soon-to-be-crowned homecoming queen would pull.

Safely down, I scoot up next to my nemesis, Angel Ives. She bristles and slides over a bit as if I'm not good enough to share the same oxygen with her. *As if* I would even *want* to share her foul, regurgitated air! Since kindergarten I've known that the only thing standing between me and my tiara was Angel. I just hope my classmates can see through her evil façade and voted for yours truly. As I turn to face the entire student body, which at Comfort High consists of only 600 students, I feel dizzy. I can't believe how nervous I am. My palms are even sweaty. Gross! I wonder if Angel would get pissy if I use her ugly, horribly outdated cashmere shawl for a napkin. Probably. Not that I'd want to touch the skank anyway.

Unlike Angel, I wouldn't be caught dead in last season's fashions. Every single piece of my ensemble was diabolically planned in anticipation of this very moment. I look smokin' in my shimmery pink tank topped with my adorable pink faux-fur shrug. My favorite pair of 7 jeans, the ones that make my butt look really good, finish off the outfit. It's a fact. You just can't have a bad day if you're wearing your good butt jeans. My prized diamond high-heel charm dangles provocatively from its chain above the slight swell of cleavage (compliments of my La Perla push-up bra) above my tank top. I am *so* queen material.

It's not like I'm totally conceited or anything, but for the last two weeks I had a weird sort of premonition that I was going to be voted in. I just knew my expensive highlights would pay off. Normally I couldn't care less about the opinion of Comfort High's student body, but let's face it, when six hundred people cast a vote saying that you are one of the hottest girls in school, that's pretty cool. Tobi tried convince me that some of the vote, especially the girl's portion, is based on personality, but that's a bunch of crap. The students choose good-looking people every year. I've never seen some geeky chick with a great personality voted homecoming queen. It just doesn't happen. It's probably not PC, but would you really want to look back in your high school yearbook in twenty years (when you would be, like, thirty-eight, *Yikes*!) and see some dorks for the homecoming queen and king? Of course not, you want to see the beautiful people. That way if you are one of the beautiful people, and you gain like fifty pounds, you can always look back and know that you used to be beautiful. It works for the dorks, too. Dorks usually go on to be more successful than the beautiful people, so they can look back and laugh that the beautiful people are now big, fat losers. It's really a win-win situation.

When Miss Hott called my name, I thought I would scream with joy, but somehow I managed a little restraint. I mean, I knew there was no way I wouldn't at least get chosen as a princess, but I didn't want to appear too confident. You never want to come off as a total snob. Last Friday, during lunch period, the entire student body cast their ballots. I carefully stood at the edges of the voting line. I nonchalantly handed out compliments about good hair days, adorable purses, and to-die-for shoes to the girls, and some of the boys were lucky enough to get a little bat of the eyelashes or an upper arm squeeze followed by the always popular "Wow, you've really been working out." After an agonizing weekend of waiting, it will be just a few more minutes before I know if all my hard work paid off or if I just wasted my breath on a bunch of ungrateful losers. It's totally an honor to even be on the court, and I know I shouldn't be greedy, but I can't help it. I want to feel that cheap rhinestone tiara digging into my scalp. I've even been practicing my queen wave in the mirror at home. I've so got it down that it would be such a waste if *my* crown went to that skank Angel Ives.

I try to put the final vote out of my mind as I scan the restless crowd for my boyfriend. He is easy to spot in a cluster of turquoise-and-black football jerseys. Lucas Riley, my totally hot boyfriend. He is tan, blond, and filled out just right in all the good places. He is also the quarterback for the Comfort Seagulls. We've been dating about two months. I've always been a Comfort High A-lister, but dating Lucas Riley has catapulted my popularity through the roof.

"And our fourth homecoming princess is Tobi Groves," a deliriously happy Miss Hott announces.

Oh. My. God. Tobi just made the homecoming court with me. Tobi is just as shocked as I am as we lock eyes and she stays frozen in her spot on the bleachers. Finally, people start pushing her and she makes her way down to meet me on the floor. We hug and squeal like the girls that we are. It's not that Tobi isn't cute, because she so is, but this is just so not her kind of thing. Even so, I can tell she is totally psyched.

"They're really scraping the bottom of the barrel this year," a poufy-lipped Angel spouts with venom.

I discreetly run my middle finger up the side of my face to silently counter her response. Tobi and I hold each other's sweaty hands as we wait for the final name. When Miss Hott announces Angel Ives's best friend, Pippi Fox, as the fifth homecoming princess it is no surprise. Pippi bounces down the bleachers screaming like she has just won a million dollars or something. The girl has absolutely no control over her emotions. She and Angel embrace and Pippi bursts into tears. Sometimes I can see why Tobi has no stomach for these types of competitions. Tobi drops my hand to clap for Pippi. That's weird. Pippi is Angel's number one crony. We do not like her. I grab Tobi's hand to stop her from clapping.

Miss Hott is now announcing the homecoming princes, one of which will become king. Angel's boyfriend, Jimmy McAllister, was the first name, no big surprise there. Jimmy makes me swoon with his wavy black hair and evergreen eyes—not that I'd ever cheat on Lucas, I'm just saying. We are in speech class together and he's always really sweet, but he must have some sort of mental defect to date Angel.

"Our next little prince is none other than the Seagulls' fantastic quarterback, Lucas Riley." Miss Hott shouts over the wild crowd. Lucas throws his arms up in the air and starts chanting his own name as he makes his way through the crowd. On his way down he gets several pats on the back and a few girls grab his ass. Note to self: have discussions with a few girls about keeping their hands to themselves. I try to make eye contact with Lucas, but he's too caught up in his own popularity for the moment.

When the crowd quiets down, Miss Hott resumes calling the names of semipopular seniors Blake Mason and Lance Brown, who are greeted with much more subdued applause than Lucas was. As our principal gets ready to read the final name from her note card she hesitates, then walks to the back corner of the gym to consult with Mr. Lowe, our accounting teacher, who has the distinct honor each year of tallying the votes. I see Miss Hott ask him a question with a puzzled look on her face, he nods solemnly, unlike the usually quite humorous Mr. Lowe, and Miss Hott turns back around and makes her way to the microphone.

She clears her throat. "And the final homecoming prince this year is Rand Bachrach." Miss Hott backs away from the microphone and winces as if the crowd is going to pelt her with their shoes or something. For one second there is absolutely no sound, not even a sneaker squealing. This so cannot be happening, but then I start to hear the chant, and realize that it is. All of the guys are chanting, "Rand, Rand, you're our man," over and over again. People start to make a path on the bleachers as Rand, who by the look on his face is still unsure what is happening, slowly makes his way down the bleachers. As he nears the other princes, every single one of them big, hefty football guys, they lift scrawny Rand onto their shoulders and continue around the gym carrying him like a trophy.

Tobi squeezes my hand as we exchange glances that say, "what the hell is happening here?" Rand Bachrach is like the anti-prince. I don't know that much about him, but let's just say that his looks are not exactly prince material. He could totally double for Napoleon Dynamite. He's not like poor or anything; his family actually owns a world-famous candy company, but Rand always looks like he shopped at a thrift shop, and not in a cool vintage way. I've never really talked to him except this one time in calculus he let me copy an answer, which was way cool, but I still don't understand how something like this happens.

"Mr. Lowe must have made a mistake counting the votes or something," I whisper in Tobi's ear.

"This was no mistake. I overheard some guys talking about Lucas putting something together to shake up homecoming. I bet this was it." She raises her terribly-in-need-of-a-waxing eyebrows, already knowing that I'm not going to like the outcome of my boyfriend's prank.

Why are guys *so* stupid? Don't they realize that you only have one senior homecoming in your entire life? A prank is running down the hallway in your jockstrap, not altering Comfort High history by voting a D-lister to the court. And, how mean is it to do this to Rand? To get the poor guy's hopes up about being thrust into popularity just to find out it was a joke.

Miss Hott finally manages to get the festivities under control. Lucas and his clan gently lower Rand back to the floor. Rand still looks dazed, but from the smile on his face, he's enjoying himself.

The princesses, with the exception of Tobi, are standing here horrified. I am personally trying to take back every wish I ever made to be homecoming queen. I feel bad that Rand is probably going to get his feelings hurt over this, but I still don't want to spend the entire week being some nerd's fantasy date.

Mr. Lowe saunters up and hands Miss Hott two sealed envelopes and the student body, knowing what they contain, quiets down.

Miss Hott rips into the first envelope and pulls out a white sheet of paper, I squint my eyes trying to read the large black print backward through the paper to no avail. "It is my pleasure to announce this year's Comfort High homecoming king," she says, then seems to slightly shake her head in confusion, clears her throat, and says, "*Rand Bachrach.*" The crowd goes wild, the male portion of the crowd—the girls are just sitting there looking confused like we're all on some noncelebrity episode of *Punk'd* or something. Like any minute Ashton is going to walk in and be like, "*Dude, you guys totally fell for it, Rand isn't really your king, duh, it's Lucas. Man, that was so dope. You should have seen the look on your faces. Swaaeeet!*"

But as the princes once again lift an ecstatic Rand on their shoulders, and parade him around the gym, Ashton never shows. I am making serious bargains with anyone holy who might be listening at this time. *I so do not want that tiara now. Please don't let me win.* I feel almost sick just thinking those things after wanting this dream for so long. But seriously, who wants to be homecoming queen if the king is a total nerd? The king is supposed to be handsome and charming, not scrawny with frizzy hair and glasses. This is turning into such a nightmare. Tobi is shaking she's laughing so hard. I can't believe she doesn't recognize how traumatic this is for me.

"I don't see a single thing funny about this situation, missy."

"Aspen, look at him." She points at Rand riding high on our best Seagulls. "He's having a blast. Rand is a really great guy. He deserves to be king."

"Whatever, just wait until he finds out it was all a joke. How much fun will he be having then? And what if you get chosen as the queen, you'll have to spend all week being his escort to the bonfire, the football game, riding with him in the parade, there's the carnival . . ."

"And this year's homecoming queen is Angel Ives." I was so busy sparring with Tobi that I didn't even see Miss Hott rip open the envelope.

I breathe a huge sigh of relief then glance over toward our queen. Angel is turning different shades of purple as Amy and Pippi shove her toward the microphone to accept her tiara from Miss Hott. I'm no girl detective, but something tells me that Angel isn't too psyched about holding court with a geek. Poor Rand is completely oblivious as he stands next to Miss Hott, his disheveled curls holding his crown high in the air.

Miss Hott sticks the combs on the ends of the tiara deep into Angel's scalp, making her wince; either that or standing so close to Rand is actually causing her physical pain.

"Okay, congratulations to our royal couple. Tonight is the bonfire so everybody dress warmly." The final bell cuts off Miss Hott, and the entire student body erupts into screaming and rushes out the door.

Angel spins on her heels and rushes toward me. She gets right into my face and starts yelling at me. "I'm going to destroy you." She's so close I can feel her spit landing on my perfectly applied MAC makeup.

"Say it, don't spray it, psycho." I hop back, hoping to avoid any more of her germ-filled spit spray. She turns and runs into the sea of students piling out of the gym.

"Angel, my ass. More like Demon Spawn." Tobi wipes my soggy cheeks.

"What the hell was all that about?"

"Oh, don't worry about it. She's just got her panties in a bunch because her Prince Charming turned out to be a frog."

I try to brush off Angel's comment like Tobi suggests, but her annoying voice keeps ringing in my ears. Lucas comes up behind me, looking visibly shaken. He looks like he has just realized the gravity of the situation he created. He is *so* slow!

"Are you responsible for this?" I demand, glancing over my shoulder at Rand, who is getting several pats on the back from his dorky entourage. Part of me feels a little bit sorry for Angel, even if she is a total lunatic. How bad would it suck to spend the entire week dragging around some nerdy guy? Thank God it wasn't me.

Lucas just stands there looking like a brain donor. He doesn't even need to tell me he did it. This brilliant handiwork has Lucas stamped all over it.

"It wasn't supposed to work out this way." Lucas finally mumbles.

"What the hell does that mean?" I ask, glaring daggers at him. I swear, I don't know why I keep sticking around and putting up with his immature shit.

"You were supposed to be queen, not Angel." He keeps repeating.

"*Tell me something I don't know, Lucas!*" I shout at him, attracting glances from the few stragglers left in the gym.

"You guys are so perfect for each other," Lucas says sadly.

Lucas isn't making any sense and his stupidity is making my head hurt. I just can't deal with him right now.

I stomp out of the gym, dragging Tobi with me and leaving Lucas eating my princess dust. We get to my locker and I pop it open and grab my periwinkle Dooney Doodle banana bag. I know, I know, periwinkle is a spring color, making it a total fashion faux pas in the fall, but it totally matches my eyes. Besides, people like me don't have to worry about pushing the fashion rules a little bit. By next week a dozen girls will have purses exactly like mine.

I slam my locker shut. I'm not even going to bother locking it since I have my purse. Who's going to steal a bunch of textbooks? Tobi is showing considerable restraint, but I can tell this whole debacle has amused her. She would be all for anything that turned the whole popularity contest that homecoming is on its nose. I swear, sometimes I do not know why I am friends with this girl. We are such polar opposites. I am all about looking hot in the latest fashions. She is all about throwing on whatever is on her floor that doesn't smell. I spend most of my free time shopping for previously mentioned luxuries and she volunteers at a soup kitchen. I have a wicked IQ. Tobi will be lucky if she doesn't end up graduating with the juniors. I push her into the bathroom.

On the way in we nearly collide with a disheveled Angel. Her pixie haircut is sticking up punk-rock style around her crooked tiara. The green eyes that normally shoot holes through me are bloodshot and remnants of mascara are smeared down her cheeks (silly girl should have used waterproof, what an amateur). A cloud of hideously cheap perfume surrounds us as Angel rushes by.

"Ya know, Angel, you won't actually become Britney Spears no matter how much Curious you put on?" Tobi shouts at Angel's hastily retreating backside while holding her nose. I laugh and rush into the first stall. Only Tobi could make me laugh at such an emotionally trying time. Even though we are like night and day I'm lucky to have Tobi for a sidekick. She has the best sense of humor and seriously quick wit. She is a loyal friend who would do anything for me and vice versa. Even though Tobi isn't exactly royalty at Comfort High, like yours truly, nobody messes with her because they know better than to get on my bad side.

As I start unbuttoning my jeans I hear Tobi scream. I quickly unlock the stall door, expecting to find her murdered by some demented bathroom serial killer, but instead find her pointing at the wall-length bathroom mirror with glazed-over eyes. As I turn my eyes toward the mirror I hear myself start screaming. On the mirror in huge block capital letters written in bloodred lipstick is a message: ASPEN BROOKS IS A LESBO WHO WEARS KNOCKOFFS.

Two

"Everyone knows that I don't really wear knockoffs, right?" Tobi is doubled over with laughter, as I precariously prop my butt up on a sink while swiping at the mirror with a damp paper towel trying to erase Angel's pathetic attempt to humiliate me.

"I think you're safe, Aspen, but some people might think you're a lesbo." She's laughing so hard she starts snorting.

"I would rather them think that than that I wear knockoffs. What is this shit?" I scrape at the lipstick with my fingernails. "Omigod, Tobi, I think she used Wet n Wild lipstick. It figures, that skank doesn't even have enough class to use decent lipstick for graffiti." I shake my head as I wipe away the rest of the message and jump down off the sink.

"You're just secretly pissed because she got queen and you didn't. I told you to get that tramp stamp last summer.

That would have cinched it for you." Tobi says referring to our inside joke about girls with lower-back tattoos being scary überskanks. Angel, of course, has a tramp stamp.

"Over my dead body would I ever deface this work of art," I say, running my hands down my body. We both burst into giggles again. No wonder Angel was in such a hurry to get out of here. Too bad I foiled her little scheme and no one but Tobi and I got the pleasure of seeing her little message. Tobi was right, Angel is all talk. This was the poorest attempt at revenge I've ever seen. Angel is so off my radar screen.

Lucas still needs to be dealt with though. Thankfully for him I didn't get queen or this dumb-ass stunt would have really cost him. Even so, I think a token of his deep regret in the form of bling is appropriate.

"Let's get out of here." I'm anxious to find Lucas and tell him what I want. We push open the bathroom door, and to our surprise, the halls are still filled with students. It seems the surprise homecoming vote is a good enough gossip topic to keep everyone from bolting home like they usually do. Clusters of students fill the hall as Tobi and I make our way back to my locker. As much as I would love to blow off my homework tonight, I have a huge accounting test tomorrow, and I'm not going to fail just because of this retarded drama that Lucas started.

As we reach my locker I yank on the lock, which I expect to pop open since I was too lazy to lock it before, but now it's locked. Some concerned teacher must have come along and locked it. They just can't keep their hands to themselves. I quickly spin the dial as Tobi waits patiently, leaning on my neighbor's locker.

"Lucas really started some shit. Even the teachers are down there talking about it," she says, glancing toward the teacher huddle forming outside the school office.

"Those losers probably love it. You know most of them were total geeks in high school," I say, spinning to the final number in my locker combination. I pull up on the latch and the locker door suddenly swings open and a burst of papers comes cascading out onto me.

"What the . . ." I don't even get out the full sentence as I stare unbelievingly around my feet at the naked girly pictures. Pictures of women topless, bottomless, or both are all over the hallway floor, like *Girls Gone Wild* has taken up residence in my locker.

"Holy crap," Tobi yells, dropping to her feet and trying to grab some of the flyers before this scene gets too out of control. Unfortunately, she's way too late. Lucas and the rest of the football team are already drooling over a girl-on-girl pic. Students are scrambling all over trying to get to the pictures. People are even pushing me aside to grab them out of my locker.

"Damn, babe, why didn't you tell me you're bi?" Lucas mumbles, ogling a glossy photo of a topless girl with pigtails.

"I didn't tell you that because I'm not!" I yell, starting to get very angry. "Somebody is sabotaging me and I know exactly who is it." I slam my locker door, catching a casualty in the side of the door with her crotch hanging out. I'm about to declare war on Angel Ives when Mr. Lowe taps me on the shoulder.

"Aspen, I need to see you in the office immediately." The office? Puhlease! The only reason I ever get called to the office is to pick up my flower deliveries. Angel's gonna pay for this.

Tobi makes eye contact with me and I mouth that I'll call her later. I don't even bother looking twice at Lucas who is busy trying to pull the crotch shot out of my locker.

Mr. Lowe has me take a seat inside Miss Hott's office, then he says he'll be back. He tried to be stern, which isn't a good look for him. I bet he's headed back out to the hallway to confiscate all the pictures to take home for himself tonight.

Why in the world would Angel want everyone to think I'm gay? I mean seriously, is that the best revenge she can think of? She is so going to pay for this.

The sounds in the hall are getting more faint, meaning that everyone has finally decided the excitement is over and it's time to go home. I'm getting a little nervous because I've never been in trouble before. The cinder-block walls in this place aren't doing a whole lot for me either. In a completely misguided attempt to make this space her own, Miss Hott has painted the walls a freakish pink color. I feel like I'm in Pepto-Bismol prison. She has a huge black-and-white picture of a couple kissing, which is kind of cool, even though I think it's a bit hypocritical since she's all over the students for any kind of PDAs whatsoever. Her desk is adorned with several tiny picture frames in the shape of high heels. Miss Hott is definitely a girly girl.

I turn one of the pink high-heel frames around. A young blonde smiles back at me. She's pretty in a completely out-of-style kind of way. She has feathered *Charlie's Angels* hair and her dress is a scary Laura Ashley floral print, circa the 1980s. The longer I stare at the poor unfashionable girl I can see slight similarities to Miss Hott. They have the same hair and eyes. This must be her sister. Wow! I bet Miss Hott needs a skycap for all her baggage after trying to compete with her sister all her life. I'm so thankful to be an only child. Any sibling of mine would have had a serious inferiority complex, and that's just no way to live.

Just when I am about to doze off, because I have been contained in this unventilated room for so long, Mr. Lowe and Miss Hott finally make their appearance. I sit up straight and prepare myself for battle. There is no way I'm going down for this.

Mr. Lowe takes the seat next to me while Miss Hott plops down into her big leather chair. For a second I'm actually afraid that the chair may collapse. To say that Miss Hott would be an ideal candidate for gastric bypass surgery would be the ultimate understatement. She tries crossing her legs, but can't get her big ham hock of a leg over the other one. She finally gives up and scoots her legs under her desk. Even though I'm sure that Marc Jacobs or Ralph Lauren sizes don't go up that high, Miss Hott does *try* to look stylish.

I notice Mr. Lowe looking her over, then I see a look of total revulsion cross his face. Bummer! It would have been kind of cool if they could have hooked up. After all, big girls need love, too. As far as I know neither one of them has a significant other, but they probably shouldn't since they work together. "Don't shit where you eat," as my dad so eloquently puts it. It doesn't really matter anyway since Mr. Lowe obviously isn't a chubby chaser.

"So, Aspen, what do you have to say for yourself?" Miss Hott asks me as she precariously tilts her chair back and folds her chubby sausage fingers over the shelf her gigantic boobs create across her chest. I bet Lucas and his boys wouldn't mind seeing her topless. Ewww . . . that was a gross thought. I better quit screwing around and start defending myself.

"I would hope that after my exemplary record at this school that you two would know enough about my character to realize that I would never bring pornographic material onto school grounds."

"But you keep it at home, right?" Mr. Lowe asks, stifling a laugh.

"Bob, that's not funny," Miss Hott says, but laughs anyway. "Of course we know you didn't bring it, Aspen. But do you have any idea how it got into your locker?"

I blow out a huge sigh of relief. I'm not going to have to defend myself after all. Angel is going to be in deep shit when I bust her out for this. "It was Angel Ives; she's pissed, oops, I mean mad because Rand got voted homecoming king. She said she was going to destroy me. Then me and Tobi practically ran into her coming out of the bathroom and once we got inside we saw that she had written a horrible message about me on the mirror. She's crazy." By the look on Miss Hott's face, I'm pretty sure I've convinced her.

"What was the message?" Crap. Am I really going to have to repeat this to her? I'll just leave off the part about the knockoffs.

"Um, well, it said, 'Aspen Brooks is a lesbo.' " I can tell Mr. Lowe is trying very hard not to picture me involved in a little girl-on-girl action. What a freaking perv! I turn back to Miss Hott.

"Is that all it said?" What is she, psychic?

"Um, well, it also kind of said that I wear knockoffs," I unwillingly admit, hanging my head. This is so humiliating even if it isn't true.

Both supposed distinguished members of this fine learning institution completely lose their minds. They both start howling at the top of their lungs like I've just told the funniest joke in the whole world. So much for compassion.

"That isn't even the worst part. She used cheap lipstick for her graffiti." I say, making them laugh even harder; I figure I might as well use their insanity to my advantage. Finally after several minutes of deep breaths and wiping tears away they manage to remember that they are supposed to be setting a good example for me. Ha, fat chance of that happening anytime soon.

"Angel's had her fun. She'll get over it once the homecoming festivities start. Besides, Rand is a very charming young man. She'll have a blast with him this week."

"So that's it? You're not even going to call her in here?"

"Aspen, we don't have any witnesses. It's your word against hers. Just be sure to let me know if anything else happens. Oh, and I have a feeling that this wouldn't have happened if someone had locked their locker." She raises an eyebrow at me. "You're dismissed now."

I get up to leave and before shutting the door I peek my head back in and say, "Totally cute office," which gets a proud look from Miss Hott. You never know when a little ass kissing might come in handy. As I shut the door and walk out into the main office I hear them start to howl with laughter. It's nice that I could provide these middle-aged losers with some entertainment today.

⊙

By the time I get done being humiliated in Miss Hott's office the school hallway is deserted. I hurry to my locker, which has been picked clean of any nudie pics, and grab my accounting textbook. Throwing my purse over my shoulder, I walk briskly to my car.

My car . . . I love saying that . . . my beautiful, shiny, fast car. My teal Explorer is easy to spot since it is nearly the only vehicle left in the parking lot. Every time I look at my gorgeous SUV, I get butterflies. After eighteen months, we are still completely in love with each other. It's my longest relationship yet. My SUV takes me wherever I want to go, whenever I want, and provides an oasis when I need to escape any kind of school or home drama. It may not be skanky Angel's brand-new Mustang, but my SUV still rocks.

I get close enough to run the tips of my fingers along the smooth blue-green hood.

"Hey, Cookie, did you miss me?" I call my car Cookie. I felt that she needed a name and Cookie, for some reason, seemed appropriate. "How's my baby today?" Okay, I know she's not going to talk back or anything, but I haven't had a single breakdown so I think a little TLC goes a long way.

I hit the button on my remote to unlock the driver's side door when something near the back left tire catches my eye.

Cookie is sitting much lower in the back with a huge pair of scissors sticking out of what used to be my back left tire. Now it's just a shredded pile of rubber. I can't believe this. Angel had the nerve to slash my tire. This is no cheap lipstick graffiti or nudie pics. This is serious shit. At least I've got my proof now. Just wait until Miss Hott sees this, Angel will probably get expelled. Kiss your tiara good-bye, beyotch!

I stomp back into the school and down the hall to the office. I try turning the doorknob but it is locked. Quickly, I run to the front doors just in time to see Miss Hott's car pull out of the front driveway. So much for busting Angel. I grab my pink RAZR from my purse. I'll just have to call Mom to pick me up. It beeps angrily then dies. Shit. I'm horrible about charging this stupid thing. I put the phone back into my purse and head for the pay phone. A snack machine now blocks where I remembered the phone being. Vaguely, I remember the pay phone being removed since every single student has a cell phone now. Damn technology.

"Hello? Anybody here?" There has got to be some random janitor somewhere who will let me into the office to make a phone call. I peek into the classrooms to try to find someone but it is looking more and more like I'm going to have to suck it up and walk home. This could, quite possibly, ruin my new boots. This has truly been the day from hell.

Suddenly I get an idea that brightens my mood. Since nobody is around, nobody would witness a certain somebody defacing a certain skank's locker. Yeah! I rush down to locker number sixty-six, which belongs to Angel. I quickly pull out my purple Sharpie and add another six next to her locker number, now it fits her perfectly. I can't resist the urge to also add a little message to greet Angel in the morning. I bite on the Sharpie cap while trying to come up with something perfect. I have to admit that Angel's mirror graffiti was witty. I don't want to write something totally lame. After careful consideration, I decide on "Angel Ives has three nipples." I check again that the coast is clear, then quickly jot it on her locker while trying to disguise my handwriting. I step back and admire my handiwork. I would love to see Angel's face in the morning.

"Does she really?" A male voice asks, causing me to scream and jump a foot into the air.

"Omigod, Rand, you scared the shit out of me." It's none other than our newly crowned homecoming king minus the crown.

"What'cha doing?" he says, laughing, knowing he totally busted me.

"Now listen, normally I would be the first to condemn this type of behavior, but she has completely tortured me today. First, she wrote something horrible about me on the bathroom mirror, then she filled my locker full of porn, then she slashed my tire," I spout, suddenly exhausted.

"I knew about the porn. Compliments of Lucas." He holds up a picture of some topless chick. "She slashed your tire? That's kind of serious. Why do you think it was her?" I realize that after attending school with Rand for twelve years this is the longest conversation we have ever had.

"She told me today at the assembly she was going to destroy me." Crap, I shouldn't have said that. Now he's going to ask me why. I'm not about to tell him that Angel thinks I was in cahoots with Lucas. I do not want to be the one to break his heart and tell him that his nomination was just a joke.

"I hate to break it to you but your little message might actually make Angel more popular. With the males anyway, present company excluded of course," he says, laughing. "So why does she want to destroy you?" Shit.

"I don't know. I . . . I . . . think she wants Lucas all to herself." This is the best I could do on short notice, besides, it's not totally untrue. I've seen the looks Angel gives Lucas when she thinks I'm not looking.

"I'm guessing you think that would be a bad thing?" He tilts his head to the side causing his curls to tumble.

"Um, yeah, considering he's my boyfriend," I reply snottily, tossing my hair back while putting the cap back on my Sharpie and dropping it back into my purse.

"That's right, I forgot you two are an item now. I would have never put you with a guy like Lucas, but hey, what do I know?"

I'm not sure what he means and I am about to unleash a string of very unladylike profanities when he grabs my arm and starts walking me toward the west doors near the student parking lot. I knew he was a nerd, but I didn't know he was a total freak. He is actually going to kidnap me.

"Let go of me!" I yell, trying to wrestle free of his surprisingly strong grip.

"The janitor's coming. He'll tell Miss Hott you defaced Angel's locker, then you'll get kicked off the court. Run."

I glance quickly behind me and sure enough our older-than-dirt janitor is taking in my message about Angel. I break into a full speed jog next to Rand.

"You kids get back here!" the janitor yells as we both burst thru the west doors together.

"Over here," Rand yells, running toward a tiny, egg-shaped, blindingly yellow car. He hops in and unlocks my side. I'm trailing a bit behind because these boots were definitely made for walking, not running. I open the passenger side door and slide in, instantly bashing my knee on the dashboard.

"Why is this car so small?" I yell, hugging my knees, not out of choice, but because I have no room to actually stretch them out.

"Some of us actually care enough about the environment to give up some luxuries." He says giving my gas-guzzling SUV a snarl as we drive by it.

"What? Sacrificing leg room makes you an environmentalist?" I ask, getting a little defensive since he had the nerve to insult Cookie.

"This car is a hybrid, I only have to fill it up about once a month. We're just trying to do our part, aren't we, Buzz?" He taps gently on the dash while maneuvering his FryDaddy on wheels onto the highway.

"You named your car?" I'm in amazement that Rand and I would have something in common.

"Yeah, kinda weird, right? Buzz just kind of fits him."

"That's totally weird." I feel a little guilty not fessing up about Cookie, but I don't want Rand to get the wrong idea. If he thought we had something in common, it might get his hopes up that we could be friends or something, and that is so not happening. "My car may not run on French fry oil, but I still do my part," I say instead.

"Oh, really? Like what?"

Shit. Now I have to lie so I don't look like a total natural-resource hog. Oh, well. Here goes.

"I'm a vegetarian," I state proudly.

"That's kind of hypocritical, don't you think? I mean considering how many cows had to die for those boots of yours." He glances over at my boots that are practically sitting in my lap courtesy of this joke of a car of his.

"I wear animals, I just don't eat them," I say, clarifying my made-up vegetarian status for Rand.

"Huh? So I guess that must have been a double tofu burger you were eating today and not a double cheeseburger?" He laughs.

I narrow my eyes into slits and give him one of the dirtiest looks out of my arsenal. He continues laughing. His behavior is completely outrageous. A D-lister making fun of an A-lister? I swear the whole world has gone insane today.

"Whatever." Not exactly my wittiest comeback, but it's been such a crappy day that I'm in no mood to spar with the biggest geek in school. I'm starting to think I should have just let the janitor bust me. He chuckles as he makes a left on Spruce Street, heading for my house.

"How do you know where I live?" Eww, I hope he's not some psycho A-list stalker.

"Aspen, everybody knows where you live. This is Comfort, population twenty-five hundred, not New York City. Don't worry, I'm not stalking you," he says, reading my mind.

"Well, I sure don't know where you live." This, of course, is kind of a lie; after all, this is Comfort. But I've never actually seen his house; I just know that he lives a little outside of town, off a dirt road. But between this car and Rand's atrocious outfit, I'm starting to think all these rumors about him being rich is a bunch of shit. There is probably a double-wide at the end of that dirt road instead of some mansion.

Oh. My. God. It just occurred to me that I am riding around town with Rand Bachrach. If anybody sees me, I will never live this down. I try to slouch down in my seat, but with my legs pushed up against the dash it doesn't really work so well. I just end up with a huge wedgie.

"Don't worry, Aspen. Nobody's going to see you. Oh, and you're welcome by the way."

Okay, so maybe I've been a little rude. I guess it's not Rand's fault he's a dork. You don't really get to pick your social standing in life. Although getting a stylist wouldn't kill him either. But he did give me a ride home, and he didn't bust me out with the janitor, so I guess he's kinda cool.

After what feels like an eternity, we pull in the driveway of my parents Cape Cod–style home. I'm so not looking forward to this awkward good-bye. I mean Rand seems like an okay guy, but we are just from two different worlds. Just as I am about to give him a big fake smile and thanks, I remember, that like a total dumb ass, I forgot to get my garage door opener out of Cookie and since I never carry keys and my parents won't be home for another hour I would only be able to run to the front porch and stand there looking like an idiot.

"Listen, I'm sorry for being a jerk before. I just get really sensitive when it comes to environmental issues," he says, running one of his hands through his unkempt curls.

I totally don't get people who get worked up about dwindling oil supply or a hole in the ozone layer. I mean, we can totally start drilling in Alaska if we need to and it's not like any of us will be around when the sun's rays start melting people so let future generations worry about that stuff. Jeez!

"I'm sorry you didn't get queen. I know you really wanted that tiara," Rand says.

How in the world would he know what I want? He doesn't even know me. It was kind of sweet of him to give me his condolences though.

"The girls are going to be lining up now that you're king," I tell him. Of course I know that's total BS, but I felt like I should say something nice back. After all, it was my dumb-ass boyfriend who did this, so I do feel a tiny bit responsible.

"The one I really want won't be." He answers back, giving me a funny look. I wonder who he's talking about? Before I can ask, he says, "I'm sure you have better things to do than sit here chatting with me. Besides, I need to get home and call Angel to tell her what you wrote on her locker." He laughs, giving me a wink. His smile shows off a really great set of pearly whites. He almost looks cute, not that I'd ever admit that to anyone, not even Tobi. But, just for a split second, I saw potential.

I'm obviously just overly exhausted. I've still got the bonfire tonight. I'd rather just go inside, take a hot bath, climb into bed, and forget this horrible day ever happened. But, I'm locked out and sitting in the freezing cold waiting at least an hour on my parents doesn't sound appealing so I'm going to have to ask Rand for another favor.

"Very funny. Um, actually, Rand, I'm kind of locked out. I left my garage door opener in my car and I never carry keys," I confess, rolling my eyes.

"Your parents aren't home either, huh? I guess we're stuck with each other for a little bit longer then. I'd offer to take you back to the school, but that renegade janitor may still be on the lookout for us. You'll just have to come home with me."

"No, that's okay. My parents should be home any minute. Can we just wait here?" I ask, a little nervous. Rand seems nice, but what if he's really a freak. I mean he must be on the D-list for some reason. He could slip me a roofie, take my picture on the sly, and then show all of his geeky friends how much of a stud he was snagging a homecoming princess. It would be like *Sixteen Candles* when Anthony Michael Hall drives the drunk popular girl home. No way. That may sound extreme, but the way this day has gone nothing would surprise me.

While I am daydreaming about how Rand would love to take advantage of me, he has pulled away from the curb and starts heading away from my house. I'm nervous, which is not a common emotion for me. I contemplate jumping from the car, but road rash would not be a good look for my flawless complexion.

"It wouldn't be very gentlemanly of me to leave you out in the cold, now would it? Let's go get some coffee while we wait for your parents."

"Oh, okay." I try not to laugh out loud at how dramatic I was being just a second ago.

As Rand navigates the streets of Comfort he suddenly turns to me and asks, "So what is someone like you doing with Lucas Riley anyway?" He says Lucas's name like it is some sort of sexually transmitted disease.

"What do you mean, someone like me?"

"You know, beautiful, smart, could choose anyone?"

He said I was beautiful. I can't help but smile and feel a little more relaxed. I never tire of compliments on my looks even if they are coming from someone who wouldn't know beauty from a hole in the ground. "Lucas is handsome, popular, and he's the quarterback of the football team."

"Those are all superficial things," he says sarcastically. "By the way, I noticed you didn't say anything about intelligence."

This guy doesn't miss a trick. Is there such a thing as an overly observant male? If so, Rand Bachrach definitely fits the part. "No, he definitely isn't the brains of the operation, but it's just a senior year thing. Next year we'll be going off to college and we'll forget all about each other."

"That's the weirdest thing I've ever heard. Why would you want to waste your senior year with someone you're planning on forgetting in nine months?"

"I'm just saying, it's not that serious."

"Aspen, I've got to tell you. I had you all wrong. I took you for someone so passionate she wouldn't waste one ounce of herself with the wrong guy."

"I'm not saying he's the wrong guy. You're twisting my words. He is special, okay? Let's just leave it at that."

"Okay, sorry. It's really none of my business anyway."

"I know you think I'm shallow," I hear myself saying.

"That's one thing I've never thought," he says, gazing deep into my eyes. I feel my stomach drop, probably because I've only had a bag of Cheetos and a Coke to eat today.

"What's your poison?" He asks, confusing me until I realize we've arrived at the drive-thru of the local coffee shop.

"Oh, just a hot chocolate. But I want it made with two percent milk, not water, and topped with whipped cream and chocolate shavings. And don't forget a straw."

"You drink hot chocolate through a straw?"

"What?" I give him a playful dirty look, challenging him to make fun of my drinking habits. "It's just that I always dribble on my shirt if I don't use a straw. Look at this outfit, it would not look good with chocolate dribbled all over it," I explain as Rand raises his eyebrows and tries not to laugh. He gives the voice in the speaker our order, then pulls around to the window. I reach my hands through my legs to try to grab my purse. Rand realizes I'm going for my money and stops me, gently grazing my hand. He jerks his arm back like touching me burned him.

"It's on me." He turns his attention back to the window and hands the girl a twenty. I'm still stuck back on that touch because I felt something, too. It must have just been static electricity, but I wonder why I have butterflies in my stomach. As I push this thought aside Rand hands me my drink. I stick the straw through the tiny opening and sip. And as usual, my order is wrong. You always get screwed at the drive-thru. I could make a big fuss, but Rand probably already thinks I'm a total snob, so I'm just gonna keep my mouth shut for once.

"Did they get your order right?" He places his coffee in the miniscule drink holder. There is definitely no room in here for a Big Gulp.

"Um, it's fine. Thanks."

"What's wrong?" He takes my drink from me, pops the lid to find no whipped cream, no chocolate shavings, and a very obviously watered-down hot chocolate. He bangs on the window and the girl returns.

"Hi, miss, I ordered this with two percent milk, whipped cream, and chocolate shavings. None of those things are present. Would you be a sweetheart and fix this for me?" He blinds her with the same smile I saw just a second ago. A smile I wouldn't have thought him capable of. She starts to blush, and then guiltily glances at me. She must think I'm his girlfriend or something. *As if!* She scurries off to hopefully fix my hot chocolate. I would never have taken Rand for an order returner. It takes balls to return an order, and most people just don't have 'em. Just the other day, Lucas took me to McDonald's and I ordered a cheeseburger with no onions. Of course, there were onions on it. When I asked Lucas to complain, he drove off and told me to just scrape them off. Ugh, as if the onion juice hadn't already polluted the entire burger.

Maybe there is a little more to Rand Bachrach than I thought. I start doodling in the condensation on the window and before I know it I've drawn a huge heart.

"Gee, thanks, Aspen. Now I've got to clean my windows." He hands me my new and improved drink, pulling me out of my daze.

I snap back and admire my artwork. "Oops, sorry. It's been a long day. I guess I'm sort of out of it." I take a sip of my drink and I swear it is the best hot chocolate I've ever had. "Yum, I think I'll take you with me in the drive-thru more often," I say, then immediately regret it, afraid that Rand will think I'm hitting on him or something.

"Shoot, that's nothing. You should taste my mom's. She uses our company's chocolate and some other secret ingredients. She could patent it, I swear. You'll have to try it some time." He gives me a little wink while sipping his black coffee.

"Yeah, sure." I'll go have hot chocolate with you and your mom right about the time monkeys fly out of my ass. I have to admit Rand seems totally sweet, but I seriously doubt that our orbits will ever cross again after today.

As Rand steers his hybrid banana of a car out of the coffee shop drive-thru his headlights flash on a familiar vehicle.

"Hey, drive over there for a sec," I say, pointing in the opposite direction.

Rand cranks the steering wheel and the car spins around toward the deserted parking lot of the local mini-mall. Rand's headlights illuminate the familiar license plate confirming my suspicion.

"Is that your mom's car?" Rand asks, coming to a stop.

"Why?" I ask, defensive.

"The license plates say Aspen's Mom so I just thought maybe . . ." Rand trails off.

I don't hear him because I am scanning the darkened storefronts trying to figure out what Mom's car would be doing here. There has to be a reasonable explanation, but for some reason I feel nauseous.

"Are you okay? You look kind of green," Rand says, concerned.

"Can you just take me home?" I plead.

When we pull up to the house Dad's side of the garage is open and his prized pickup is pulled inside.

"Do you need a ride to the bonfire tonight? It would be no problem to come and get you," Rand offers, his eyes filled with hope. I hate to crush him, but I can't be getting his hopes up by telling him yes. Besides, how would it look if I showed up to the bonfire with him? I should do it just to piss Lucas off, but I'm a bigger person than that.

"No, thanks, Rand. Lucas had already planned to come pick me up." Which is a total lie but won't be once I get inside and call him.

"Well, okay. I guess I'll see ya tonight then." And before I can respond he has jumped out of the car and is rushing around to open my door. I'm not going to lie; it is kind of cool to be treated like such a lady. Lucas could definitely take some lessons from Rand on how to treat women. He wouldn't open my door for me if his life depended on it. But I guess Rand probably doesn't get girls in his car very often, so he's thought things out a lot.

I grab my purse in one hand and my drink in the other and lift myself out of the car. My legs are wobbly from being scrunched up for so long and Rand steadies me as I start to fall against the car. There's that spark again. Weird. There must be tons of static electricity in the air tonight.

"Thanks, Rand. This was supercool of you. I'll see you tonight." I start to turn and walk through the open garage, then I turn back around. Rand is already back inside the car when I approach him. He lowers his window.

"I'm sure it's nothing, but could you maybe not say anything to anyone about seeing my mom's car tonight?" I ask him.

He clenches his lips together then uses his fingers to act like he's zipping them shut. He tosses the imaginary key over his shoulder, waves, and backs out of the driveway. He beeps his cheesy hybrid horn and waves goofily as he drives away. I can't help but laugh and realize that I had Rand Bachrach pegged all wrong.

Three

Pumpkin isn't normally a color I would choose for myself. But Mom, being the fashion guru that she is, thought I needed a fallish-type sweater for the bonfire tonight. I'm modeling it for her now. With my blonde hair and periwinkle eyes I'm definitely a spring, but as I gaze at my reflection in a full-length mirror I realize that someone like me doesn't have to be restricted to one season. I look pretty great in every color.

"I'd kill for your complexion, Aspen. You look amazing in any color," Mom gushes, while pulling the price tag off a new pair of khakis to go with my sweater. "Your boots will look really good with this outfit," she adds, jealously eyeing my new leather boots and making me glad that we don't wear the same shoe size.

"I wore those today so I can't wear them again until at least Thursday. Besides, these are more comfortable for outdoors," I hold up a pair of brown suede clogs.

"Maybe you should think about putting some of your allowance in your college fund instead of buying more shoes and purses. What do you think?" Mom says, not taking her eyes off my boots. I just know she's going to be shoving her size-ten hooves into my perfect size-six boots the minute I walk out the door. Maybe I should hide them before I leave.

"Oh, you're a good one to talk, Little Miss Has-the-Credit-Card-Bill-Sent-to-a-Post-Office-Box-So-Her-Husband-Doesn't-See-It."

She whips her head up with so much force I'm afraid it might come off as she stares at me with huge eyes. "H . . . H . . . How do you know about that?"

"I'm wise beyond my years, and I don't miss a thing that goes on in this house, Mother dear."

"In my defense, most of the stuff I buy is for you." She pushes her new Coach bag behind her back.

"Oh, the sacrifices you make." I dramatically hold my hand across my heart. We start into one of our famous mother-daughter fits of laughter.

"Judy, where have you been?" my dad asks, busting into my room looking flustered. Mom quickly bends the price tags in her palm. My dad is like a total cheapskate. An example would be the time he tried to make us reuse paper plates by turning them over. My mom threatened to divorce him. He would shit himself if he found out that she bought me a new outfit just to go hang out by a gigantic pile of burning wood.

Or that her new purse would probably pay for the textbooks my first semester of college, but what he doesn't know won't hurt him. Men just don't understand the price you have to pay to look good.

"Don't you remember me telling you that I had to work late tonight?" Mom asks him.

"Oh, that's right," Dad says, slapping his forehead. "I just get nervous when I can't find my girl." He wraps his arms around Mom's tiny waist and gives her a squeeze. I swear, they are the cutest old couple ever.

"So, let me see it," Dad says to me.

"See what?" I ask, confused.

"The tiara that you've been coveting for the last year of your life."

"Oh," I say, disappointed. "I didn't get it."

"Oh, babe. I'm so sorry," Dad says, squeezing my arm.

"It's no biggie," I lie. I am still disappointed about losing to Angel, but right now my mind is back on why Mom just lied to Dad about where she was tonight.

"I'll give you two some girl time," Dad says, kissing me on the forehead. Dad always makes a quick getaway when he thinks Mom and I are going to start talking about periods or cramps. I guess tiaras fall into that category now, too.

Besides my dad's massive hang-up about money, my parents are like the coolest. They completely trust my judg-ment so I don't really have a curfew. They give me a decent allowance (although I've been lobbying for a cost-of-living increase lately) that requires almost no actual chores, and they don't give me the third degree about my life. They show just enough interest without being overbearing. I consider myself lucky, especially when I think that I could have ended up with Tobi's parents. I pretty much had to pass a background check when we started being friends, and she can only stay out until ten on weekends. Her parents are lame with a capital L.

"Do you want to talk about it some more?" Mom asks, hiding the price tags in a tissue, then tossing it in my garbage can.

"I think we pretty much covered every angle." We completely dissected my loss before Dad came in. We finally agreed that the contest was fixed, and tiara or no tiara, Angel is still a super skank. I love that my mom will call some girl she doesn't even know a skank just to side with me. We have such an awesome relationship. I love that I don't have to hide things from her like my friends do with their parents. We have the most honest mother-daughter relationship of anyone I know.

Mom moves to step out my doorway.

"Mom, did you go anywhere after work tonight?"

"Nope. You know me, I'm a slave to the grind." She laughs and closes my door.

I hereby request that the last statement about honesty be stricken from the record.

I decide to put the mama drama on the back burner for tonight. I have more pressing concerns right now as my car is seriously out of commission. I'm going to be forced to rely on Lucas and his hoopty to get to the bonfire. I grab my now-recharged phone (not making that mistake twice in one day) off my dresser and dial his number. It goes straight to voice mail, again. This is the third time I've called him since Rand dropped me off. I'm starting to get a little pissed. I even called his home phone and his mom said she gave him the message that I called earlier. He's probably off planning another one of his retarded pranks. I still can't believe he pulled that shit with voting Rand in. Sometimes I wonder why I'm dating such an idiot.

My cell rings in my hand and Tobi's number pops up. Sometimes I think she has some sort of weird ESP when I need her.

"Can you come get me?" I whine, not bothering to say hi, because I mean really, why even bother with that anymore when everybody's got caller ID.

"What happened to Lucas and his busted-down chariot?" Tobi counters, not missing a beat.

"Listen, don't give me any shit, I've had the worst day ever. Angel slashed my tire and I had to bum a ride with Rand in his FryDaddy on wheels. My legs still haven't recovered."

"He's sweet, isn't he?"

Thoughts of Rand's hand on the small of my back leading me out of the school fill my mind and I quickly push them out. "Yeah, I guess. Whatever. So can you pick me up or what?"

"Sure, I'll be there in ten," she says, clicking off.

I hang up and start to reapply my lip gloss. I purposefully left out the part about getting butterflies when Rand touched me. I mean, I can't be attracted to him or anything because that's just crazy. I think I was just feeling grateful, plus I'm just so tired from the day from hell. But even if I had told Tobi, she would never judge me. She's all about people of different social status intermingling.

⊚

Tobi and I pull up to the school and see the obvious handiwork of Comfort High's rival, Maroon High. They have used black spray paint to scrawl "Flock the Seagulls" in huge letters across the entire brick front of the school. I bet Miss Hott is freaking out. I think it's kind of funny actually, but I wouldn't want to be the one standing outside in this freezing weather for hours sandblasting the message off the school. Tobi pulls her red pickup truck next to Rand's joke of a car.

"Can you believe this thing? He calls it Buzz." I lay my hand on the hood of his car as we walk toward the giant fire in the sky.

"That's so cute that you both name your cars," Tobi gushes as we near the outer edges of the massive crowd of hyper students. I put my arm out to stop her. I can't stand it. I have to tell her about Rand's strange comment.

"He's got a major crush on somebody," I say, remembering Rand's strange comment about not getting the girl he wants.

She just stares at me. Then she pushes her neck forward and bulges her eyes out, not a good look on her.

"What?"

"You're freaking kidding me, right?" she asks.

"Tobi, what is your major malfunction tonight?" I am seriously starting to regret bringing this up with her.

"*Oh. My. God!*" She flings her arms around dramatically. This is very un-Tobi-like behavior. "Aspen, for somebody with a photographic memory, you are the dumbest person I have ever met."

"Hey, I don't have to put up . . ."

"*It's you! He has a crush on you!*" Tobi screams while still flinging her arms around wildly. Seriously, I don't know what has gotten into her.

"You're crazy." I glance around to make sure no one is overhearing this absurd conversation.

"Rand has been completely infatuated with you since you convinced him in first grade he was lactose intolerant so you could have his chocolate milk. He studies every move you make. He adores you! How can you not have known this?"

"I think I would know if someone had been in love with me, for like ever."

"One would think," she replies sarcastically.

"I don't want to talk about this anymore. We never had this conversation."

"Fine, but you be careful with him. He's got it bad," she warns me.

This whole conversation is disturbing on so many levels. Rand in love with me for years? How could I have been so unobservant? I guess it does explain how he had the cheeseburger info and the strange comment in the car. I hope I didn't get his hopes up by letting him spend time with me today.

I drag Tobi over to Cookie so that she can see the damage Angel did with her own eyes. When I circle around to the left rear tire, it has already been replaced with my spare. How weird. My dad was with me the entire time and he hadn't planned on changing out the tire until morning. Aww, it was Lucas. How sweet. That's why he didn't have his cell on, because he was out here freezing his butt off changing my tire. I'm so lucky to have such a caring boyfriend. I hope he doesn't think this gets him off the hook to buy me something though.

"Look, Tobi. Lucas changed my tire for me. Isn't he sweet?"

"If he were any sweeter, I'd be diabetic," she answers back in a sugarcoated sarcastic voice. Tobi doesn't have much use for Lucas. She thinks he is a brain-dead jock who thinks with his penis. I remind her that describes half of our school.

"Be nice." I shove against her. "Let's go find Lucas, so I can thank him properly."

"Actually, I think I'm going over this way for a minute." She turns into the crowd leaving me by myself. Great, is anyone not going to ditch me today? I circle the outer ring of students, trying to find Lucas. I'm not big on crowds, and tend toward massive claustrophobia in certain situations, so I'm not going in until I spot him. While scanning the crowd I make eye contact with Rand; he smiles and holds up his hand. I put on a plastic grin and wave back.

He's decided to conform to Miss Hott's request that everyone wear school colors. Somehow this does not surprise me. I don't have respect for people that violate rules of fashion just to conform for others. And let's face it, wearing a summer color like turquoise in the fall just isn't right unless you're me. Fashion-wise, I can get away with anything. But I have to admit that turquoise isn't a horrible color for him. As my eyes move up, I see his ridiculous black stocking cap pulled down over his ears and forehead. Jammed atop the curl-filled hat is his gold crown. He puts his finger up as if signaling me to wait. I stand still until I see him turn around to make his way over, then I bolt. After the bomb that Tobi just dropped on me, it would be totally awkward talking to him. Besides, I don't need to be seen chatting it up with the biggest geek in school. Angel would have a field day with that whole scene. Speaking of Angel, I wonder where that scary bitch is? We need to have words about my tire.

"Let's hear it for the Seagulls," Coach Buchanan screams as the entire football team breaks through a huge paper likeness of a Maroon Bulldog. The first stud pushing through the paper pup is none other than my AWOL boyfriend. I forgot all about the stupid football introductions, like everyone here doesn't already know all the players. Lucas looks hot, as usual, in his number ten football jersey.

The cheerleaders, affectionately known as the Seagals—I usually just refer to them as the sluts—fan their pom-poms out for the boys to run through and that's when I spot her. Angel, head cheerleader of the Seagals, looking quite the picture of innocence. To an outsider she would appear to be a fun-loving, hurkey-jumping, perfectly normal member of our student body. But I know the truth. That Seagal is a psycho. As I'm plotting how to confront her, I notice her expression change from innocent to a sexy smirk. She and Lucas have their eyes locked on each other. If I didn't want to completely destroy Angel before, I sure as hell do now. I try making my way closer to the line of football players to make my presence known and interrupt the "fuck me" eyes these two are giving each other. I can't seem to break through and there are so many people I'm starting to freak out a bit. I decide to edge closer to the fire to get warm. I'll just have to deal with Lucas later.

"Pretty chilly tonight, huh?" I hear a familiar voice ask from behind me.

"Illinois weather, what are you gonna do?" I answer back to Rand, who is now standing beside me.

"I can't believe you didn't wear a coat. Here, take mine." He tries to hand me the black fleece jacket he has on over his turquoise crewneck sweater.

I put my hand out to stop him. The last thing I need is to be seen exchanging clothes with Rand. It would probably end up on the front of the school newspaper with some witty caption like "Princess warms up to king." Besides, I so don't do fleece. "I'm fine, really." This is a total lie. I'm freezing my ass off. I scoot closer to the fire.

"Helluva a fire, huh?" Rand is obviously trying to make small talk. But he does have a point. The flames from the fire are at least ten feet tall. Someone has suspended a stuffed bulldog above the flames and the fire licks at its paws.

"Pretty amazing what you can do with wood and a few matches these days."

"You don't want to be seen talking to me, do you?"

God, when he puts it that way he makes me sound like a bitch. I am not a bitch; I may be a little bit materialistic with a tendency to place a person's value on their outward appearance, but I'm not a bitch. A bitch is someone who is just downright mean for no good reason. I'm being mean to Rand because he is geeky and being seen talking to him is likely to affect my popularity. But . . . he fixed my hot chocolate . . . and he did let me stay warm in his car until my parents got home . . . plus he knows I defiled Angel's locker . . . and as far as I know he hasn't told anyone about seeing Mom's car . . . so I guess I could be a little bit nicer. Besides, nobody is paying any attention to us now anyway since Coach Buchanan just started lowering the poor stuffed canine to his fate toward the flames. Everyone is chanting "Burn the Bulldogs" over and over like possessed zombies. I guess I just don't have enough school spirit.

"How about those Seagals, huh? They're like Energizer Bunnies on crack." He points to the five pigtailed bimbos in the shortest cheerleading skirts imaginable, jumping up and down. Angel even tried to put pigtails in her short black hair. They look more like horns. How can Lucas find her even remotely attractive? It's revolting.

"What? You mean I've found a man who is immune to the charms of Angel and her zombie cult of Seagals?" I ask, amazed.

"I don't have anything against her personally, but I've seen her do things to purposely get under your skin. You definitely have reason not to like her."

Wow, it feels so great to be validated in my hatred for Angel. Maybe Rand isn't so bad after all.

Rand gently takes my arm and guides me over to sit on a bale of hay.

"No, I really shouldn't." I continue standing next to him while he sits.

"Just when I thought we were getting to be friends," he replies, looking sad.

"No, I just meant I shouldn't sit on the hay. I'm deathly allergic to it. To all of this stuff actually. I've also got asthma and it doesn't mix well with my pea-sized lungs." I point to the smoke from the fire and the corn husks twirling above the flames and the hay. "I'm usually okay if I take a shower as soon as I get home, but I've broken out in hives from sitting on it before."

"That sucks. So no hayrides for you at Halloween, huh?"

"Not unless I want to end up in the ER with an oxygen mask strapped around my face."

"You'd look kind of cute in an oxygen mask." He gives me a cheesy grin.

I decide to ignore his comment even though he is obviously hitting on me. It's not his fault. I look exceptionally good tonight. This pumpkin-colored sweater is just really doing it for me.

"Shouldn't you be getting up there?" I remind him, pointing toward the stage where Angel is standing. The smile she has plastered on her face actually looks real. Maybe she's accepted Rand being king after all. Her tiara is crooked from too many hurkeys. She blows the crowd kisses as Coach introduces her as this year's queen. Yuck, what a waste of a tiara!

"Oops, don't want to miss my intro. By the way, I threw your old tire in the school Dumpster. I hope that was okay. See ya." He goes flying past me practically tripping and landing in the fire.

Then suddenly his words sink in. *I threw your old tire in the school Dumpster.* Rand changed my tire, not Lucas. This officially puts Lucas back into the doghouse big-time.

"And now the moment you've all been waiting for, this year's king, Rand Bachrach," Coach screams into the microphone with bulging eyes. I guess that burning pup got the coach all riled up. It's kind of fun sitting back watching everyone make total asses out of themselves. Students buzzing on school spirit are dancing dangerously close to the fire. The school will be lucky if someone doesn't get maimed tonight. Rand bounces on stage just in time. Angel bolts off the stage as soon as Rand gets on. How rude! Rand doesn't seem to notice or if he does, he doesn't care, which is pretty cool. Everyone starts his signature chant again, "Rand, Rand, you're our man." He stands there, looking embarrassed and pulling on his stocking cap. I have to admit he is sort of adorable, for a geek.

"Where's all your school spirit?" Tobi slams against my shoulder.

"This is about as excited as I get. Don't get me wrong. I want the Seagulls to beat the crap out of the Bulldogs. I just don't think me painting my face is gonna get the job done." We both start cracking up at the mere thought of me wearing face paint. *As if!*

Tobi suddenly gets serious, and says, "Aspen, don't kill the messenger, but I saw Angel locking eyes with Lucas during the intro . . ."

"Oh, I know. I saw it, too. They're both going to get it."

"That's not the worst part. I just saw them heading toward the school."

"What? Are you kidding me?" I shove my way through the crowd. Claustrophobia be damned. I've got a Seagal to exterminate.

"Do you want me to come with you?" She pulls on my sleeve.

"No, I need to do this alone." Unfortunately for Lucas and Angel it is a rather long walk back up to the school. I am pretty much plotting their deaths the entire way. I know Lucas wouldn't cheat on me. I mean, please, who in their right mind would cheat on me with her? But I'm also not blind. I recognize the powers that females wield over horny teenage boys. I've been known to wield my own powers from time to time. I can't wait to see the look on Angel's face when I break up her little attempt to make Lucas stray. Damn. She really has it out for me.

As I reach the parking lot I start to feel a familiar tugging sensation in my chest. My asthma. The smoke, hay, and all the Lucas drama have wreaked havoc on my mediocre respiratory system. But I'm no amateur; I've been dealing with this since I was seven. I know that I just need to calm down and pace myself until I can get to my locker to get my spare inhaler. Damn that Angel for getting me so upset.

As I breathe in the cold October air it refreshes me a little, but I hear a tiny whistle when I let it back out. It's never good when I start wheezing. I try to distract myself by thinking about something pleasant like my fabulous new homecoming dress. A simple black velvet tank dress with a pale pink ribbon weaved through the waist. I'm going to look fantastic. It's not working. I'm almost to the west entrance of the school. I'm wheezing heavy now, and with the little strength I have left, I fling the door open.

I don't even care about finding Lucas and Angel now. I just want to get to my locker. The lockers are assigned in alphabetical order. I entered the school on the Z end, and I'm a B, so I've still got to make it down the long hallway. The school is deserted even though I know that Lucas and Angel are in here somewhere. I hope they come out right this minute and see me struggling for every breath, wheezing like I smoke three packs a day, and feel eternally guilty for whatever they're up to. But they don't, and it's starting to feel like someone is sitting on my chest. My legs feel rubbery, and my vision is starting to get blurry. I've never had an attack like this before. I wonder briefly if I might die as I struggle to get air into my tightened esophagus. I hope Mom buries me in my homecoming dress. I hope Angel feels so responsible for my death and has so much self-loathing that she becomes a stripper. I hope Lucas picks up dog poop for a living. Finally, I stumble to my locker. I rest my face against the cool metal knowing everything is going to be all right. I remove the unlocked padlock and slide the handle up. I reach on the shelf above my books where I always keep my inhaler and feel nothing but picture frames.

I'm overcome with fear because I feel like no air is getting into my lungs. I panic and start throwing things out of my locker searching for my precious inhaler but it's not here. Fatigue overcomes me and I slide down my locker onto the floor. A horrible noise fills my ears. It sounds like a wild animal. The wild animal is me. I realize that I really might die. I curse myself for not having any purses to match this outfit therefore deciding not to bring one, resulting in not having an inhaler. Death by lack of accessories, the horror! I'm close to passing out when a picture passes through my mind of Lucas pulling a nudie pic from the top shelf in my locker earlier today. I remember when he did that my inhaler was lying where it always is. I didn't forget it. Someone took it. Angel.

Suddenly Rand is bending over me with his cell phone in one hand brushing my hair from my face with the other. As he hangs up I hear him tell me to try to relax. He kneels down on the floor and takes me in his arms. I have to tell him Angel did this to me, but I can't get anything out except large gasps. I hardly even know Rand, but I can tell by the expression on his face that he's scared shitless. I wonder if he'll come to my funeral? I really want him to see me in my awesome black dress. Rand and I are flying down the hallway. He's telling me to hang on so I wrap my arms tighter around his neck. He smells so good. It's getting really dark now.

Four

I must be in hell. There is no other explanation for this hideous gown I'm wearing. Mom and Dad are asleep on a leather couch in the corner, and Rand is coming into focus beside me. I guess I'm not in hell, just the hospital, wearing a garment from their fabulous fall line.

My hand is throbbing. I look down to see an IV protruding from the top of my left hand. I despise needles, and I can tell that this one is going to leave a huge black-and-blue mark. That's going to be a real cute accessory to go with my homecoming dress. I guess it's better than being dead though.

"You tell anybody you saw me wearing this, and you're dead meat," I tell Rand, but the harsh scratchy voice that comes out I don't recognize.

"Don't try and talk. They had to do some serious *ER* shit on you. Just relax and get some more rest. You're okay now."

For some reason I believe him, and I'm already feeling tired again, so I close my eyes. Before I drift back to sleep I feel Rand stroking my hair. It feels really good. There's nothing like a good hair rub. Even after a near-death experience, I've never felt so safe before. Then I remember I've got to tell Rand that Angel's the one who took my inhaler. My eyes pop open, and I jerk my head up at the same time that Rand is leaning in to kiss my forehead. His lips land square on mine. Instead of pulling away from him I wrap my IV-free arm around his neck and pull him closer. A few delicious seconds later, I realize that I'm in the hospital, wearing a butt-flashing gown, kissing the biggest geek in school. Either I'm in the psych ward or they gave me some serious freaking drugs. The weirdest part of all is that I don't want to stop kissing Rand. But I am Lucas's girl-friend and cheating is so white trash. Once our tongues take a rest I sort of roll onto my side without opening my eyes. Maybe Rand will think I was asleep the whole time and didn't know what I was doing. If he tells anybody we kissed, I could be like, "They had me so doped up I didn't know which end was up." Rand would look like a big perv who took advan-tage of a sickly girl. Oh, yeah, my alibi is so covered.

Rand lets out a loud breath and begins to stroke my hair again. I hope my eyes aren't fluttering and giving it away that I'm not really sleeping. Who could sleep after a kiss like that? It was perfect combination of lips and tongue. No slobbery mess to wipe off my chin like with Lucas. It was like one of those perfect kisses at the end of a chick flick. Who would have guessed Rand could kiss like that? I guess I should probably feel guilty cheating on Lucas and all, but Rand did save my life so the kiss was just a total obligatory one. Now that I think about it, the kiss doesn't really even count. It's like that whole "it's okay to kiss somebody else when you're in a different zip code than your boyfriend" thing. I guess when I was kissing Rand subconsciously I knew that. I feel so much better now that I know I didn't really cheat on Lucas.

The next morning, Mom is fussing over me like I'm a baby or something. She helped me get dressed, and now she is insisting on humiliating me by wheeling me downstairs to the car in a wheelchair. I tried to get up, but a nurse who looks like she might be on the women's weight-lifting circuit shoved me back down, muttering something about "hospital policy." I don't know what everybody's drug is, I feel totally fine. I stand up and open Mom's car door and get a bit woozy. Nurse Schwarzenegger grabs my arm and helps me into the car. Okay, maybe I'm not so fine. Mom thanks her and runs to get into the driver's side.

Flowers, balloons, and stuffed animals fill the backseat. I was only in the hospital for twelve hours, but I had like ten deliveries. The candy stripers, boy, were those a surly bunch, just kept bringing them in one after another. Most of the stuff is from Rand and Tobi. Lucas sent absolutely nothing and didn't even bother to call. If he isn't at least maimed, we are so broken up.

Rand kept popping by every couple of hours. He was always cracking jokes to pass the time until they released me. I can't believe I never knew how funny he is. There wasn't even any weirdness about the kiss. If I hadn't been obsessing half the night about how good it was, I might have thought I just dreamed it. Plus the nurses all treated me like a queen (or should I say princess, since my peers obviously don't think I'm queen material. Yes, I still have issues about losing the tiara). I overheard them talking about Rand's family donating a wing of the hospital. I guess that's what you have to do to get an extra blanket and a cup of ice chips around this place.

I think my almost-dying episode really scared Mom. I'm bracing myself for a lecture.

"Aspen, for the life of me, I cannot understand why you are so careless with your inhaler. You know you should have it with you all the time."

"I know, Mom. I'm sorry I worried you."

"It's okay, sweetie. I'm just glad you're okay." She softens while reaching over to gently touch the bruise my IV left on the top of my hand.

It takes every ounce of energy I have left not to defend myself, but if I tell Mom about all the crazy stuff Angel's been doing, she'll stomp right down to Miss Hott's office causing a big ruckus. And I've decided that I would rather handle Angel myself.

⌒

Against my will, I spend the rest of the day in bed. Luckily, today was an in-service day so I only missed a half day of school. I hate getting too far behind with my homework, plus I'm itching to get a piece of Angel Ives. My parents seem to think I'll be spending a few more days in bed, but I plan to convince them at dinner that I'm well enough to go back tomorrow. There is no way I'm missing homecoming week. I'm sure that is just what Angel had hoped for. *Think again, skank!*

Tobi's kept me updated on school news through e-mails and phone calls today. She said that I made the front page of the school newspaper with my near-death experience. They used this awesome picture of me in jean shorts and a bikini top from a charity car wash last year. I look so hot in that picture. If somebody took a popularity poll right now, I would knock Angel on her ass. I told Tobi about my suspicion that Angel stole my inhaler. She's going to put out a few feelers and see if she can get the 411. I have visions of holding Angel down and shaving her head before the dance to get even with her. I'm pretty strong, I could definitely take her. But until I have solid proof, I'm not going to indulge in any more fantasies.

Rand sent me another dozen light pink roses, in addition to the yellow ones he had delivered to the hospital, and the biggest box of chocolates I've ever seen in my life. The card just said, "Get some rest," and it was signed from "The King." He's really getting into all this homecoming stuff. He's definitely growing on me. Maybe I should try to hook him and Tobi up. She needs a boyfriend and Rand seems like he'd be a really great one. She doesn't even need to know about our kiss since it didn't really count.

Lucas is still AWOL. No flowers, candy, not even a free e-mail. I don't know what he is smoking lately, but if he thinks he can treat me this way, he's got another thing coming. I still haven't found out what happened between him and Angel, but I'm going to get to the bottom of it eventually.

I hear our doorbell ring. A few seconds later Tobi busts into my room. She looks uncharacteristically adorable today. Not that she isn't always cute, but today I can tell she *tried* to look cute. She's wearing a tartan plaid jumper with a navy turtleneck peeking out the top. Thick cream-colored tights cover her legs and penny loafers adorn her feet. Her magnificent auburn hair is loose in fat ringlets around her face instead of her trademark ponytail. Her midnight blue eyes are sparkling. I can tell she's got serious dish. I decide that grilling her about her appearance is going to have to wait, but I take a moment to feel proud as my great sense of fashion is obviously wearing off on her.

"Wow! These are the most beautiful roses I've ever seen." She says, tracing her finger along one of the outer blooms. She grabs the card and scrunches her face up. "Elvis is sending you flowers now? So he really is still alive? My mom's gonna be so excited." She laughs as she places the card on my vanity.

"So, what's going on?" I ask, distracting her so she doesn't question me again about the flowers. She doesn't need to know her soon-to-be boyfriend is sending me roses.

As if suddenly remembering her hot gossip, she gasps, "It's Angel. She's missing."

○

Tobi explains in great detail how right before the last bell rang, Miss Hott made an announcement that anyone who had seen Angel Ives since the bonfire should report immediately to the office. It didn't take long for the school grapevine to figure out that Angel's parents reported her missing. Lucas was the last person to see her, and he's not talking.

"You know what this is about, don't you?" I ask Tobi, still unfazed by her supposedly shocking news.

"That there is some psycho serial killer in Comfort kidnapping teenage girls?" She looks visible shaken by her own assessment.

"Tobi, come on. Comfort is the safest place in the world. Nothing ever happens here. Angel just knows that she's in deep shit because of everything she's done to me. But she can't run forever." I smirk.

Tobi gets an angry look on her face. "You know, Aspen. Not *everything* is about you." She spins on her penny loafers and rushes out the door, slamming it behind her.

Jeez! What's up her butt? I can't help it if Angel is jealous of me, and created this situation, and isn't a big enough person to deal with it. Now Angel's got everyone in Comfort panicked for no reason, and Tobi thinks I'm the bad guy. *Whatever.*

A few minutes later a knock on my door tells me that Tobi has come back to beg for my forgiveness. I'm going to overlook her harsh tone because she's obviously PMSing this week.

"Come in." I prop myself up in bed against my pillows and brace myself for her apology. The door opens, but it's not Tobi. Rand saunters in wearing a huge grin. I sink back into the pillows as I realize that my hair is greasy and I haven't even brushed my teeth today. The Nick & Nora pj's I'm wearing are adorable, but I'm not exactly making a fashion statement. Why am I even stressing? It's only Rand and he's already seen me today at the hospital.

"Hey there, pretty lady," he says, immediately putting my lack-of-hygiene fears to rest. He shuts my door and takes a seat at the foot of the bed. He playfully grabs my foot through the comforter until I squeal. It's weird how comfortable we are together after only one day.

"I don't think pretty would describe my unhygienic condition today, but thanks. And thanks for the flowers, oh, and the chocolate. I've never seen a box of chocolate that big before."

"My mom insisted on the chocolate. She says its good for the soul."

Hmm. So his mom knows about me. Very interesting.

I watch him shrug out of his jacket as his eyes take in the photos taped to my vanity. They stop on a photo of Lucas and me at a carnival taken just a few weeks ago. He doesn't say anything, but I get the feeling he's a little jealous. I don't know why, but I kind of like it. But the most Rand and I are ever going to be is friends. Not that I'd ever want more or anything.

"So, I hear Angel Ives is missing. What a shame," I say sarcastically.

"Oh, you already know about that, huh?"

"Yeah, Tobi told me. It's obviously all a bunch of garbage though. She's just knows she is going to be in deep shit when everybody finds out it was her who took my inhaler."

Rand's eyes bulge out behind his thick glasses in disbelief. "Angel stole your inhaler out of your locker? How do you know?"

"Oh, please. This has got Angel's name all over it. I bet that's why she was going into the school last night. Lucas was probably just following her to use the bathroom." Rand's eyebrows shoot up.

"What?" I ask.

"Nothing, you're probably right. I don't think it's a good idea for you to tell people she's done this stuff without having some proof though, especially now that she's missing." He pulls his coat back on and I'm disturbed at how disappointed I feel knowing he's leaving soon. What is my problem?

"Where are you going?" I ask, hating that I sound like a jealous girlfriend.

"Some Detective Malone down at the police station wants to question me." He drops his eyes to my bedspread.

"What could you know? You were with me the whole time."

Rand starts fidgeting with the zipper on his jacket and scoots toward my door. "It's just routine, I guess," he answers without looking up. He begins twisting my door handle until I'm afraid it might break off in his hand. This is not the Rand I know. He's definitely hiding something.

Why on earth would Comfort's doughnut-eating civil servants want to question Rand? What could he possibly know about Angel's supposed disappearance, and why is he suddenly acting so strange? I may not be some fancy girl detective, but I've been known to get things out of people, especially people of the male persuasion. I think it's time to bust out some of my girly charms.

"Can't you stay for just a few more minutes?" I plead while patting my side of the bed for him to come sit by me. His eyes dart to mine, soften, and then dart away again. He moves slowly toward me and gently lowers himself down beside me.

I reach up and take his glasses off, which is a serious improvement. He definitely needs to invest in contacts. I start to run my fingers through his unruly curls working my way down to his neck. I start to massage his neck and feel him relax again under my fingers. I hear him start to breathe quicker, then he closes his eyes.

I lean in so close that I can feel his breath on my top lip. I started out seducing him to get the 411 on Lucas and Angel, but now I just want to feel his lips on mine and I don't really care what he knows. I close my eyes and softly place my lips on top of Rand's, praying I don't have funky breath.

He immediately stiffens and pulls back.

"You don't really want to kiss me. This is just a means to an end," he says, jumping off the bed.

Why did he have to go and get all philosophical on me? I want to tell him that I really did want to kiss him but I just can't admit that. Admitting to wanting to kiss a geek? That would be like admitting that I think Paris Hilton is talented. Even if they are true, some things just shouldn't be said out loud. So I sit stunned and don't say anything.

After staring each other down for a few seconds he moves to the door.

"Take care of yourself, Aspen," he says, not bothering to look back.

❍

Did he actually just turn down kissing *me*? No guy has ever turned down kissing me! I even know some girls who want to kiss me! Who does he think he is? It is absolutely infuriating when I don't get my way and I really wanted to kiss Rand. Well, he's never going to get the chance again and when he realizes that he could have had seven minutes in heaven with yours truly he'll be begging for some lip action. And I will so tell him it's not happening. Maybe. Depending on what mood I'm in and if he smells as good as he did today.

He must be kind of mental. It's the only explanation. He got so weirded out when I asked what he knew about Angel. Surely he couldn't have had something to do with her disappearance?

All these high-maintenance visitors have worn me out. Mom brings me a tray of chicken and stars soup, Goldfish crackers, and a frosty cold mug of milk, all my favorites when I'm sick. After eating, I bury down into my covers and drift to sleep with a smile on my face, dreaming about Angel making her grand entrance at homecoming with her tiara taped atop her shiny bald head.

What feels like several hours later, but a quick glance at my bedside clock is really only forty-five minutes, Mom comes into my room waking me up and telling me to get dressed and come downstairs. She has a worried look on her face when she closes my door behind her. I pull back my shade to see a police cruiser in our driveway. Jeez! What now? Can't a person be allowed to recuperate from a near-death experience in peace? I slip into my most comfortable jeans, a pale yellow fisherman sweater that brings out my highlights and slide a headband thru my shoulder-length hair. A few swipes of lip gloss later and if it wasn't for the ugly bruise on the top of my left hand, you wouldn't have a clue anything was ever wrong with me.

I start my normal bounce down the stairs, then suddenly feel light-headed. Maybe I'm not feeling as great as I thought. I slow my pace and eventually reach the bottom of the stairs to see my parents gathered at the kitchen table with a uniformed officer. I was expecting a Rick Schroeder look-alike but this guy is tall, lanky, and extremely hairy. The scary thing is that I know this even though he has a long-sleeved shirt on. Thick black hair is escaping from the cuffs of his sleeves, the neck of his shirt, and even from his nostrils. He holds his hand out for me to shake, and it is only the fear of being arrested that makes me touch him even for a millisecond.

"Hi, Aspen, I'm Detective Malone. I'm just here to ask you a few questions about Angel Ives. Can you tell me about the last time you saw Angel?" He asks, immediately starting a barrage of questions.

I move over to an empty seat and settle myself, trying to stop my head from spinning. I think my body needs more sustenance than soup. Maybe Mom will make me a cheese toastie when this hairy guy leaves.

"Aspen, honey, he asked you when you last saw Angel?" My mom interrupts after I've waited too long to answer. "You'll have to forgive her, Harry. She's had a rough night."

Ha! His name is Harry, that's classic. I wonder how Mom knows his first name?

"So I heard. It sounds like you were lucky Mr. Bachrach found you when he did."

I smile at him and nod my head yes. He's fishing, I can tell by the look in his eyes. I've got this gift of having a sixth sense about people. He probably thinks this is going to be the big break that bumps him up to sergeant. He'll be so disappointed when Angel returns home with her hands full of shopping bags.

"Your father and I went to high school with Harry . . . uh, Detective Malone." Mom babbles nervously. The detective nods his head and smiles.

"Oh, yeah. Your parents and I go way back." He throws his head back, laughing.

"Hey, now. It hasn't been that long," Dad jokes.

"I can't believe you guys have a daughter old enough to be a senior. Man, I feel old. Here's my family." He whips out a wallet and shows us a picture of him surrounded by a tall, beautiful blonde and three tiny versions of her. How in the world did this guy snag a hottie? If he wasn't in the picture, I would have sworn he was lying and that this was the picture that came with the wallet when he bought it.

"They are so beautiful, Harry," Mom coos.

The detective turns to me and asks, "Can you believe I used to be in love with your dad's girlfriend?" He laughs hysterically.

"Mom?" I ask with a twinge of horror in my voice.

The three of them get a good chuckle out of this. Mom composes herself first and answers. "No, sweetie. It was a girl Dad dated before me."

I was gonna say. As if my mom would ever give this guy the time of day.

"Wow, Harry," Dad pipes up, "I forgot all about that. Did you guys ever get together?"

"Nah, I was too shy to approach her. Thankfully I grew out of that." He says tapping the picture of his wife.

Okay, I already know way too much information about this guy. I decide to interrupt their little trip down memory lane. "So, you're here about Angel?"

They all look guilty remembering that this isn't a social call. The detective quickly slips back into his stern I'm-all-business mode.

"Yes, Aspen. When was the last time you saw her?"

"The last time I saw Angel was at the bonfire. She's a Seagal and she was cheering. A few minutes later, I saw her heading toward the school with Lucas Riley. I was on my way to find them when I had my attack."

"Why do you think they were headed toward the school? Everybody else went to the football field for doughnuts and hot chocolate, right?" He pulls out a tiny spiral notebook from his front pocket and starts jotting down notes.

"I have no idea what they were doing. That's what I was going to find out."

"Do you normally stalk people?" He gives me a challenging look. I don't like this guy. He's trying to get a rise out of me, and it's working. I'm just going to give it to him straight.

"Only when they're trying to steal my boyfriend."

"Lucas Riley is your boyfriend?" He looks genuinely surprised.

"Yeah, why?"

"Aspen, honey, let the detective ask the questions," my dad chimes in nervously.

"It's okay, Dan. I was just under the impression that you and Rand Bachrach were kind of an item. I just got done talking to him and it was pretty apparent how much he cares for you . . ."

"Now listen here, Rand and I are so not an item!" I yell, suddenly getting an adrenaline rush. "You make sure and write that down on your little paper. Lucas Riley is my boyfriend, not Rand Bachrach. Seriously, write that down and tell everybody." Detective Malone just stares at me with his pen paused in midair.

"Aspen," my parents both shout in unison. Detective Malone holds up his hand to signal that my outburst is not a problem.

"Well, miss. I'm afraid I have some bad news for you then. Your boyfriend was the last person to be seen with Ms. Ives, so he is a prime suspect in her disappearance. We don't have enough to charge him yet, but we will."

"This whole thing is so ridiculous. If you knew Angel, you would know that she's only doing this because she stole my inhaler, and now she's scared she's going to get into trouble. The only reason this is a big deal is because her family is richer than Bill Gates."

"Do you have proof that she stole your inhaler?" he asks, suddenly very interested in what I have to say again. I explain to him about the cheap lipstick message, the nudie pics, and the slashed tire. He is completely unconvinced that even if Angel was responsible for the aforementioned acts that she would deliberately try to harm me by stealing my inhaler.

"That's the point. I've never had an attack like that before, she couldn't have known it would happen." I hate that in a way I'm defending Angel. I just don't want homecoming week ruined any more than it has been because of her. "Can't you dust my locker for prints or something?" Maybe all those *CSI* episodes I watched are finally paying off.

"Even if her prints were there, she goes to your school. They are supposed to be there. Right now we are more concerned with finding Angel safe. Then I can question her about the inhaler." He answers, rising from the table. I see where I rate. I can't wait until Angel comes breezing back home, arms full of shopping bags, then I bet Detective Malone will be so pissed at her for wasting his time and blowing his promotion that he'll take me seriously.

"Thank you all for your time and if you think of anything else give me a call." He places a business card on the table.

"I'll show him out," I say, slowly rising from my chair so that I don't get light-headed again. I walk the detective to the front door, now safely out of my parents' hearing range.

"What did Rand say that made you think we were an item?" I ask, opening the front door.

"He didn't really say anything, I just thought I detected something more. Obviously I was wrong," he says, sarcastically, while patting the notebook in his front pocket. What a wise guy!

"Aspen, if you think of anything else, give me a call." He turns away from me and walks onto the front porch.

Suddenly he turns around and says, "By the way, Rand probably didn't mention this, but he was the last one to see Lucas and Angel together. From the way Rand described it, Angel had a mouthful of your boyfriend, and it wasn't his tongue in her mouth. It sounds like maybe you need to get a new boyfriend." With that he gets into his squad car and drives away while I'm left to pick my chin up off the front porch.

Five

"We are so broken up!" I scream into the phone. It took me about five seconds to get back to my bedroom and speed dial Lucas's cell phone after Detective Malone dropped his little bomb on me. I am so pissed at Lucas right now I think I could kill him. And why the hell didn't Rand tell me that he saw them together? This is beyond humiliating. Now everybody in school is going to know.

"Aspen?" a bewildered Lucas asks back.

"No, it's fucking Angel. Yes, of course, it's Aspen. As far as I knew I was still your girlfriend and now I find out from some hairy police detective that Angel was giving you head at the same time that I almost died in the hallway."

"Listen, Aspen, I've got to keep this line clear. Angel might be trying to call." And with that he has the colossal balls to hang up on me. I am so done with Lucas Riley. I hope they throw him in jail and some guy makes him his bitch for the rest of his life. I've got to call Tobi and tell her all of this. Oh crap! I keep forgetting. She's mad at me.

I suppose I should call and apologize even though I totally didn't do anything wrong. But I don't like fighting with Tobi and I need her help because now I'm not going to have a date for the homecoming dance. Which I guess isn't such a big deal because Tobi doesn't have a date either. I guess her and I could just go together. That kind of blows since it's my senior year though. Maybe I should try and seduce Jimmy McAllister since Angel's "missing." Nah, it wouldn't be any fun if Angel couldn't see me steal him away from her.

I suppose Rand would trip over his own feet to be my escort. Part of me feels like showing up with Rand just to shock people. But he knew about Lucas and Angel and didn't tell me. So no way is he getting off that easy. Besides, I'd look like a joke if I showed up at the dance with geeky Rand by my side. I've got a reputation to uphold. Even though he's kind of cute, and funny, and an amazing kisser.

I knew Tobi was crazy for thinking that Rand had a thing for me. If he did, he would have spilled the beans about Lucas's BJ to get his foot in the door with me. Instead he didn't even tell me. The really weird thing about all of this is that I'm more upset that Rand didn't tell me than that Angel blew my boyfriend. I thought Rand was so sweet. I mean, we kissed. Doesn't that automatically make him obligated to disclose any humiliating information he knows about me? Why am I obsessing about King Geek Rand anyway?

Determined to force all thoughts of Rand and his perfect lips from my mind, I jump off my bed and pull the picture of Lucas and me off my vanity mirror. I carefully rip it in half, throwing the Lucas half in my garbage can and sticking the half of me back on the mirror. Lucas is an idiot. I could get practically any guy in school to go out with me. He's going to realize what a skank Angel is and come crawling back on his knees. Then I'm going to kick him in the face.

I still have to convince my parents that I'm well enough to go back to school tomorrow. I put on my best fake smile and join them in the living room. I plop down next to Mom on the couch. Dad is dazed out watching something horribly educational on the History Channel and Mom is busy reading her Oprah magazine. Oprah is the God my mother worships. This gives me an idea.

"We should go to Chicago sometime, just me and you. We could get tickets to Oprah's show and go shopping. You know, just do the whole girl thing." I get an immediate reaction of elation from my mother, which is exactly what I was expecting. I feel a tiny twinge of guilt, but hey, sometimes a girl's gotta do what a girl's gotta do.

"Aspen, that's a great idea. Maybe we could get on her favorite things show and get a bunch of free stuff."

"I'll check her website and see about getting tickets," I answer back, knowing my foot is firmly in the door. "Actually, I could do that tomorrow during computer lab. I always finish my assignment early, so I'll have a little time to browse the Web." My parents are the only people in the free world who don't own a computer. Of course, I've got a laptop and the neighbors have wireless Internet so I connect here all the time but my parents don't have a clue about that. I wouldn't even try to explain it. They just totally don't get anything that doesn't have wires. They're still amazed by the remote control and our cordless phone.

Mom gets a worried look on her face. "I don't know, Aspen. You gave us a real scare. I think maybe you should rest a little more. Besides, now a girl is missing. That really scares me. What if it would have been you? It's scary. Her poor parents." Brilliant, why doesn't she just hand it to me on a silver platter? I suppose I should feel guilty about using my parent's naivete against them, but I just don't.

"Yeah, I've been thinking about that. You and Dad will both be gone to work and I'll be here all alone. I think I'd rather be around a bunch of people. I think I'd just feel more comfortable." I try to look terrified at the thought of being alone.

Mom looks to Dad, who just shrugs his shoulders, giving Mom permission to make the final call, as usual. She turns back to me, narrows her eyes, and starts jabbing her index finger toward me. Uh-oh. I've taken it too far this time.

"Don't think I'm not on to you. Because I am. I used to pull this shit with my parents, too. Okay, you can go to school, but if you start feeling bad, you call me immediately. And don't forget your inhaler and no overdoing it."

"I won't. I promise. Maybe you should write me a note to stay out of gym for a few weeks, too."

Mom nods her head in agreement and adds, "And Aspen, I don't think it's a good idea if you go around telling people that Angel stole your inhaler. Just keep that to yourself until they find her. Okay?"

I know that I have to agree or I'll be locked in my bedroom for the rest of the week. So I nod my head like a good daughter, give her a peck on the cheek, and start to run back upstairs to patch things up with my best friend.

Mom calls to me when I get halfway up the stairs. I peek my head over the banister, hoping she hasn't changed her mind.

"Don't forget about the Oprah tickets," she says, not even glancing up from her magazine.

Tobi answers her cell on the third ring. She was probably debating on whether to answer it or not. She must be super-pissed at me. I'm constantly pissing her off. She's always lecturing me about not appreciating the people in my life and being too self-centered. *Hello*, I'm the one who almost died and she's mad at me? But I'm going to be the bigger person and not remind her of that.

"What do you want?" she answers, obviously still very pissed.

"Tobi, I'm really sorry. Please forgive me. I should have taken Angel's disappearance seriously." I'm actually cringing as I say these words. It's a good thing I didn't have to apologize in person or I never could have done it with a straight face. "Have they found her yet?"

"I just got off the phone with Pippi and no one has heard anything yet. Her family thinks it might be a kidnapping because they're so rich, but no one's gotten a ransom note yet."

I know I should be focusing on what Tobi is telling me, but I can't seem to get past the fact that Tobi said she just got off the phone with Pippi. What in the hell is she doing cavorting with the enemy? I can't make an issue of this though or Tobi will go off on me again. I might be self-centered, but I'm not stupid.

"But why now? I mean Angel's family has been rich since her great-grandfather made up that Christmas song a million years ago. Why would someone want to kidnap her all these years later?" I delicately try to poke a hole in Tobi's theory without her realizing it.

Tobi lets out an exasperated sigh, and then says, "Aspen, I know you think she took off, but I really don't think she did. Lucas was the last one to see her, and that was when he walked her back to her car in the school parking lot last night."

"Oh, he did more than walk her back to her car." I'm feeling her out to see if she's already got the lowdown from Pippi.

"Yeah, I heard about the BJ. Sorry about that."

I have to bite back my anger. The total outrage. Tobi was trading gossip about me with Pippi. So far today, I've been screwed over by Rand, Lucas, and now Tobi. Who's next?

In a dignified tone, I ask, "So everybody knows already, huh?"

"Yeah, pretty much. But Lucas told everybody he had already broken up with you."

"What? He did not and you know it . . ."

"I know. I told Pippi that Lucas did no such thing, so even though Angel is missing, everybody knows that she's still a boyfriend-stealing ho bag."

"Thanks for defending me, Tobi." I breathe a sigh of relief.

Too bad the homecoming vote wasn't this week. I bet I could have swayed the girl vote once they found out Angel was sucking my boyfriend off while I was nearly dying.

"Aspen, could you just try to think of someone besides yourself every once in a while?"

I can't believe Tobi is talking to me this way. I can tell Pippi's got her brainwashed so I'm going to have to spend several days deprogramming her. I'm too tired to start right now, so I just agree and offer to pick Tobi up for school tomorrow.

⊚

Rand fixed Cookie up like new. I haven't gotten over being mad at him, but I do have to admit it was nice that he fixed Cookie. I haven't talked to him since his visit yesterday. Surprisingly, I really wanted him to call last night. I think I probably just wanted to bitch him out for holding out on me about Lucas and Angel.

I pull up in front of Tobi's house and she is already waiting on the front porch. Again, she looks like she jumped from the pages of a moderately fashionable magazine. She probably thinks I need cheering up about my breakup with Lucas. What a sweetie!

"You look adorable," I tell her once she's safely in and buckling her seat belt.

"You have taught me well, Master," she says in a fake Chinese voice while putting her palms together and bowing her head.

"I never thought you were actually paying attention."

We giggle and it feels good to have lost the friction between us.

"So who's going to be your victim for the homecoming dance?" she says playfully, messing with my radio stations.

"You know I've thought about it, and there really isn't anybody I want to go with. I thought maybe you and I could just hang out together."

I see her stiffen out of the corner of my eye. "Don't tell me you went and got yourself a date?" I tease.

"Not really, but I did tell Pippi she could ride with me. But all three of us could go."

I have to concentrate very hard not to drive my car right into a brick wall I'm so mad right now. My senior homecoming was supposed to be stellar. First, the insanity of Rand getting king totally blew. Then I lost my date to the person I detest most in the world. Now my best friend is ditching me for some redheaded freckle-faced freak show. This is not my idea of stellar. Maybe I should just stay home. I slowly take a few shallow breaths and shrug my shoulders like it's no big deal. "Don't worry about it, I'll figure something out." Tobi glances at me with shock. I can tell she expected my head to explode. The smile widening across her face tells me that she's proud of me for taking her news in stride. I smile, pushing back the tears forming in the corners of my eyes. Everyone seems to think I'm made of stone, but I'm actually pretty sensitive and I've just about had my fill the last few days.

We pull into school and part ways inside the door. I grab a newspaper out of the bin on the way to my locker. On the front page is a huge picture of Angel from last Halloween dressed up like an angel, complete with halo. The caption reads, "Where has our Angel gone?" *Please, freaking spare me.* I toss the paper into the garbage without even reading it.

Reaching my locker, I notice that it is disturbingly free of fingerprint dust. I thought maybe Detective Malone would reconsider, but obviously an "angelnapping" ranks higher than attempted murder.

As I pull open my locker door all my belongings come spilling out. Someone obviously just shoved everything back in after Monday night. Now, as if my day hadn't started out bad enough my entire locker contents are spilled onto the hallway, and the first bell just rang, making me late for first period. Fabulous. Maybe I should have stayed home today.

I figure if I'm already late, I might as well take my time, so I carefully stack my textbooks. I replace my picture frames on their shelf, but not before removing the picture of Lucas from one and throwing it into the hall.

"I could give you an after-school detention for littering, you know?" Rand's voice cheerily jokes behind me.

"Whatever," I respond, determined to give him the cold shoulder.

"Are you mad at me?" He leans on the locker beside mine, trying to make eye contact. I'm not in the mood for games this morning so I'm just going to let him have it.

"Um, yeah, you could say that. I had a Detective Malone question me last night and he dropped a little bomb on me before leaving. Something about you seeing Angel with a mouthful of Lucas. You wouldn't happen to know what he was talking about now, would you?" I cross my arms over my chest finally meeting his gaze.

As I do, I'm surprised at how cute he looks. I wasn't prepared for this and he smells incredible. I feel myself start to sweat even though I know the hallway is never over sixty degrees due to Miss Hott's new energy conservation program. My eyes fall to Rand's perfect pillowy lips. I have to remind myself I'm furious with him as I force thoughts of kissing him from my mind. He's wearing a tight black crewneck sweater and fitted khakis. I always thought he was scrawny, but he isn't. He must usually wear really baggy clothes because his physique really isn't that bad, especially his chest. What am I doing? I definitely should have stayed home today, I am not well.

Rand drops his gaze and I see the slight bit of pink start to tinge the skin on his neck above his sweater. "I was afraid you would think I was lying." He looks past me to avoid my eyes.

"Why would I think you were lying?"

"You know," he says, fidgeting. "I thought maybe you would think I was trying to steal you away from Lucas or something."

I start to laugh hysterically. From Rand's shocked face I can tell he has no idea why I'm laughing. "You," I say, pointing to him, "steal me away from Lucas. Are you kidding? Lucas is the quarterback of the football team. You're . . . wait, how should I say this . . . you're not really a threat to someone like Lucas Riley."

Why am I being so mean? I sure as hell don't think that cheating bastard of an ex of mine is better than Rand, so why in the hell did I just say all that? I'm just so mad at Rand for not telling me about Lucas and Angel. But mostly I just want to grab him and kiss him. I'm so confused. I wonder if Angel spiked my lip gloss with some mind-altering chemical. It's the only explanation.

His green eyes meet my violet ones again. I see the slightest flash of anger.

"Well, if that's really true, then why did you kiss me twice?" he replies, grinning devilishly.

I whip my head from side to side to make sure no one is in the hall with us. Luckily, the coast is clear. If that news got out, I'd be the laughingstock of the school. "Will you shut up? That whole thing was a big mistake, and you better never tell anyone. It's not like anyone would believe you anyway." I narrow my eyes at him, giving him my bitchiest expression.

We stare each other down in silence for a few seconds. Then Rand says, "I was so wrong about you, Aspen." The look he gives me nearly causes me to double over in pain. I want to take back every word. I want to defend myself and tell him that Lucas is pond scum compared to him. But I don't say anything.

Suddenly Rand grabs my waist and pulls me to him. His lips come crashing down on mine and I'm happy because I know I don't have to explain myself to him. He already knows. Our tongues move expertly in and out of each other's mouths. One of his hands rests at the base of my neck while the other runs down my back. I've never been kissed like this. It's hot. So hot that I see a flash behind my closed eyes. Rand is literally making me see stars. Suddenly, cruelly, he pulls away.

Holding my face in his hands, he says, "I was so crazy about you." Then he turns and walks away. What have I done? I stand paralyzed with shock. What is happening to my life? A few days ago I couldn't have picked Rand out of a crowd. Now, watching his gorgeous butt walk away, I feel like I've lost everything. And even though I can still see him walking down the hallway, I miss him already.

Six

I'm sitting in accounting class trying very hard to focus on Mr. Lowe's incredibly mind-numbing lecture about straight-line and accelerated depreciation. I am borderline low A/high B in this class and a B will not cut it. My mind is not cooperating and it just keeps playing back the kiss Rand and I just shared. I can safely say I've never been kissed like that. If I could bottle the feeling that kiss gave me, I'd be a freaking millionaire. Now I've gone and screwed things up royally. Maybe I'll just break down and finally tell Tobi about the kisses and see what advice she has for me. Surely I can think of something to get Rand to forgive me. I'm a very resourceful girl when the situation calls for it.

With that settled, I'm ready to start learning. I crack open my textbook and as I do a note comes flying out. It slides to the front of the room and lands right under Mr. Lowe's shoe.

Crap. I don't even remember any notes being in my book. Lucas usually just texts me and Tobi and I have practically all the same classes so we just sit next to each other and chat whenever we want.

Mr. Lowe gives me an evil glare as he bends to pick up the note. He carefully unfolds it and begins reading it aloud. This is his standard practice. He has no life so it gives him great pleasure to completely humiliate his students. I slink down in my seat and pray that the note is some kind of shopping wish list or something.

"Okay, class, let's see what Aspen has to say that just couldn't wait until the end of class." He clears his throat then begins, "Tobi, what's up?" Okay, so far so good, nothing incriminating. It does bother me that I have absolutely no recollection of writing this note though. "Doesn't Mr. Lowe look totally hot today? I want to have sex with him *so* bad!" My scream reverberates around the classroom as Mr. Lowe just realizes what he read. The class erupts into hysterical laughter. I look over to Tobi for sympathy and I could swear that I see her wink at Pippi. What is happening to my world?

"Aspen, go to Miss Hott's office right now," Mr. Lowe shouts above the laughter. I gather my books and flee out the door. I rush to my locker and jam my books inside then head to Miss Hott's office. Surely she will see that there is no way that someone like me would be writing dirty notes about Mr. Lowe. Just the thought of it makes me want to hurl my breakfast.

When I get there, her office door is cracked. I knock gently, hoping she doesn't hear me—then maybe I can just skip out of school for the rest of the day.

"Come on in," I hear her perky voice chirp. Damn. I walk in and shut the door behind me. I sit down, take one look at Miss Hott, and burst into tears.

"Aspen, honey, what's wrong?" She pulls her bulky frame around the desk to take a seat next to me. She hands me a tissue and pats my shoulder trying to be consoling. I milk the crying session for a bit because I really don't want to tell her about the note. But I can't just sit here bawling forever or she might send me to the school shrink.

"Mr. Lowe sent me down here because he found a note. It fell out of my book. But I didn't write it, I swear."

"That doesn't sound like such a big deal. We should be able to tell from the handwriting that it wasn't written by you."

"That's not the worst part. He read it in front of the whole class. It was horrible. Everybody is going to make fun of me." I start getting misty-eyed again.

"I highly doubt it's that bad. What did it say?"

I bury my face in my hands because I can't bear to face her while I say this. "It said that I wanted to have sex with Mr. Lowe." The tears are flowing freely now as I heave in and out hysterically. My life is ruined. The entire student body thinks I want to have sex with a teacher. Not even a hot teacher, a gross one.

"Oh, dear. Why would anyone want to write a note like that?"

I didn't have an answer. Normally I would have blamed it on Angel, but my textbook was only in my locker for a few minutes while I went to the bathroom before class. If it were Angel, somebody would have noticed her, and some huge announcement would surely have been made about the queen's miraculous return. *Gag!* I've really got to start locking my locker.

Realizing that Miss Hott is waiting for an answer I respond, "I don't know. In the last few days I've had my locker filled with porn, a nasty message written on the bathroom mirror, my tire slashed, my inhaler stolen, and now this. Somebody wants me to suffer, but I don't know why."

"Don't worry about the note. I'll talk to Bob and let him know that you didn't write it. Maybe everything else is just a coincidence." Great! So much for getting help from the leader of this fine establishment. It looks like I'm going to have to figure this all out on my own.

"Okay, thanks," I answer, knowing that this is a dead end, and if I'm going to start figuring out who is torturing me, I better get started right away.

I get up and start toward the door when Miss Hott says, "Aspen, it's okay to be worried about Angel. We all are. I hope I'll see you at the candlelight vigil tonight." I nod my head yes and close the door.

So now they're having a candlelight vigil? My life is falling apart and I'm expected to stand outside freezing my ass off while hot candle wax drips onto my perfect French manicure? I don't think so.

I was only in Miss Hott's office for a few minutes, but as I get near my locker I can see that someone had enough time to seriously defile my locker. People are standing around because there are still a few minutes before second-period bell rings. Everyone is pointing to what I can now see. As humiliated as I am by the scene depicting me having sex with Mr. Lowe, I have to admit that someone has got a promising career in caricature.

"What the hell is everybody staring at? Does anyone here honestly believe that someone like me would have sex with someone like Mr. Lowe? I mean, seriously." The group seems to agree that the very idea of it is ludicrous and they start to scatter about their business. Relieved, I open my locker, grab my English text and a fresh notebook and jog to class to avoid another tardy.

Luckily, Tobi sits next to me in this class, too, so I can get to the bottom of that little wink she shared with Pippi. Could Tobi possibly be behind some of these horrible intrusions into my life? Maybe she's tired of being the sloppy sidekick and wants to ruin me. It could happen. They make movies about this stuff all the time.

"So, you wanna get it on with Bob, huh?" Tobi asks, barely able to contain herself. I narrow my eyes into slits and slowly look her up and down. Yet again she has pulled together a stylish ensemble. I haven't seen her wear her signature outfit of holey jeans and T-shirt proclaiming some smart-ass slogan for more than a week now. Something's going on and it smells fishy.

"*You* wouldn't happen to know anything about that note, would you, Tobi?" I don't bother to hide the suspicion in my voice.

"Are you on glue? How would I know anything about it? I kinda thought you did it as a joke."

"Oh yeah, it's real funny to make myself look like a total ass in front of the entire school. Why were you winking at Pippi anyway?" By the look on her face I can tell my question surprised her.

"I wasn't winking at anybody. You're seeing things." She drops her eyes while doodling on her notebook. She is *so* busted. How could she team up with Angel and Pippi? We've been best friends for years, and this is how she repays me. Just the thought of the three of them huddled together plotting my takedown is enough to make me lose it. I gather my books and approach Mr. Hamilton's desk. I mutter something about not feeling well. He doesn't question me since the whole school knows about my near-death experience. I'm out the door, ignoring Tobi's fake looks of concern.

I shove my books into my locker and race outside to Cookie. In a few minutes I'm safely home with a pint of Chubby Hubby consoling me.

Between spoonfuls, I alternate between rage and desperation. Everyone I know has betrayed and abandoned me. My boyfriend dumped me for a total skank. My best friend is trying to destroy me. And the boy who kisses better than anybody in the whole world hates me. My life is over.

I'm about to wing my spoon into the sink when I hear a noise coming from upstairs. I freeze, holding the spoon in midair. My parents are at work and no one else has a key to our house. Hurried footsteps creak above me. What if Comfort really does have a kidnapper and he's come for me next?

I gently place my spoon on the countertop and reach for my keys. I'm so scared I don't even worry about leaving my Dooney behind. I tiptoe through the living room and am almost to the front door when someone comes barreling full speed down the staircase.

I hold my key out to try to jab them in the eye and scream at the top of my lungs.

"Aspen, what are you doing here?" I hear Mom ask in a snippy voice. My heart rate instantly lowers as I realize I'm not about to be kidnapped.

"What are you doing here?" she repeats, much louder this time.

Great. Lucas cheated on me. Rand hates me. The whole school thinks I fantasize about Mr. Lowe and now Mom is yelling at me. I'm almost ready to burst into tears when it clicks in my head that *she's* not supposed to be here either. And why is she so defensive? It isn't like this is the first time I've skipped out of school. Then I remember how she lied to me about being at work. The pieces start to snap into place.

As she stands with her fists on her hips waiting for me to answer I search her face. She's a brick wall. But my gut tells me I'm right. A noise comes from upstairs and her eyes give her away.

I turn and run up the stairs as fast as I can. Mom's having an affair. She actually brought some stranger into our home to have sex on her lunch hour. My parents are going to end up another sad divorce statistic and I'll be a latchkey kid.

"Aspen, I can explain," Mom shouts, coming up behind me breathless.

I get to my parents bedroom and expect some Fabio-looking character to be sprawled out naked on the bed. But the bed is made, military corners and all, just like Dad leaves it every morning.

"Come out here and face me like a man, you freaking coward," I say, flinging the closet door open.

I don't see a man, but I suppose he could be hidden under the mountains of shoeboxes and shopping bags in here. Mom must be getting some serious kickbacks from her personal shopping job.

"There's no man in here." I say, stunned, shutting the closet door behind me.

"Why would there be a man in here?" Mom asks, sinking down onto the bed.

"Duh, because you're cheating on Dad."

Her gasp is so heartfelt it gives me goose bumps. How could I have ever thought she would cheat on Dad? It's official. I've totally lost my mind.

Mom sits on the bed with her face buried in her hands, sobbing. I can now add "shattered Mom's feelings" to my list of horribly shitty things I've accomplished today. I sink down next to her and wrap my arms around her.

"Let's not tell Dad about this, okay?" I plead.

Mom looks up at me, her mascara running down her cheeks, and nods her head violently. She must think I'm horrible for accusing her of doing something behind Dad's back.

I keep forgetting how stressful her job is; she's a personal shopper for senior citizens, and those are a cranky bunch. It's such a relief to know that she was just home blowing off some steam and not some guy.

◎

"I'm sorry, Aspen, but I just don't think Tobi could possibly be involved in all of this. She's been such a good friend to you. I think you should hold off on falsely accusing her until you have more evidence." Mom says, always the advocate for innocent until proven guilty.

"I just can't figure out any other way that the note could have gotten into my book. But I'll hold off on jumping down her throat. At least for now."

"Okay, so what else is bothering you?" She pitches the empty ice cream container I left sitting on the counter into the trash. She can always tell when something is wrong. It's genetic. We both hit the ice cream when our lives are turned upside down.

I pull the blanket from the back of the couch and wrap it around myself. Mom sits down across from me in the recliner. She's changed out of her suit and into a ratty flannel shirt and sweatpants. Amazingly, she still looks incredible. There's no doubt about it, I've got good genes.

"What?" She sticks her tongue out at me.

"I was just thinking that it's good to know I'll still be hot when I get all old." I laugh.

"Watch it." She wags her finger at me. "I may be old but I could still kick your butt." She thinks she's a badass just because she took some self-defense class. "Seriously, Aspen, what's wrong? Are you still bummed because you didn't get queen?"

"No. I mean, I am. But it's just lots of stuff," I answer back vaguely.

"Do I have to beat it out of you?" She jumps off the recliner, coming toward me. Before I can move she's got one of my arms twisted behind my back and is pointing two fingers in my face to gouge my eyes out.

"You're a total psycho." I wriggle out of her loosened grip. "But I guess you're a little tougher than I thought." Satisfied at my compliment she plops back down in the recliner.

"Now spill before I really do some damage."

"Lucas cheated on me with Angel the night I had my asthma attack."

"That little shit. Wait. Do you think he had something to do with her disappearance?"

"I'm telling you, Angel isn't missing. She's just doing this for the drama. Even if she was missing, Lucas isn't smart enough to pull something like that off."

"Amen. I never knew what you saw in him in the first place."

"Thanks for clueing me in. So now I don't have a date for the dance. It's my senior year and I'd rather skip the dance than go stag."

"Isn't there anyone else you like?"

"Well, there is someone. But he isn't the type of guy I usually go for. He's . . . kinda of . . . well . . . he's a nerd," I say, cringing. My mom has never had an uncool moment her entire life so I know she has to be screaming inside right now. She's been behind me all my life helping me achieve the status I have and now I thank her by trashing it all to fall for a geek.

"What do you mean? He's a geek?" She looks confused. I didn't think she would take it this hard.

"You know, he kind of falls at the lower end of the high school social food chain."

"So why do you like him?" She sounds angry. I knew I shouldn't have told her this. It was probably hard enough on her that I didn't get homecoming queen, now I go and dump this on her, too.

"I didn't really know I did until just now. We've kissed and it was just different from any of the other times I've kissed guys before. Rand is just really funny and sweet . . ."

"Wait a minute. Isn't Rand the boy who saved you?"

"Yeah, why?"

"I forgot all about him. He was so sweet. We talked for hours while you slept."

"You did? About what?" I hope the answer isn't going to completely humiliate me.

"Everything really. He's a very well-read young man. And he's crazy about you."

"Yeah, well, not anymore. I was really mean to him today."

"So just call him and apologize."

"There's more to it then that, Mom. We're from totally different classes. People would totally freak out if they saw us together."

"You know, I've gone along with the homecoming queen stuff because I knew how bad you wanted it. But, Aspen, I didn't raise a snob. You may be better-looking than a lot of people. But that doesn't make you *better* than them. I need to show you something." She quickly runs up the stairs and a few seconds later I hear her rummaging around in her closet.

A few minutes later, she comes back down the stairs with an armful of books. She deposits them onto the island in the kitchen. I get up to join her.

"What is all this stuff?" I ask, sitting cross-legged on a padded barstool.

"This is something I've hid from you for far too long." She leafs through what appears to be her high school yearbook.

"I thought you said you lost these." I try to look over her shoulder.

She looks up and has big tears forming in her eyes. She looks terrified. I'm scared to know what she's going to tell me. Is she really a man? No, it can't be that, I've seen her naked. Maybe Dad is a chick. No, he grows facial hair by the minute. Before I can imagine anything else she spins the book around to face me and gestures to a photo.

In the grainy black-and-white photo a young girl stares back at me. The girl has a serious unibrow, her makeup looks to have been applied by a blind person, and she has enough hairspray in her five-inch-high bangs to be held personally responsible for the hole in the ozone layer. I don't get it. Why would my mom be showing me some picture of the next contestant of *Extreme Makeover*?

"That's me," she whispers, then buries her face in her hands. I hear myself scream for the second time that day.

I've studied the picture for a full five minutes. I still can't believe this person is my mother. My "makeup always applied lightly to look natural, eyebrows waxed every other week, hair kept in place perfectly with barely any product" mother was originally a total geek! I feel like she's just told me I was adopted or something. It's all so scandalous.

"Does Dad know about this?" I ask, suddenly worried that she may have tricked my dad somehow.

"That's my whole point." She grabs the book back, flipping frantically through the pages. I can't say I'm disappointed to see her turn the page. Looking at that picture was very unsettling. She finally finds what she was looking for and spins the book around again to face me. She points to a candid photo of my dad with his arm draped around a good-looking blonde. My dad looks almost exactly the same. He was adorable even way back in the eighties. I guess I know where I get my looks from now.

"Wow! Dad looks exactly the same. He's always been a hottie, huh?"

"Your dad was very popular in school, and obviously, you can tell the same wasn't true for me. But he didn't care what people thought. He knew he was in love with me, and that was all that mattered to him. I just want you to realize that in a couple of months you aren't even going to see half of those people again until your twentieth-class reunion. Do you really want to miss out on the love of your life because you were afraid of what those people thought?"

She's absolutely right. To hell with my status, I'm going to start dating a geek. But first I have to get that geek to forgive me.

"Mom, I've got a phone call to make." I bolt up the stairs to my bedroom.

I rummage through my junk drawer for the mini-directory the school hands out at the beginning of every school year. It conveniently lists everyone's cell phone number. I page through the B section until I finally spot Rand's number. I frantically dial not even sure what exactly I'll say. After four rings it rolls to his voice mail. This is not something I want to leave on his voice mail, so I hang up. I try the number listed for his home phone and a polite older gentleman tells me, "Mr. Bachrach is gone for the evening," in a very stiff voice. Crap. I bet he's at the vigil for Angel. I'm not going anywhere near Pippi, Tobi, and fire (they're probably planning to singe my eyebrows off or something) so I'll just have to tell Rand tomorrow.

Exhausted from a long day, I climb into bed, but after a few minutes my mind is still racing. I switch on my bedside lamp and grab a notebook and pen. I quickly jot down a little note to Rand. I'm afraid if I wait until tomorrow to tell him how I feel, I might chicken out. But if I wake up in the morning and see this note, I'll remember the same feelings I have tonight. The note isn't some mushy piece of garbage proclaiming him the new owner of my heart. It's just me telling him that I think he is really cool and I'd like to hang out more. Nerd or not, I don't want to give him the upper hand. After reading the note over, I'm satisfied, I shut off the light, and fall asleep imagining Rand and I slow dancing at the homecoming dance. I look so good in my dress . . .

I had a nightmare that I woke up and had my mom's unibrow. I nearly screamed until I looked into the mirror and my own perfectly sculpted brows stared back at me. I woke up early so I took extra care getting ready. I laid out a black cashmere V-neck sweater, a pleated red plaid skirt, black tights, and black Mary Janes with a kitten heel to make my legs look longer. Rand won't be able to resist me.

The stars are aligned and my hair turns out perfect. The weather is even cooperating with little wind and no rain. I jump into Cookie and head toward school. This afternoon was supposed to be the homecoming carnival, but Miss Hott felt that we should cancel it in light of Angel's disappearance. So instead of having a half day of classes and a half day of fun now we have a full freaking day of classes. *Thanks for ruining something else, Angel.*

The local television station has been running constant coverage of Angel's disappearance and they have camped out across the street from school. As I drive by I see the familiar face of the news anchor. It's almost like seeing a celebrity. She's holding a microphone and I realize she's live as I drive by. I get excited thinking that Cookie and I may be on the evening news. This day just couldn't get any better.

As I glide to my locker I notice that everybody is buzzing around whispering about something. A couple of people point at me, and I figure it's just because I look so good and they're jealous. As I pull my twenty-pound accounting book out to get ready for first period I try to be subtle about looking around for Rand. I want to get him alone once everybody else goes to class. Maybe we can even sneak in another one of those delicious kisses. Just the thought of it gets my body tingling.

"You're all dolled up today," Tobi says, sneaking up on me.

I shrug my shoulders, like my appearance didn't take me an extra hour and mutter, "Whatever."

"Somebody said there was a new kid. I've overheard the adjectives—gorgeous, beautiful, totally fucking hot, and loaded. I'm thinking he's a keeper."

The entire student body goes into heat whenever we get a new student. We rarely get fresh meat so everybody goes on the prowl, especially if the person is at all attractive. Angel will be so disappointed that she isn't getting first dibs. For the first time ever I don't care about turning the new guy's head. I just want to talk to Rand.

"Whatever." I'm hoping she'll get bored and leave. I so don't trust her anymore.

"You need a new line, Aspen. By the way, I can't believe you didn't tell me about this." She throws a school newspaper at me before storming off.

I look down at the front page of the paper. It's a picture of Rand and me kissing yesterday at my locker with the caption, "While the queen is away, the king will play."

Holy shit!

Seven

If this had happened a few days ago, I would have completely lost it. Tangible evidence, in the form of our cheesy school newspaper, that I've swapped spit with Rand is in the hands of every student right this very moment. But after Mom's revelation and some soul-searching, I realized that sometimes you just can't help who you fall for. I'm not saying that I love Rand, but I know I'm in serious like. Even if he doesn't fit the Blaine prototype I usually go for. He's adorable. I want to be with him, and I don't care if everybody knows about it. Actually, I want everybody to know about it. Now I just have to convince Rand that I'm for real.

I'm a little disappointed that Rand isn't waiting at my locker for me. But I don't blame him for being mad. I was a total beyotch yesterday. I've got some serious groveling to do. First, I want to put our first official picture on display in my locker. I wonder what Rand thought when he saw it? I carefully rip the newspaper along the outlines of our intertwined bodies. I stick the picture into a pink heart frame and prop it up on my locker shelf. The black and white photo of our passionate kiss is so romantic. It reminds me of the poster in Miss Hott's office. I trace the outline of Rand's body with my fingertip. He looks so sexy with his arms around me. Tobi is right about one thing. For somebody so brilliant, I can be extremely dense sometimes. How was I so oblivious to Rand for so long? I'm not wasting another second. Screw accounting class, I don't want to look at gross Mr. Lowe anyway. I'm going to hunt Rand down and tell him how much I want him.

As I slam my locker shut, Amy, one of the zombie Seagals, comes rushing toward me. At the last moment she makes a beeline around me. I turn to see where she's going. She drapes her arms around an absolutely beautiful male specimen who is headed straight for me.

This must be the new student that everyone was in such a twitter about. Except the "new" student is Rand. Either that or Rand has a totally freaking hot twin. When Amy finally moves to the side, I can finally take in his miraculous transformation. His glasses are gone, but I recognize those dazzling evergreen eyes. Eyes that seem to display disgust. Yep, this is definitely Rand.

He's still really pissed at me, but I'm too amazed at the moment to care about the dirty look he's giving me. Clay Aiken must be somewhere crying because Rand obviously stole his stylist. Short, spiky, strawberry blond locks replace his previously unruly curls. The form-fitting navy blue sweater and tight khakis cling to a body that I just can't wait to get my hands on. He is gorgeous. I am speechless.

"This is what you wanted, right, Aspen? Someone who would look good on your arm? Someone you wouldn't be embarrassed to have your picture taken with? Someone who treats you like you're garbage?" He's right in my face now. Amy is pawing all over him. Seeing her touch him is making me crazy. Could this possibly be what jealousy feels like?

Hot Rand obviously still has serious' tude about me dissing our exchange of spit. Normally I wouldn't have any problem coming up with something witty to say to win him over. But the alluring musky scent radiating from Rand is slowly working its way to my nostrils, overpowering my olfactory sense. I just want him to grab me and kiss me like he did yesterday. Leaning against my locker I try to form cohesive sentences. I can't let Rand see how his new look has affected me or he will never believe I already liked him.

His head is tilted to the side and he is waiting for me to respond. I look from him to Amy then back again.

"Hey, Amy, make like a tree and leave," I say, glaring at her. She looks to Rand who nods his head. She sticks her tongue out at me and spins on her heels. She takes off down the hallway muttering under her breath. The first-period bell rings and the final stragglers rush to class. It's just me and Hot Rand alone in the hallway.

"Listen, Rand, I know I've been a jerk. I don't blame you for being mad, but I really like you. You're funny, smart, and I just really feel good when we're together. So I was thinking maybe we could start seeing a little bit more of each other." I manage to spit out my confession without hyperventilating, so far, so good. But . . . man, smells so good . . . trying to control impulses to . . . cover his neck with kisses.

"I figured this is what would happen. This is so typical, Aspen. You wouldn't give me the time of day until I looked like a Ken doll. Now you want to 'hang out'?" he says, angrily making air quotes. Ouch, I'm pulled harshly out of my fantasy.

"Blaine," I answer, still in a bit of a hottie stupor.

"What?" he asks, looking confused.

"You look more like Barbie's new boyfriend Blaine then Ken. It's a joke." I smile, trying to lighten him up. Surely he can't really believe that I'm so shallow that I'd like him now just because he looks good. I mean, I am shallow, but I'm not that shallow.

"Go ahead and make your jokes. Everything is a joke, isn't it, Aspen? I suppose Angel missing, that's a big joke, too, huh? I can't believe how wrong I was about you." He laughs, sounding deranged.

"So why did you do it?" I ask, gesturing toward him.

"I wanted you to prove me wrong. I wanted to see for myself how shallow you really are. I wanted so badly to believe that you would treat me the same way. But you didn't. Now you want me. Now I'm good enough. I just wish you would have wanted me yesterday."

"But I did. I do. I tried calling you last night, but some old guy said you were gone."

"It's not going to work, Aspen."

Great. For once in my life I was ready to base a relationship on something besides looks. Now the guy doesn't believe me. How am I ever going to convince him he already had me? The thought of losing him to someone else now, especially Amy, is inconceivable. As I run my finger over the cool spiral binding of my notebook while trying to figure out what to say next, I have a total epiphany. The note. Yes! Rand is so mine. I am so going to have the upper hand once he reads my note.

"This is how much your new look means to me." I thrust the note at him.

His eyes soften as he unfolds the note. Just as quickly they turn hard again. "This will come in really handy when I don't buy any of it for you for Christmas." He throws my current designer label wish list back at me. Crap. I gave him the wrong paper.

"Shit. Hold on." I rummage through my notebook.

Rand starts drumming his finger against my locker door and tapping his foot impatiently while I search desperately for my note. I just had it. Now I can't find it anywhere. I'm starting to freak out. I don't want to lose him. And it's not just because he's a total hottie now, even though he is. It's because I know I'm supposed to be with him. I can feel that now. I hate that he's mad at me. I've got to make him understand I really like him.

"Why are you doing this? Just admit it, there is no note."

"There is a note!" I scream. I'm starting to get really pissed. Why won't he just believe me? He thinks I'm nothing but a shallow label whore. I wonder why he even liked me in the first place? Wait a minute! He's no better than what he's accusing me of.

"Rand, I'm curious. You've supposedly been carrying this torch around for me for years. But until a few days ago we had never even talked. So you were basing your feelings on my looks. How does that make you any better than what you're accusing me of?" Ha, gotcha, buddy boy. Now Rand will admit that I'm right and that we are made for each other. He will dazzle me with those delicious kisses any second now. I wet my lips and rub them together in anticipation.

Rand slowly bends down and places his books on the floor. He raises back up and gets right into my face. I can feel his breath. I swear if he doesn't kiss me soon, I'm going to faint. Is this what it feels like to fall in love? I feel like I just can't get enough of him. I want to savor every touch, every kiss, every moment. He places his palms against the side of my face.

"Aspen, I'm not going to lie. I used to think you were the most exquisite creature on the face of the earth."

Used to? I don't think I want to hear the rest of this. I can't stop the fat, salty tears from streaming down my cheeks.

"But your looks weren't what made me fall in love with you. I loved that you convinced Molly Davis she would never get a date to eighth-grade graduation if she didn't stop wearing white socks with black shoes. I loved that you spent an entire class period convincing Big Luann that Diet Pepsi tastes just as good as regular, helping her lose twenty pounds. I loved that you could spend all hour in calculus painting your nails, then the minute you get called on, you could rattle off the answer like you've actually been paying attention. I loved that every time I saw you eat applesauce, you put salt in it. I could go on for days. But none of that matters now. I want someone who reciprocates my feelings. I want someone who notices little things about me. I just can't love you anymore,

Aspen." He wipes my now free-flowing tears, kisses my cheek, picks up his books, and walks right out of my life.

❧

My makeup was completely ruined from crying and there was no way I could stay at school in that condition. I haven't stopped crying since Rand walked away. I feel like a huge hole resides where my heart used to be. Is this what it feels like to pine for someone? Has Rand been feeling this way about me all these years?

I'm just about to dig into Dad's Karamel Sutra since I already ate all my Chubby Hubby when Mom busts through the front door, her arms full of shopping bags. Again, we nearly give each other a heart attack. She looks exquisite in a burgundy DKNY pantsuit. I swear it seems like she never repeats an outfit.

"Aspen, aren't you going to get in trouble for skipping school again?" She asks, sounding nervous. She's probably worried I'm not keeping my grades up.

"No. My principal is totally cool. She even offered to drive . . . Oh, crap." I told Miss Hott I had terrible cramps and she was so cool about me leaving. I swear, she's the most understanding principal ever.

"What's wrong?" Mom asks.

"She wanted to drive me home because I was so upset. She went to get her car and I walked to my locker and totally forgot. I just got into Cookie and drove away." Classic! I stood up my principal.

"I'm sure she'll understand, sweetie."

"Could anything else go wrong today?" I sob, dropping my head on the kitchen island. Mom drops her bags and rushes to me. She throws her arms around me and begins stroking my hair.

"You can just call her and tell her you forgot. It's not that big of a deal."

"It's not that. Rand's a hottie now and he hates me." I sob, wiping my nose on her shoulder.

"Oh, honey, I'm sure he doesn't hate you. You just need to convince him that you had feelings for him before he got handsome. What about the note you told me about this morning?"

"I can't find it. And even if I could, he'd never believe that I wrote it before I saw him. What am I going to do? And why do I care so much about him after only spending like two days with him?" I wail into her shoulder.

"That's how love is. It might take a lifetime to find you but once it does, you get hooked fast. He'll come around. Let's go shopping and get you a new outfit he won't be able to resist."

"I don't want to go shopping! Are you even listening to me?" I scream. "He said he can't love me anymore." I sob.

She takes one look at my face and says, "Oh, dear. You've got it bad."

Mom and I are sitting at the dining-room table brainstorming about how I can win Rand back.

"He knew all this cool stuff about me. He's been watching me for years. Not in a creepy stalker kind of way, but in a lovesick puppy way. He even knows I put salt in my apple-sauce."

"You do? Gross," Mom says, turning her nose up.

"I don't know anything about him. I'm just not that obser-vant," I whine.

"Aspen, please. You can spot a fake Fendi from a mile away. Surely you can think of a few things about him."

Exhausted, I bury my head in the folds of my arms resting on the table. My brain is fried. The only thing I can remember about Rand right now is how delectable his lips are and how I may never get to kiss them again. I groan in physical pain at the thought. Wait . . .

"He cares about the environment," I blurt out, star-tling Mom.

"Okay, that's a start," she says, looking unconvinced.

"I could sell Cookie and get one of those awful looking cars that get a hundred miles a gallon."

Mom puts her hands up. "Whoa, let's not get in a big hurry. You need to start out slow." She taps her finger against her temple as if willing a good idea to surface. "I've got it. You could start riding Dad's bike to school."

My eyes widen and my mouth drops open. "Seriously?"

"How bad do you want this guy?"

A few seconds later, I call Dad at work and beg him to air up the tires when he gets home. He agrees, but not before ask-ing me if I'm feeling all right.

The only other things I can remember about Rand is that he likes chocolate and he is annoyingly involved in school activities.

"Are there any games tonight or anything going on?" Mom asks.

"They are building floats for the homecoming parade."

"Aspen, you have to be there. Let him see you getting involved. Show him a different side of yourself. Oh, and make sure you look hot."

I hurry upstairs to get ready. I actually decide to go against Mom's advice about looking hot. I'm going to go more casual to show Rand that I'm not all about looks all the time. I pull on a glittery pink Hello Kitty T-shirt and a pair of frayed jeans. I pull my hair into a simple ponytail. I take a less-is-more approach with my makeup. I slide my RAZR in one pocket and my inhaler in the other, slip into my Nikes and I'm ready to go. I catch my reflection in the mirror. I look adorable. It's impossible to doll myself down.

Mom holds up crossed fingers as I open the front door. Dad has his bike propped up in the front yard. I hop on and take off down the road. The temperature went from freezing at the bonfire to a sunny seventy-five degrees today. It's perfect weather for building a float. Not that I've ever built one, but how hard can it be?

Thankfully, my house is only a few blocks from the school so it doesn't take me long to get there. I ride through the parking lot at the perfect time. Rand is climbing out of a black Jaguar and spots me immediately. It seems Hot Rand ditched the FryDaddy on wheels. The look on his face when he sees me is priceless. If I were keeping score, I definitely just got a two-pointer, or a touchdown, or whatever it is they use to keep score in sports. I'm ecstatic that my plan is working so well until I see Amy jump out of the Jag's passenger side.

"Nice wheels, Brooks," she smarts off.

I have to fight the urge to make tire tracks on her face with my bike. Instead, I wave pleasantly to both of them and head toward the bike rack.

Rand and Amy start walking behind the bus garage. I follow them, making sure to keep a good distance. Four flatbed trailers, one for each class, are set up behind the bus garage. I continue following Rand and Amy to the senior float. Tobi and Pippi are sitting on the trailer with their legs dangling off. When Tobi sees me, she jumps off the trailer and bolts to my side.

"Aspen, are you okay? I was really worried when you left early today."

I put my hands on my hips and look her up and down. "Yeah, you look pretty broken up about it."

"Come on, Aspen. I don't want to fight with you."

As hard as it is to be mad at Tobi, I'm still not convinced she isn't behind some of these horrible things that keep happening to me.

"Tobi, come over here," Pippi says, patting the spot next to her. Jealous much, Pippi? Whatever, I don't even care. If Tobi wants to be b/f/f with Pippi, she can go for it.

Tobi gets big tears in her eyes and says, "Aspen, I have room in my heart for more than one person." I don't respond and eventually she turns and goes back to her new b/f/f.

Rand and Amy have huddled in a corner with Blake and Jimmy. I scan the remaining seniors to see who I can hang with since I would rather die than share Tobi with Pippi. I spot Melinda Paxton and head her way.

Miss Hott waddles up with float supplies and dumps them on our trailer. She's flushed and out of breath. After catching her breath, she says, "It's so exciting to have such a good turnout. I see some new after-school faces." She looks my direction and winks. "Okay, we need floats that will blow Maroon High out of the water. I'm giving you full creative reign. Just keep it clean, and have fun."

"Hi, Melinda. Is it okay if I work with you?" I ask.

Melinda turns and looks at me and for a moment I'm afraid she might be having a stroke. I touch her shoulder and ask, "Are you all right?"

"Fine, just a little shocked. I didn't know you even knew my name."

"Of course I do. We're in the same English lit class."

"Right? But you've never actually talked to me before."

She's right, I haven't. I've never been a mean girl, but I have been indifferent, which I'm starting to realize might just be worse.

"I'm sorry, Melinda. I'll just go over here." I start to walk away and she touches my arm.

"No, stay. I want you to." We grin at each other and get busy.

After examining our "supplies" and watching Amy fawn over Rand, I'm feeling like I could hurl.

"You're really into him, huh?" Melinda asks, grabbing a can of spray paint.

"It's that obvious?"

"Only to those with the gift of sight." She laughs. "Plus, I saw the paper today. That picture was hot. You've got to get him away from the Evil Princess though," she says, gesturing toward Amy with the paint can. I'd love to hold Amy down and spray paint her face green. I wonder if Melinda would help me?

"Believe me, I'm trying."

"Damn, girl, you're the great Aspen Brooks. You can get any guy you want. Let me see you work it," she says, snapping her fingers. Who knew Melinda Paxton was such a crack-up? I've really been missing out by closing my world off to so many people, but not anymore.

Melinda's right. I need to quit sitting here like a victim and start working it. I laugh loudly and toss my ponytail around. I can see Rand watching me out of the corner of his eye. There is no way I'm letting him fall out of love with me.

I help Melinda collect our supplies, which consist of chicken wire, a bag of sand, tissue paper, and ten cans of spray paint.

"Omigod, is she serious? Who does she think we are, MacGyver?"

Melinda starts snorting with laughter getting Rand's attention again. Amy is getting frantic because she knows she's losing him. I see her turn sideways and undo another button on her shirt. Pretty much everything but her actual nipple is visible now. I can't blame Rand when I see him staring at her chest. A blind man would be gawking at that fake rack. Amy's fighting dirty.

I turn back to Melinda, who is miraculously forming a seagull out of chicken wire.

"Holy shit. That looks awesome. What can I do to help?"

"Why don't you start pulling tissue paper through the holes. Just leave a little bit sticking out then we'll spray paint it gray."

I gladly start following her orders. Surprisingly, this whole float-building thing is kind of fun. Maybe there is something to these extracurricular activities after all. It helps that Melinda is such good company. I'm still periodically sneaking glances at Rand. I've caught him looking at me, too. If Tobi and Pippi were any closer, they'd be Siamese twins. Before long they'll have matching tramp stamps. One will say "best" and the other "friends." Losers.

"Stop eye-fucking Rand and help me," Melinda jokes.

"Hey, I wasn't even looking at him. I was just checking out my traitor ex-b/f/f over there."

"Aspen, I don't think Pippi is trying to compete with you for Tobi's friendship."

"You're right. She's already won."

"Um, well, I don't want to tell you your business, but maybe you should just talk to Tobi about it." She hands me a roll of chicken wire and starts to unroll it. A jagged edge of metal catches the skin on my index finger and rips it open.

"Oh, shit," I yell, dropping the wire. Miss Hott glimpses the blood spilling over my fingertip. She screams for no one to move or touch me while she rushes into the school to get the biohazard kit. The exchange of bodily fluids amongst students is highly frowned upon these days. She's not even to the door yet—at this rate I'll bleed to death.

"I'm so sorry, Aspen." Melinda says.

"It's not your fault . . ." I trail off as I spot Rand walking toward me. Never in my life would I have thought that a guy dressed in blue jeans, a wife-beater, and flip-flops would reduce me to a quivering mass of Jell-O. As a rule, open-toed sandals make me gag. But Rand has the cutest little toes. His second toes are so long that they curl over the third ones. He grabs my hand and puts my bloody finger in his mouth. He starts to suck on my finger. I start getting light-headed and it's not from losing blood. He is gazing seductively at me and the pressure of his tongue against my finger feels so disturbingly intense. If Rand were a vampire, I'd have no problem letting him suck me dry. Everyone around us is guiltily watching, but it feels like we are in our own parallel universe. I wonder if I would get expelled for having sex on the senior float behind the bus garage?

"Oh, my," an out-of-breath Miss Hott interrupts. Rand immediately releases my finger from his mouth and gently drops my arm. I smile at him, but his eyes go cold.

"Don't go reading anything into this, Aspen," he says, walking away.

Yeah, right. You don't just go around sucking somebody's blood unless you are seriously into them. He still wants me. He just doesn't want me to know it.

Miss Hott hands me a bandage, then busies herself looking for any traces of blood-borne pathogens she might need to sanitize. Satisfied there are none, she waddles away.

I am still trying to catch my breath when Melinda whispers, "Holy shit. That was so *hot*! I'm going to have to wring out my panties when I get home." We both start giggling and try to get back to decorating. My mind keeps floating away to Rand wearing nothing but his crown. When I finally come back around, Melinda has managed to create a fantastic float displaying giant seagulls mauling a bulldog.

Everyone starts heading home. To my horror, Rand and Amy leave together. He doesn't open her door for her though, which is a good sign. Tobi climbs into Pippi's yellow Xterra and waves good-bye to me. I raise my hand in a very unenthusiastic wave. I tell Melinda good night and head toward the bike rack. It's pitch black out now and I'm glad I don't have too far to go. Especially now that I realize someone has stolen Dad's bike. I'm too exhausted to even be pissed. I could call Mom to come and get me, but it's only a few blocks. Besides, it will give me time to fantasize some more about Rand.

As I cross the street in front of the school, Miss Hott pulls her car up beside me and rolls the window down.

"How about that ride now, Aspen?" she says, throwing a turquoise pom-pom into the backseat.

"Hey, sorry about earlier. I was all messed up." I'm about to open her passenger door when a red Mini Cooper pulls up behind her and honks. It's my new friend, Melinda.

"Thanks, Miss Hott, but Melinda will take me home." She gives me a smile, then peels away like Mario Andretti.

Eight

The next morning I'm busy picking out another scorching ensemble when my cell phone rings. I bet it's Rand; he's finally come to his senses and he's calling to say he can't live another minute without me. Nope. The screen displays a local number I don't recognize. Maybe he's calling to say he still loves me from a pay phone.

"Hello," I answer, using my best sex-kitten voice.

"Hi, Aspen. It's Miss Hott. I was wondering if you could meet with me before school this morning? I have something that I want to discuss with you. Privately."

Why do I have the distinct feeling it's going to be a lecture on teenage sexuality? After the show Rand and I put on yesterday I guess I can't really blame her. But this isn't the time to be rushing my appearance. I've got to make sure I'm a masterpiece everyday if I'm going to win Rand back.

"I really don't have time this morning, Miss Hott," I answer, switching back to my normal tone.

"I really hate to tell you this over the phone, but it's about being homecoming queen. It's tragic about Angel, but with the parade and game being today, we need a queen. You only lost to Angel by a few votes so I want to give you the tiara."

Holy shit! I'm the homecoming queen! Holy shit! Rand is my king! This couldn't be more perfect if I'd orchestrated it myself. Now he'll realize that we are meant to be. It will probably only be a few hours until I get to kiss those sweet lips again. Yum!

"Where do you want to meet?" I ask, excitedly.

"How about that little diner outside of town. I'm jonesing for some bacon and eggs."

Yuck! How can she think about food at a time like this? My stomach is churning just thinking about having that tiara placed atop my head and taking my rightful place next to Rand as his queen. A salty taste fills my mouth and I drop my cell and rush to the bathroom to hurl.

As I rest my head against the cool porcelain bowl, that I pray has been disinfected recently, I realize it's not nervousness that made me puke. It's guilt. I brush my teeth to get rid of the nasty taste, then go back to my room. My cell shows the call was dropped. I scroll through the list of incoming numbers, find Miss Hott's, and dial her back. She answers on the first ring.

"Sorry about that, Miss Hott. And I can't believe I'm actually saying this, but I can't accept the tiara. I just don't feel right about it." I do feel guilty about taking the tiara off a missing girl's head, but I'm also not going to be queen by default, that's just tacky. I didn't get the most votes so I didn't win. Period.

"Are you sure? If you don't take it, I'll have to give it to the girl with the third-highest amount of votes, and that's Amy. Which I guess would work out pretty good now that she and Rand are a couple."

Her words twist in my gut. She just sits there waiting for my response for what feels like an eternity. It practically kills me not to scream, "All right, give me the freaking tiara already." But I don't. She finally hangs up. She must think I am completely mental after everything I've pulled this week.

Fabulous! I just handed Rand to Amy on a fake-gold, rhinestone-embedded platter. It's only seven o'clock in the morning. I just can't wait to see what the rest of this day has in store for me.

An hour later the school hallway is buzzing as I stroll to my locker. It must be the new queen gossip that's got everybody hyped up. I'm only halfway to my locker when I notice Rand waiting for me. My stomach drops like I've just gone upside down on a roller coaster. Nobody has ever made me feel like this before. I smooth my pink-and-gray-plaid pleated skirt. I peek down to make sure my pink cashmere V-neck sweater is showing just a hint of cleavage. My hair is hanging in fat ringlets framing my perfectly madeup face. I'm kind of glad that Dad's bike got stolen because I don't much care for the windblown look. I put on the biggest smile possible and aim it directly at Rand. This is it. He's going to confess that he just couldn't stop loving me and we are going to live happily ever after.

"Morning, Rand," I say, purposely invading his personal space so he gets a whiff of my new irresistible perfume.

He moves back a little then pushes a school newspaper at me. "Listen, Aspen. I just wanted to be the one to show you this." So much for him scooping me up and us riding off into the sunset together.

I look down at the black-and-white photograph on the front page of the paper. My eyes must be playing tricks on me. I bring the paper closer to my face, but it's still the same image. How can this be? The picture is of Tobi and Pippi behind the football concession stand, kissing. I'm not talking an innocent little Madonna/Britney Spears kiss. This kiss involves the sharing of tongues, spit, and possibly even cavities from the looks of it. The always-witty caption reads, "Which one's the princess?"

My mind just refuses to process what I'm seeing. I must start shaking because Rand takes hold of my shoulders. I know I shouldn't be thinking about how good it feels for him to touch me, but it does. I search his adorable face, confused. He nods his head yes.

"Pippi's a dude?" I ask.

He shakes his head no.

"Somebody Photoshopped this, right?"

"No, Aspen." God, his answers are so irritating. Why can't he just cooperate and let me stay in my little bubble? I don't want to know this. How could I have *not* known this?

"Tobi's gay?" I squeeze my eyes shut hoping that will make this whole drama just disappear.

Rand says softly, "Yeah, she is."

"Duh, Aspen. How could you have not known that? Everybody knew. You're so clueless." I open my eyes to see Amy, tiara and all, standing there mocking me. I pull my arm back to punch her in the face, but Rand sees me and gently lowers my fist. Damn, I would have loved to see her wearing her tiara with two black eyes.

"Amy, go to class," Rand yells at her. She huffs loudly, then stomps off.

"Sorry about that," he offers apologetically.

"Actually, Rand. She's right. Tobi has been my best friend since kindergarten. How could I have not known this? What kind of a friend am I?" I shake my head, full of disgust for myself.

All of the pieces start to snap into place like a puzzle. Tobi's never had a boyfriend. She has a boy name. The wink I saw between the two girls in class. All the time they've been spending together, and Tobi's sudden interest in her appearance. She drives a pickup truck, for God's sake. I have been clueless. My best friend has been wrestling with lesbo issues and I've been obsessed with matching accessories.

"Where is she?" I ask Rand.

"She ran out of here pretty fast once she saw the paper." He realizes he's still touching me and drops his hands. I really want to savor the way he is gazing at me, but I have to find Tobi.

"I'm sorry, Rand. I have to go."

He smiles wide and says, "Yes, you do."

❧

I pull into Tobi's driveway parking behind Pippi's Xterra. I have no idea what I'm going to say to get Tobi to forgive me. I don't blame her if she doesn't ever want to see me again. As

I approach the front door it flies open. My hostess is Pippi and she doesn't look happy.

"Did you stop by to torture her some more?" She says trying to sound sarcastic, but it ends up sounding like a cheer. Pippi is just naturally enthusiastic and sarcasm just doesn't work for her. I don't have anything against her personally. It was just hate by association because of her affiliation with Angel. I'm going to have to win her over first to get to Tobi.

"Pippi, I've been horrible. I'm not going to stand here making excuses for myself because there are no valid ones. Somewhere along the way I forgot that the most important things in life aren't made of diamonds, leather, or cashmere. I just want to tell Tobi that I love her no matter what, but if she doesn't ever want to see me again, I understand."

"Omigod, Aspen. That was like the sweetest speech ever." She cheers jumping up and down. "Tobi is going to be so happy that you're here." She pulls me into the house and points up the stairs. I start the familiar route to my best friend's bedroom that I've taken so many times before.

Tobi's door is cracked and she is lying on the bed curled in the fetal position. I hear her sobbing. I creep into her room, climb into her bed, and wrap my arms around her. I let her sob until her tear ducts are empty.

Once Tobi stops crying I get off the bed and plop down in her hot-pink beanbag. I've been in Tobi's bedroom a million times but everything looks different now. I feel like I don't even know her. My black leather boots knock against a guitar case.

"You play the guitar?"

"Only for about three years now. I want to be a songwriter, remember?" she asks, her eyes questioning me.

"No, Tobi. I didn't remember that. I haven't been a very good friend to you lately. I had no idea that you were having all these lesbo issues. Is it okay to call you that?"

"We prefer dyke, but I'll make an exception for you." She laughs.

"I just want you to know that I don't care what you're into. I love you and I'm going to be the best friend ever if you'll give me another chance."

"Aspen, you'll always be my best friend. You've just been a little preoccupied lately." She moves from the bed to the beanbag to hug me.

A thought hits me and I jerk back. "Why haven't you ever hit on me?"

She chokes on her own spit before answering, "You're not exactly my type."

Not her type? *Hello!* I'm everybody's type. I decide it's not worth debating. We've both found love in the most unlikely places. That's all that matters. We sit hugging for a long time, in a best friend way, not a lesbo way. Jeez!

The three of us are sitting around Tobi's kitchen table sharing a pizza. I'm filling them in about Rand touching my shoulders earlier. It turns out that they both thought Rand and I would be perfect for each other, but they knew I'd never even consider it.

"This is really hard for you, isn't it?" Tobi asks me.

"What do you mean?" I answer with a mouth full of cheese.

"You've never really had to earn anything before."

She's right. I've been skating by on my beauty, intelligence, and addictive personality that people just can't get enough of. I've pretty much had everything that I ever wanted dropped right into my lap.

"You're right. I never realized how lucky I've been," I finally answer.

"He's so in love with you, Aspen. He'll come back," Pippi says. "I can't believe how Amy has been all over him this week," she adds, dropping a piece of pepperoni on her tongue.

"I know. It's revolting. Now that she's queen she'll be with him all the time."

They both drop their pizza and their mouths telling me this is a news flash.

"But you should be queen. Angel only beat you by three votes!" Pippi shouts.

Tobi whips her head around, facing Pippi, "How do you know that?" I'm glad she asked because I was wondering the same thing.

Pippi's normally perfect-except-for-the-occasional-PMS-zit complexion starts getting all red and splotchy. It gets so bad that she could be the "before" model for acne medication. She knows something. Uh-oh. Something tells me that Tobi and Pippi are about to have their first girl fight.

"I said, how do you know that?" Tobi asks, blue eyes blazing.

"We . . . we . . . we . . . kind of . . . helped Angel . . . ch . . . ch . . . cheat." She hangs her head in shame.

"What? Are you fucking kidding me?" Tobi puts her fingers below Pippi's chin to lift her face back up. "Are you telling me that Aspen was supposed to be the homecoming queen and you helped Angel cheat her out of something she's wanted her whole life? Please tell me you aren't capable of something so evil."

Pippi's silence reaffirms her guilt. When she finally speaks, she says, "I'm so sorry, Aspen."

Angel the Super Skank strikes again. The tiara was mine after all. I wait for the intense craving to plot revenge against Angel to hit me, but it never does. Instead, I almost feel grateful. Besides, Angel's plan backfired on her when Rand got voted king so that was punishment enough for her.

They are both waiting for me to explode. I can see Tobi physically bracing for it. Pippi has her eyes closed.

"You know what, Pippi?" Pippi opens one eye to look at me. "I think you did me a favor. If I would have gotten queen, I would have been mortified just like Angel was. I would never have taken the time to get to know Rand. Angel is actually responsible for bringing Rand and me together. I'll have to thank her when she gets back."

"Who are you? And what have you done with Aspen?" Tobi asks in amazement.

It takes a few minutes to convince Tobi that it really is me. But when she witnesses me shudder as I spy Pippi digging around in her obviously fake Prada purse, she's knows it's me. I sneak out when I notice the girls making googly eyes at each other. As comfortable as I am with Tobi being a lesbo, I'm not interested in being a voyeur.

As I drive back to school I think about how different things were just a few days ago. When Angel finally does come out of hiding, her mind will be blown. Her best friend stole her tiara. Her other best friend is gay and in love with one of her biggest enemies. But when she finds out that I'm in love with Rand, she'll be the one thinking aliens abducted her.

⊚

I sneak back into school. You would think security would be a little tighter around here with a student "missing," and all. I guess it's a good thing its not with all the skipping I've done this week. I'm almost to my locker when the intercom clicks on.

Miss Hott clears her throat, then says, "Due to recent events, the faculty has made the decision to cancel the homecoming parade and the football game." Her voice is interrupted by loud "boos," "aw, mans," and a few "that totally sucks" coming from inside the classrooms.

Once everyone settles down she begins again, "We realize that this isn't going to be a popular decision, but due to Miss Ives's disappearance, we have to take precautions. The good news is that because you can all be contained and monitored carefully in the gymnasium, the dance is still on for Saturday night." Screams of joy escape the classroom doors.

Contained and carefully monitored? What are we, endangered species? The dance should be a real blast. It sucks about the game and the parade, but I'm getting sort of numb to disappointment this week.

I'm just about to slip into Psychology for the Teenage Mind when Miss Hott appears out of nowhere. Damn, for somebody who considers Twinkies a food group, she sure is stealthy.

"How nice of you to join us today, Aspen."

"Listen, Miss Hott. You know how much I value the top-notch education here at Comfort High, but I had a total friend emergency. It just couldn't be helped," I plead.

"Oh, yeah. I saw the paper," she says, shaking her head.

I get a thought that makes me angry. "Doesn't the newspaper staff have to run its photos by you before running them?"

"I give them complete creative control. Besides, everybody already knew about those two anyway." She shrugs.

Okay, do I need to continually be reminded that I haven't exactly been the poster child for b/f/f? I'm working on it. Jeez!

"Aspen, since you're here. Can you come out to my car and help me unload some supplies for the dance?"

Hello, stay out of class with an excused absence. I'm there.

"Sure, just let me put my books away first." I turn around and walk back to my locker. I fiddle with the lock even though it is unlocked. The last thing I need today is a lecture on the importance of locker security. I shove my books in and spin around.

"Okay, I'm read . . ."

"Do you normally talk to yourself, Miss Brooks?"

Miss Hott has disappeared and in her place stands the hairiest, most obnoxious man on the planet. Detective Harry (oh, man, that still kills me) Malone.

I turn my lip up and give him a snarl. "I was talking to my principal. She was just here," I say, looking around, as if a 400-pound woman is just hiding in the hall somewhere.

"Right," he says, unconvinced. "That's why I'm here. To speak with your principal. We keep playing phone tag."

"Whatever. I am so not interested in your 'angeligation.' "

"I just didn't want you thinking I was here for your boyfriend. He's in the clear. So you guys can 'blow' out of here if you want." He retorts without missing a beat.

I narrow my eyes at him. He is seriously testing my limited patience. I've been working so hard trying to be a better person. One comment from him and I want to chuck it all and rip him to shreds with my tongue. The words "electrolysis" and "wildebeest" fight to escape my mouth.

Just when I don't think I can hold back any longer Rand comes around the corner behind Harry. Harry is forgotten. My heart comes alive to its own conga beat. Rand is wearing blue jeans that hug him in all the right places and his evergreen polo matches his eyes. I even like the Adidas flip-flops he's wearing because I can see his adorable fold-over toes. He is coming right toward me. Our eyes lock, and my stomach drops so hard Harry could probably hear it. I feel shaky. It drives me crazy that I can't read him at all. I want him so bad. Does he still want me?

Rand suddenly realizes who I'm talking to and a worried look flows over his impressive facial features.

"So. Where can I find this principal of yours?" Harry asks, oblivious to the Adonis walking up behind him.

"Hello? Aspen? Are you still with me?"

Rand comes up beside him. "Hey, Detective." He sticks his muscular hand out to shake the detective's hairy one. I'd love to feel those hands running all over my body. *Focus, Aspen, focus!*

"Hello yourself, Mr. Bachrach."

"Hi, Rand," I try to say casually, but it ends up sounding all dreamy. I am such a loser! I have absolutely no hand in this nonrelationship.

Harry, being the observant detective that he is, picks up on my total loser no-hand vibe immediately. His eyes widen as he looks back to me. I ignore him and keep gazing at my beloved.

"Hey, Aspen. Everything cool?" Rand asks, referring to the whole everybody-knew-they-were-lesbos-except-me situation with Tobi.

I smile sweetly at him and nod my head yes. He smiles back and for a second I get lost in thoughts of his lips kissing all over my body. I wish I could read his mind. He has to still want me a little bit, right? I wonder where I can get a Rand secret decoder ring?

I can almost hear Harry's inquisitive brain whirring. He's taking in all of our nonverbal communication. Rand breaks the silence. "Any news about Angel?"

Harry frowns as he remembers the reason he's here. "Nothing yet. I just have some routine questions for your principal."

Rand makes a pained look and shakes his head. I hate that all of this self-created Angel drama is worrying him. I hope Harry charges her with a crime when he finds her. Some jail time would do her good. With her coloring, she'd look like shit in an orange jumpsuit. That would be awesome.

"I better get going. Nice to see you again, Detective," Rand says, turning to go to class. He doesn't say anything or even look at me. It makes me want to cry. I watch his sweet ass until it disappears around a corner.

"My, my, my. This is one for the books," Harry says, dripping with sarcasm.

"Gimme a break, okay?" I am so not in the mood to trade barbs with him anymore.

"It's not easy, is it?"

"I'm sure I have no clue what you are talking about."

"Fighting for something you could have had and wondering if maybe it's already too late."

Damn, he's annoying and he can read minds. I'd rather die than let him know he's right though.

"The office is that way, Dr. Phil," I say, pointing him in the direction of Miss Hott's office.

Nine

Somehow Tobi managed to wrangle me into joining her and Pippi for dinner at Ravioli's. While I hate the thought of being a third wheel, Ravioli's is a paradise for carb junkies like me, and I am in need of some serious breadstick therapy. Besides, if I stayed home, I would just be driving myself crazy wondering what Rand and Amy are doing. Now I can drive Tobi and Pippi crazy instead.

My closet is in need of a serious overhaul. I can't find one decent thing to wear. Just as I am about to ignore my own advice of "always dress for the part you want to play" and throw on jeans and a T-shirt, I remember a delectable suede jacket Mom was wearing the other day. I usually never raid Mom's closet even though we are the same size, but tonight I'm desperate. I think about calling her cell to ask if she cares, but she's at a chick flick with a friend since Dad's out of town and I don't want to interrupt her movie; besides, she won't care.

I pull on her closet doorknob, but it's locked. That's weird. Mom must have accidentally pushed the button in on her way out. I retrieve a wire hanger from my closet and bend the top out straight. I stick the now-straight metal piece thru the hole in the doorknob until I hear the lock pop open. I toss the deformed hanger on the bed, then open the closet.

Before I can even turn on the light I am immediately assaulted by a cascade of shoeboxes toppling down on my head. I bat them away and turn the light on. When I do, I can hardly believe my eyes. It looks like Neiman Marcus exploded in here. Mom's closet has three times more stuff than it did when I was looking for the man the other day. The metal clothes bars are sagging in the middle from the weight of all the clothes. I run my fingers over the rainbow-colored garments. Almost everything still has the tags hanging from their cuffs or hems. The shelves above are stuffed with shoeboxes, purses, scarves, and belts. Unless Mom is planning on opening her own store, this is very strange. I slowly back out of the closet and relock the door.

Where in the world did Mom get all that stuff? I know my parents don't make good enough money to afford all that. If Mom did buy all that stuff, I'm definitely going to be looking into student loans next year. But why would she buy so much stuff just to let it hang in the closet? I wonder if she is a kleptomaniac? I'm glad that Dad is gone tonight because when Mom gets home (unless I stay out later than she does) I am planning a serious intervention.

I return to my own closet and decide on a crème-colored cashmere sweater, black wool pleated skirt, and knee-length kitten-heeled black leather Gucci boots.

My blonde hair is down and rolled into my big, smooth, signature curls. My eyes are done up with dark gray shadow, black liner, and tons of jet-black mascara making them smolder. I paint my lips bright cherry. A glance in the mirror verifies what I already knew. I look totally freaking hot and I'm spending the night with a couple of lesbos. What a waste of makeup!

I pull open my closet again and survey my choice of Dooney bags. Dooney & Bourke is the God I worship. They understand me. Somehow they just know that I need different types of bags for different occasions. Sometimes I'll go classy and I'll need my ivory-and-pink mini tassel Bubble bag. Other times I'm feeling fun and nothing will do but my bubble-gum-pink Heart mini gym bag. If I'm feeling really eccentric, I'll whip out my black drawstring Doodle. And then there are times like tonight when my makeup and outfit don't really fit into any of those categories. Tonight I need something sexy. I pull down my Tattoo bucket bag, it's the perfect combo of trashy and sexy. Those Dooney people really know what they are doing!

I'm switching my goodies from Dooney to Dooney when I get a fabulous idea. I flip through the school directory, find Melinda's phone number, and dial it.

"Hello," she answers before the first ring is even complete. It breaks my heart that the poor girl is just sitting there on a Friday night waiting for the phone to ring.

"Hey, Melinda. Do you want to go to Ravioli's with me?"

"Who is this?"

As if she has so many people calling her. "Duh, it's Aspen."

"Sure," she says excitedly. "Just give me fifteen minutes to get ready." She clicks off.

I'm frozen in place still holding my cell phone to my ear. Fifteen minutes? Who can get ready in fifteen minutes? This girl is so in need of my fashion tutelage.

⊚

A half hour later we walk into Ravioli's. Tobi and Pippi have reserved a cozy candlelit table in the back. Tobi sees us and waves us over.

"Hi guys. Melinda, it's good to see you," Tobi greets us, being her natural casual self and immediately putting Melinda at ease.

"Aspen, you look amazing," Pippi says to me in awe. She's really starting to grow on me.

"Yeah, too bad it's gonna be wasted on a bunch of dykes." I laugh.

Melinda and I take our seats and start to peruse the menu. Italian food, yum!

"It might not be totally wasted," Tobi says sneakily.

"What's that supposed to mean?" I ask, curious.

"Your wonderful best friend may have called a certain royal male specimen and asked him to join us."

I drop my menu in shock. "You invited Rand?"

"Maybe," she answers coyly.

"Oh, shit!" Pippi yells, slamming her menu down.

"What?" Melinda, Tobi, and I ask in unison.

"I kind of invited Amy," Pippi answers, looking guilty. "I thought it would be okay for her and Aspen to be together if Rand wasn't around. I'm really sorry, Aspen." She gives me the most pitiful look I've ever seen and I know she really is sorry. Before I can tell her it's all right and bolt out the door, Tobi goes on a rampage.

"This was superinconsiderate of you, Pippi. From now on, you clear with me who you are going to invite. Got it?"

Pippi vigorously shakes her head up and down. Damn, I guess I know who wears the pants in their relationship. I am about to push my chair back to leave when Rand and Amy approach the table.

One look from those intense green eyes and my knees are knocking so bad there is no way I'm getting out of this chair. Rand is wearing the same jeans he had on earlier with a green and yellow long-sleeved John Deere T-shirt. The T-shirt reads, "Save a tractor, ride a cowboy." *Show me where to saddle up, big boy!* How in the hell can he make a T-shirt and jeans look so freaking hot? My hotness isn't lost on him either. He's totally checking me out.

"God, Aspen. Take a picture, it lasts longer." Amy smarts off before lowering herself into the chair Rand is holding out for her. I am really starting to despise Amy. She has slipped right into Angel's Manolos without so much as a mandatory grieving period for her missing leader. But I'm forced to admit that her clingy Calvin Klein dress looks incredible. Then I notice she's actually wearing her tiara. Someone above is testing me. Rand sees me eyeing the tiara as he takes the seat across from me. If I make a smart-ass comment, Rand will think I'm still the snotty, superficial girl he can't love anymore. If I keep my mouth shut, maybe he'll realize I'm really trying to grow for him. But how can I possibly not comment on that?

Luckily, Tobi beats me to the punch. "I can't believe you are wearing that," she says, not bothering to hide the disgust in her voice.

"I can't believe you even accepted it," Pippi adds. "What about Angel?"

Amy tries to look innocent. "I only accepted it in her honor. Angel would be mortified if she knew there was no homecoming queen. Besides, I can't help it that I got the most votes after Angel," she finishes, giving me a very satisfied look.

Bitch! She knows I can't defend myself without looking like a petty asshole. I would love to get her alone in a dark alley and beat her over the tiara'd head with my Dooney.

Pippi pipes up, coming to my rescue, "Amy, did you forget that Aspen actually won?"

Amy makes a horrified face. She can't believe that her friend just betrayed her. Go, Pippi!

"You remember. Me, you, and Angel cheated so Aspen would come in second and Angel could win. Miss Hott even offered the tiara to Aspen, but she had the class to turn it down. I guess that tells us how classy you are."

God, I just love that Pippi. The look on Rand's face goes from realization to shock.

"You turned down the tiara?" he asks in amazement. I look so good to him right now. I owe Pippi big-time.

"Yeah." I shrug like its no big deal. "It just wouldn't have been right with Angel missing."

"But you won. You could have proved to Miss Hott that Angel cheated." He is completely thrown. I can almost hear my brownie points racking up.

I put my elbows on the table and fold my hands together. I rest my chin on top of my hands and look deep into his eyes and say, "Some things are just more important than tiaras." Amy gasps as she catches the sparks I'm sending in Rand's direction.

"Come on, Rand. Let's get out of here." Amy says, trying to pull him out of his chair.

"I'm not going anywhere." He gives her a dirty look. Trouble in paradise, Amy?

"Damn, Amy. Are you going to let your boy toy talk to you like that?" Tobi jokes, clearly trying to start shit.

"Shut up, lesbo!" Amy screams.

"I'm rubber. You're glue. What bounces off me sticks to you," Tobi sings.

Amy's comment doesn't roll off Pippi so easily. I notice her stabbing the tablecloth with her fork, glaring in Amy's direction.

"As if," Amy responds to Tobi. "I don't see why anybody would want to be a freaking carpet muncher."

"That's it. It's on, bitch!" Pippi yells, jumping up from her chair.

"Calm down, sweetie. She's not worth it," Tobi says softly, reaching across the table and touching Pippi's arm.

"What are you talking about anyway, Tobi?" Rand asks, confused.

"Just ignore her, Rand. She's a man-hater," Amy responds, trying to deflect Rand's attention.

"You're not implying that Amy and I are a couple, are you?" he continues.

"If you aren't hitting that, what's with the Siamese-twin act all week?" Tobi asks.

I'm in awe; I'm just sitting here on my best behavior and my friends are collecting the 411 for me. Melinda is sitting beside me taking the conversation in with saucer-sized eyes. She probably feels like she just stepped into the real-life O.C.

"I've just been giving Amy a ride since her car is in the shop," Rand explains, causing Amy to turn scarlet.

I stare her down, but she's too chickenshit to even make eye contact with me. I so want to rip her face off right now. All week she's been deliberately making me think that she and Rand were an item.

"Her car is at my house." Pippi laughs.

"You lied to me?" Rand asks Amy, slightly raising his voice.

Amy takes a look around at everyone, except Melinda, glaring at her. She knows she's busted. She jumps to her feet and screams, "You're all just jealous of me," and storms out of the restaurant. This night is just too good to be true. Tobi, Pippi, and Melinda are busy cracking up at Amy's dramatic exit. They completely miss Rand leaning across the table, whispering, "I was never with her." Then he picks up his menu like we didn't just share a lifetime with one look. I mean, it's a good thing that he felt the need to clarify that he didn't get with Amy but I'm just more confused. Does he want me or not?

Laughter flows freely throughout dinner. Melinda is having the time of her life. I'm so glad I thought to invite her. I do wish I had met her here though because I may be able to get Rand alone in the parking lot. Shit!

Rand insists on paying for the entire dinner. None of us put up too much of a fight. On the way out Rand holds the door open for all of us. I smile sweetly as I notice him glance down at my stems. Busted! That's the green light I needed. He definitely still wants me. I see Melinda sidle up next to Pippi and Tobi and whisper something to them. A few seconds later, all three of them jump into Pippi's Xterra and drive by Rand and me, waving and honking.

"That was subtle." Rand chuckles.

"No doubt," I add, making a mental note to buy those chicks something fabulous.

We walk at a snail's pace to our cars. Neither of us wants to say good-bye. Knots form in my belly. I was so sure of myself just a few seconds ago, but now I'm a mess. I know I scored major points with Rand tonight, but I don't know if it's enough.

He walks me to Cookie's driver side door. I hit the remote to unlock her. Rand slowly opens the door for me. *Please, please, please, don't let me leave.* I just kind of stand there like a dork for a second. Nothing. I move to get in.

"That was kind of fun, huh?" He stops me.

I slam the door shut and lean against Cookie. "Yeah, I think I ingested about a thousand carbs though."

"I like a girl who isn't afraid to consume three days' worth of calories in one sitting," he jokes, in reference to the ten or so breadsticks I put away.

"Do you?"

"Do I what?"

"Do you like the girl?" I ask, seductively licking my lips. They still taste buttery from the breadsticks.

He starts nervously running his fingers through his hair. Could this be the same superconfident Rand who had no problem kissing me two (almost three, but who's counting?) times before?

I decide to help him out. I lean into him, pressing my chest against his. I run my hands up and down his back and neck. He takes a deep breath, getting a good whiff of my new, intoxicating Escada perfume. His eyes practically roll back in his head. He's trying to be so strong and resist me, but why? We are so meant to be. He has to see that.

"Don't you want me?" I ask, looking up at him with my best Bambi doe eyes.

"You know I do," he whispers, moving his hands underneath my leather jacket. He moves his face a teensy bit closer to mine. His eyes are intensely watching my lips. I counter his teensy move. This is going to be the kiss to end all kisses. There is even background music. It sounds like the theme song from *COPS*. Not very romantic, but whatever.

Rand jerks away from me and pulls his cell phone from his pocket. So that's where the music came from. I'll have to make sure and thank whoever is calling for ruining the hottest moment of my entire life.

Rand turns his back to me as he answers. I hear a girl's voice, but I can't hear what she's saying. It's probably skanky Amy trying to get her knockoff-Ferragamo-clad foot back in the door. Rand just listens, then finally says, "I'll be right there," and hangs up. Excuse me?

He turns back around to face me and I can tell he is no longer putty in my hands. His resolve to push me away for whatever reason has returned in full force.

"I've got to go, Aspen," he says, opening my door again.

I refuse to go down like this. I want an explanation. "Wait a minute, what is going on here?"

"Aspen, I know you've been trying. I saw you riding the bike and making friends with Melinda. I still can't believe you gave up the tiara. But . . ."

"But nothing? We should be together. I know you know that. Why are you fighting this?"

"Why do you want to be with me?"

Reasons? He wants me to give him specific reasons? I don't work well under pressure. "I don't know, I just do. I just know that I'm supposed to be with you." Tears start to well up in my eyes as I realize I'm not making a very good argument.

He puts his hand over his heart and says, "You have no idea how long I've waited to hear you say that."

"Good, because I mean it," I say, flinging my arms around his neck.

He gently removes them and drops them to my side. Suddenly, I feel how cold it is tonight. Rand blows out an icy breath.

"I wish I could believe you, but I don't. The only reason you want me now is because I'm a challenge. I was the first thing you ever had to work for. You'd ditch me as quick as you ditch purses."

I am beyond pissed at Rand right now. How dare he assume that I'm just interested in him because there has been a chase involved, and the purse comment was just uncalled for.

Doesn't he even notice that I only buy Dooneys? I am totally purse monogamous.

"You know, for someone who has supposedly watched and loved me from afar for years, you don't know shit about me." I slide into Cookie, start her up, and drive away without another glance in Rand's direction.

◎

"I give up!" I shout dramatically, then throw myself on Mom's bed.

"What's wrong, sweetie?" Mom asks, glancing up from her stack of mail-order catalogs.

I raise up long enough to unzip and pull off my boots, then flop back down on Dad's pillow. I'm kind of glad he's working out of town tonight. I love my dad, but he's kind of clueless sometimes, especially in the romance department.

I work up the energy to explain my mostly fantastic/slightly aggravating evening. "It's Rand. One minute I practically have him panting, and the next he's telling me I only like him because he's a challenge now."

"Is he right?" she asks, propping herself up on her elbows.

"Who's side are you on anyway?" I roll my eyes at her.

"Face it, Aspen. You've never worked this hard for anything your whole life. Are you sure you don't just want him because he's unattainable?"

"I'm not answering that." I roll over and bury my face in Dad's pillow.

"Okay, okay. So, tell me what you like about him?"

I roll back over and conjure up my favorite mental picture of Rand. It was the first time we kissed in the hospital. When he was stroking my hair. It made me feel so safe.

"He makes me feel safe," I repeat out loud. "I love the way he looks at me, like he can read my mind. When we kiss, it's like I always imagined it could be but never was before. And . . ."

"I get it. You're in love," Mom interrupts.

I stare up at the white swirly ceiling and realize that she's right; I am in love with Rand. What if he never wants to be with me? The very thought makes me want to hurl all my breadsticks. I roll onto my side and face Mom. "What am I going to do?"

"I know he's crazy about you. It was obvious that night at the hospital, and you don't just get over feelings that strong in a few days. The way I see it, he's testing you."

"Do you know where I can get a study guide because I'm fresh out of ideas to win him over?" I laugh.

"Put yourself in his shoes for a minute. He's had a crush on you almost his whole life. Suddenly you drop right into his lap. He probably never thought he was good enough for you to begin with. Now he's scared that you might get sick of him and then he'll lose you forever."

"Nah, that doesn't make any sense. If he's wanted me for so long, shouldn't he be dying to be with me instead of pushing me away?"

"Okay, let me put this another way. Do you remember your first Dooney bag?"

Just the mention of my first Dooney practically gives me goose bumps. "Of course, I do. It was a white buckle satchel It bag covered with the rainbow-colored Dooney insignia. I lusted after that bag for months." I'm not getting what this has to do with Rand, but purse talk is never a bad thing.

"Right. So, what did you do when Dad and I bought it for you?"

"I nearly broke my ankle jumping for joy."

"Right, but what did you do with the purse?" she says with the slightest hint of irritation.

"I took really good care of it, and resold it on eBay for more money a year later?"

"Exactly. You were so enamored by that purse that you wouldn't even use it. You just sat it on your dresser and stared at it. We begged you to enjoy it, but you were so afraid that it would get dirty or someone would steal it that you never even enjoyed it."

"I'm Rand's first Dooney?" I ask, hoping I'm finally getting her brilliant analogy.

"Yes," she says, relieved. "Well, kind of. He's loved you for so long that he's put you on a pedestal. Now that he can have you he's afraid he'll screw it up or worse, he'll lose you to someone else."

"So am I supposed to sell myself on eBay?" I giggle.

"Hmm . . . I wonder how much we could get?" She cracks up.

"I want to prove to Rand that I'm here for good," I say, getting serious again.

"Then we need to come up with something drastic."

"Speaking of drastic," I say, creating a segue into the intervention portion of the evening. I so don't want to have this conversation, but Mom's mental health might be at stake. I'm crazy about Rand but he's going to have to wait.

"What?" She drops her eyes back to her catalog.

"I was in your closet earlier," I say, softly.

She doesn't look up from her catalog but her eyes get glassy with tears. As the tears spill over onto her cheeks, she drops the catalog and buries her face in her hands, sobbing.

"Aspen, I'm sick." I can barely make out what she said through her sobbing. But I did make it out and I wish I wouldn't have. Mom, sick? Breast cancer? Leukemia? Brain tumor?

"I'm a shopaholic." Mom sobs.

A huge sigh escapes me. "Is that all? I thought you were dying." I laugh.

☺

It turns out that being a shopaholic is pretty serious business. Especially when you've charged $11,000 to your credit card like Mom has. I agreed not to tell Dad for now just for the fact that he would have a stroke and my parents can't afford the hospital bill.

The next morning Mom and I sort everything into piles broken down by store. By the time everything is returned to its appropriate pile we have twenty different stores to visit. Agh! I never thought I would actually dread a shopping trip!

Thankfully Mom was with it enough to save her receipts. We carefully load Cookie and drive to Comfort's two-level shopping center where Mom did most of her damage.

"Why did you buy all this stuff?" I ask her on the drive there.

She contemplates her answer for a moment, then begins, "In the beginning, it felt good, like a rush. I'd just buy something small as a reward to myself. But then it got to the point where small things didn't work for me anymore. I had to start buying more expensive items and more of them to feed my unquenchable thirst. I think it has something to do with being such an outcast in school most of my life. All I ever wanted to do was fit in," she says sadly.

It's weird to hear Mom talk like this. I've always sort of had her on a pedestal. Now I realize that she isn't perfect and she has issues just like everyone else. I'm going to help her beat this no matter what I have to do.

"You do fit in, Mom. You fit perfectly with me and Dad." I reach over and squeeze her hand and notice that she is trembling. She smiles at me but she almost looks like she's in pain.

We pull up to Coldwater Creek and approach the cash register with four full shopping bags of returns.

"Hey, Judy. How are you?" a tiny red-haired woman wearing lots of turquoise jewelry asks Mom.

"Hi, Flo," Mom answers back timidly. I realize as I watch Mom's eyes dart from rack to rack that I've made a terrible mistake. I never should have brought her with me. You wouldn't take an alcoholic to a kegger or an overeater to Krispy Kreme so what in the world was I thinking dragging her in here?

"We just got these new winter sweaters in that you're going to fall in love with," Flo rambles on.

"Mom, go wait in the car," I say, dangling my keys out to her.

Flo stands frozen with her mouth halfway open. Mom stares me down and just when I think she is going to fight me, she drops the bags she was carrying, grabs my keys, and walks out the door without another word to Flo.

One by one I turn the bags over on the checkout counter and let the contents spill out.

"I just have a few things I need to return, Flo." I smile.

It takes her fifteen minutes, but the end result is a credit for $876 back on Mom's credit card. Not a bad start.

Flo doesn't say one word to me during the entire transaction. I get the distinct feeling that she's known about Mom's problem for a while but didn't want to screw up her commission.

She hands me the receipt and I walk toward the storefront. I abruptly spin around and say, "Oh, Flo? If you ever sell my mom anything again, I'll tell the whole world that Coldwater Creek is pulling a Kathie Lee. Enough said?"

Her eyes bug out upon hearing my threat and her turquoise drop earrings swing like pendulums as she agrees to ban Mom.

I happily swing the front door open. One down, nineteen to go.

Ten

We spent the rest of the day returning stuff. We were so not popular with the sales clerks. Hauling Mom's addiction around all day made me realize that she truly does have a problem. I counted seventeen black turtlenecks alone. Even buying one turtleneck is a cry for help, but *seventeen*? Mom was screaming!

Dad isn't coming home until tomorrow so we have made the dining-room table our headquarters.

I just finished tallying up all the returns from today. The total, disappointingly, only came to a little over $6,000.

"You said you spent eleven thousand. We returned everything in your closet. Where's the rest?" I ask, agitated after such a long day.

"I don't know," Mom replies, hugging her knees and rocking back and forth in her chair. I keep forgetting how hard this must be for her. I'm expecting a "junkie" to go cold turkey.

"Why don't you go take a nap?"

She nods her head in agreement and slowly climbs the steps to her room.

I add the receipts one more time in hopes that I made a mistake, even though I so know that isn't likely, but they add up exactly the same. I tap the capped end of my ink pen against my temple willing myself to think where she could have spent the rest of the money.

I get up from my chair to get a drink. My left leg is asleep from sitting so long and I smash into Mom's curio cabinet. Luckily, it's bolted to the wall so it doesn't move. I try to get my balance, then trip over one of her Longaberger baskets. Why is there so much crap everywhere?

A light goes on as I survey my surroundings with new eyes. Baskets, knickknacks, and pictures cover every free space of the dining room. I hobble into the kitchen and realize that it is also overflows with stuff. I guess Mom is an equal opportunity spender. I just assumed she was buying things only for herself, but she's overaccessorized the house, too!

A twinge of guilt hits me when I realize how much she's spent on me. I never questioned her bringing home new Dooneys or handing over Choo boxes. How could I not have realized we couldn't afford all that stuff? I guess maybe I did, but I just didn't care. Dad never noticed because he wouldn't know a Jimmy Choo from a Payless pump.

I need to get Mom's credit card statement to see how much of this junk can be returned. I remember her hiding it on a shelf in her closet. I tiptoe up the stairs. Even if we can't return everything, we can still sell it on eBay and get some of the money back. God bless eBay!

I gently turn the knob to Mom's room when I hear her whispering. I crack the door and peek in. Her back is facing me and she's holding the cordless phone in one hand and a catalog in the other.

"Yeah, give me one in pink and one in blue," she whispers.

"What are you doing?" I bust in, causing Mom to jump and drop the phone. She immediately starts crying.

I bend down and pick up the phone. I tell the customer service representative to cancel the order and hang up. I cross the room and wrap my arms around Mom.

"It's okay. I'm going to help you." I rub her back. I'm a little scared though. This is a lot more serious than I thought. As much as I hate it, I'm going to have to bring in reinforcements (aka Dad).

I finally get Mom calmed down enough to take a nap. How can someone who has a tornado of issues swirling inside them look so peaceful? I confiscate her cell, the cordless, her stacks of catalogs, and her credit card.

Two hours later and Mom has been removed from every mailing list imaginable. I even cancelled her credit card. I figured she had the number memorized so hiding it wouldn't do any good.

I'm exhausted. Thank God Mom has never shopped online! So much for spending the day thinking up some fabulous scheme to win Rand back once and for all. My brain is a mush of catalogs and toll-free numbers. I'll never think of anything good enough to win Rand back before the dance tomorrow.

Mom bounds down the stairs with renewed energy. I'm suspicious of her perky mood, but there is no way she could have bought anything in the last two hours unless Neiman Marcus started taking orders by smoke signals.

"I just had the best dream and it gave me a plan for you to win Rand back," she says so excitedly that her words run together.

☺

"This isn't exactly the kind of plan I had in mind." I say, fingering Mom's old prom dress.

"Do you want to win his heart or not?"

"Yeah, but . . ."

"No buts. Suck it up and quit whining."

"Jeez, chill out." I'm teasing because I actually love it that she's so excited. This is the mom I know, not some shopping addict with self-esteem issues. She is so going to beat this!

Mom's dream was about the prom she missed. She thinks this is one of her core issues. It was really important to her that the entire school see her and Dad together to validate to her it was real. But then prom got cancelled and Mom felt incomplete. Mom says that she has psychoanalyzed me and figured out my biggest fear. Public humiliation. She thought up a way for me to publicly humiliate myself and get Rand to see that I'm serious about him. If it works, she's a genius; if it tanks, she promised to pay for at least five years of therapy.

The first part of Mom's plan is in full swing. The next morning we are destroying my beautiful head of hair. Mom wrapped my precious locks in these pink and purple hot-dog-looking things that she dug out of the junk closet. She said she wants my hair to be "kinky," whatever than means. I know all about kinky sex, but kinky hair is a first for me. Apparently it was "killer" in the eighties, her word, not mine. She mentioned something about wanting it to look like Chaka Khan's hair. I don't know who that is, and I think it's best if I don't Google her. I have a feeling if I knew what she looked like, I'd be running out of the house screaming.

The second part of the plan is to completely surrender my normally wicked fashion sense. The hair I can choke down, but I have a feeling my body may actually reject anything unfashionable draped upon it.

"Can you put this away? It's giving me a migraine," I say, holding the dress out while turning my head the other way.

"Do not diss my prom dress," Mom says, delicately hanging her prized garment back in her nearly empty closet.

"I just refuse to believe that was ever in style."

"I was devastated when I didn't get to wear it." She looks sad. I'm tempted to tell her that I really think it worked out for the best, but at the last second I decide I still need her help so I better behave. Besides, her plan seems to have helped sideline any residual desires she may have had to spend money.

"Why was prom cancelled again?"

"Some asshole called in a bomb threat to the hotel where the dance was supposed to be held. They didn't have time to move the dance to another location. They never even found a bomb."

"It was probably somebody who saw your dress and wanted to save everyone's eyesight." I say, unable to control myself any longer.

"I can't wait to see you in it," she says, giving me an evil little smirk.

"Yeah, about that. Our dance isn't really formal so maybe . . ."

"Zip it. You're wearing it."

"Control freak much?"

Mom ignores me and hands me some accessories. One is a huge bowtie necklace made entirely of rhinestones.

"Please tell me you're kidding?" I say, fingering the heavy necklace. Between this thing and my hair I'll be lucky to walk upright tonight.

She doesn't respond, just hands me a pair of satin pumps (gag!) that are dyed the exact hideous hue of hot pink as her dress.

"This is for your hair." She hands me a strange-looking contraption with plastic teeth.

"What the heck is it?" I hand it back to her.

"It's called a banana clip and it works like this." She shakes out her chestnut hair. She breaks the clip apart at the top and splits it open. She puts it under her hair then with one hand on each side of the clip she pulls it to the top of her head and snaps the two ends together. The end result is a Mohawk on the back of her head.

"Hell, no!" I scream in horror.

"Don't you want to be kissing Rand later tonight?" She laughs, tossing her Mohawk around. "Look, I even hot glued lace to it so it would match my dress. I used to be crazy good with a glue gun." Her eyes get excited at the memory.

"You're really starting to scare me. Just for the record, these items will be incinerated the moment they leave my body."

She looks sad, but recovers quickly, and shakes her head accepting the demise of her eighties couture.

Her cell phone rings. She unsnaps the banana clip in a flash like an old pro and tosses it to me before answering.

"Hello." Several seconds pass of her just listening. She makes a few weird faces, then says, "Sure, no problem," and clicks off.

"Dad?"

"No, but he should be home from the airport soon. I've got to run to the senior center real quick, then do a few other errands, but I'll be home in time to help you get ready for the dance."

"Okay, but do I really have to leave these in all day?" I ask, fingering the hot dog hair thingies.

"Yes, and don't forget your makeup." She tosses me an assortment of Mary Kay compacts. I pop one open to find a color palette that I didn't even know existed, and for good reason. I slam it shut afraid I might go blind.

"Go practice making yourself look hideous," she jokes.

"It's going to take all day, and even then I'm not sure I'll be able to pull it off." I'm really scared to let her leave. What if she has a relapse? She looks okay and she hasn't mentioned shopping all day. I guess I can't watch her 24/7. I turn to go back to my bedroom.

"Oh, and Aspen?"

"Yeah." I pop my head back in her door.

"I need to borrow Cookie because Rosie needs help with a new mattress she bought. Apparently she needs a king size now that Ned is back on his Viagra."

"Gross, Mom. I don't need to know the details on the sexual habits of senior citizens. The keys are on my vanity; just don't let those two in my backseat."

"I love you, sweetie," I hear her yell on her way down the stairs.

⊚

It is now five o'clock in the afternoon and Mom still isn't home. I'm freaking because the dance starts in two hours and I have to be there early to figure out how I'm going to pull off the third stage of our plan. I've left six messages on her cell. I can't believe she left me hanging. She knows how important this is. I swear, if she is out somewhere shopping, I will not be responsible for my actions.

I can't wait for her any longer. My makeup is already done. I look like a demented circus clown. I'm hoping that I don't bump into any small children tonight because I can guarantee they would be scarred for life after catching a glimpse of me. I coated my lids with lavender eye shadow and used electric blue eyeliner and mascara. My blush and lipstick match my hot-pink dress. One by one, I remove the hot dogs from my hair, Curls spring to life all over my head. I run my fingers through my hair, trying to calm the curls a bit, but they just pouf up even more out of control. It really is scary to look at myself in the mirror. I'm pretty sure this is how I would look if I got struck by lightning. I can barely contain the curls inside the banana clip.

I fasten the ten-pound necklace around my neck. It is already straining my neck muscles and it doesn't feel good. I wonder if this is why rappers are so angry all the time? I struggle into black pantyhose then slip the pumps on. They are huge so I shove a few socks in the bottom to make them fit better. They are still a little wide, but I should be able to manage without killing myself.

I can't avoid it any longer so I slip into the hot-pink nightmare of a dress. It is made of satin featuring a fitted bodice and tiers of satin that trail to my knees. Clusters of sequins are splattered all over it. The cap sleeves are huge poufy things that make me feel like I'm about to lift off. Worst of all is the gigantic bow plastered across my ass. There is no doubt that I'm committing fashion suicide tonight. If Rand doesn't appreciate this, I might just have to kick him in the teeth with my hot-pink pumps.

I try calling Mom one more time, but there is still no answer. I laugh to myself as I picture Mom going on a shopping binge, then trying to pay for everything with a cancelled credit card. I know that's mean, but I can't believe she stood me up! I take a picture of myself with our digital camera and leave Dad a funny note telling him that I haven't seen Mom since this morning and that I think my outfit scared her off. Hopefully he'll get a chuckle after a long day of commuting home. I can barely fit my hair into Mom's Acura. It's actually a good thing that I have Mom's car instead because now I'm incognito. I don't want anyone to see me before I can make my grand entrance.

When I pull into the school parking lot there is only one other car. I don't recognize it. When I get inside, the hallway is deserted. I sneak over to peek inside the gymnasium. The freshman class spent the morning decorating for our

Hawaiian-themed homecoming. Those little frogs did a pretty good job. The gym floor is covered in sand and huge fluffy makeshift clouds hang from the rafters. All the snack tables are edged with grass skirts and tiki torches line the dance floor. Fake palm trees are scattered throughout the gym and leis cover every free surface. Huge silver Mylar balloons shaped like sharks are tied to the sides of the DJ booth. Off to the side of the sand-covered dance floor are two iron lawn chairs that have been spray painted gold. Red velvet pillows sit in the seats of both the chairs. This is where the royal couple will hold court over the rest of us peons tonight. A microphone stands in front of the chairs so that Rand and Amy can thank their adoring fans. Barf!

I'm a little caught up in a daydream featuring me as the queen with Rand by my side when I hear someone clear their throat. I jump back and bump right into Miss Hott.

"Well, hello, Aspen. You look . . ." She pauses searching for the proper adjective. "Interesting tonight." She squints her eyes, taking in my entire ensemble. I think my dress is actually hurting her eyes. She gets closer and I can see that they are bloodshot and the skin around her eyes looks splotchy like she's been crying. Her normally coiffed to perfection hair has a few wild stragglers tonight. She reeks of perfume. It wouldn't be so bad if it were something good like Angel (which I love, but refuse to wear on principle), but it's the same foul shit I've been trying to break Mom of for years. There must be some sort of gravitational pull on women in their thirties to wear White Diamonds.

"Thanks, Miss Hott. I'm trying out a new look," I say, partially shielding my nostrils from her offensive odor.

"No offense, Aspen, but you're a spring. Hot pink just isn't ever going to work for you."

"Yeah, I know," I reply, trying hard to hide my admiration for her uncanny fashion sense.

"Since you're here, I was wondering if you could help me place goodie bags on the tables?"

"Um, sure." Crap, now what? It's not like I could say no. She's my principal, and I've already blown her off a few times this week, plus she's let me skip school half the week and not been a hag about it.

"Just give me a few minutes and then meet me in the teachers' conference room. Just be careful. The light is burned out in there, so don't hurt yourself."

I nod and watch her waddle away. Shit. I can't stand up Miss Hott, but if I don't, I'll miss my opportunity to publicly humiliate myself. Okay, that sounds so wrong.

I hear the east and west doors swing open simultaneously and excited students rush in. I fling the gym doors open and head toward the giant ocean backdrop that is hanging behind the royal chairs. I grab the microphone off its stand and head to the stage behind the backdrop.

Students quickly fill the gym. My stomach is doing flip-flops thinking about all of these people seeing me dressed like a knockoff Cyndi Lauper. I peek out the side of the backdrop and see Rand enter the gym. The king looks *hot*! He is wearing a navy blue blazer layered over a white button-down shirt and khaki chinos. He looks like he just stepped off the pages of a Ralph Lauren ad. His crown fits perfectly now that he's gotten those curls under control. He smiles, making his dimples cave in and causing my heart to start racing. He holds his hand up to wave at a few people, but never stops moving. I watch his eyes scan the crowd. He's looking for someone. He's looking for me! I get a sudden burst of courage. It's going to be okay. I'm just going to go out there and profess my undying love. Rand will reciprocate and we will dance the night away as soon as I run home and change.

"What the hell are you doing back here?" a female voice asks from behind me.

I swing around and come face-to-face with the queen-by-twice-default Amy. She's wearing my dress. Not the hot pink one I have on, but the black velvet tank with the pale pink ribbon running through the waist. She's even got the shoes I wanted, but couldn't get because they were sold out. Thank God I didn't wear that dress. I would rather look like a human jellybean than be twinkies with Amy.

She takes one look at me and doubles over. It takes her a few minutes to regain her composure, but then she raises up and says, "Omigod, Aspen. Like the eighties called and they totally want their stuff back."

"Very original, Amy. Listen, I am so over this feud. Can we please just stop all this because it's really getting played out?"

She rolls her eyes, then sticks her finger down her throat. "Like gag me with a spoon." She cracks herself up.

"Seriously, Amy. I'm glad you got queen. You deserve it way more than Angel or me. I really like your dress, too." It really about killed me to say that about *my* dress, but desperate situations require desperate measures, or something like that.

She eyes me suspiciously.

"Amy, I'm serious. That's why I'm back here. Miss Hott is looking for you. She's got your homecoming queen sash and rose bouquet. I told her that I'd come find you."

"Really?"

"You don't want to go out there without being properly accessorized, now do you?"

At the mention of accessories, she instantly forgets her suspicion of me. "What does she have for me?" she asks, getting visibly excited.

"She's got a beautiful white satin sash personalized with your name and two dozen red roses for you to hold. She wants you to meet her in the teachers' conference room." As she starts to bounce up and down with excitement I kind of feel like I just kicked a puppy, but I had to do it.

"I can't believe I'm actually queen." Her eyes glaze over as her fingertips gaze her tiara.

"You better hurry, Amy. You don't want to miss the king and queen announcement."

"You're right." She turns to go out a side door leading to the girl's locker room. She turns back and says, "By the way, Rand is so in love with you it is pitiful. Aspen, Aspen, Aspen, that's all I've been hearing all week." She smiles, then disappears into the girl's locker room.

Okay, so I feel a little guilty about lying to Amy but it won't take her long to help Miss Hott. I just hope she's right about Rand still being in love with me. I have to do this before I totally chicken out. I take a deep breath and turn on the microphone.

"Hey," a voice says softly from behind me causing me to nearly tumble out of my hot-pink pumps. I turn to find a somber-looking Lucas. I flip the switch back off on the microphone so the whole school doesn't hear me ripping Lucas a new one. This is the first face-to-face we've had since the BJ incident.

"What are you doing here?" I ask, not bothering to hide the contempt in my voice.

"I thought you might need some closure," he mumbles.

I start to laugh hysterically. "Wow, Lucas! That's a really big word. Don't hurt yourself."

He raises his head up to look at me, causing his blond locks to fall perfectly across his forehead. Damn! As much as I hate to admit it, Lucas is still a hottie!

"Aspen, I'm really sorry about everything." He walks closer to me.

"Um, which part? Letting Angel suck you off, humiliating me, or making Rand the laughing stock of the entire school?" I shout. I can hardly wait to hear him try to talk his way out of this.

"I didn't do shit to Rand," he yells, looking angry.

"Oh, right. What about that little stunt you pulled to vote him king?"

"Haven't you figured it out yet? I was trying to get you guys together. Rand's been in love with you like forever, and I knew you wouldn't give him the time of day unless you were forced to. How was I supposed to know Angel was going to cheat?" he defends himself, breathless.

"So I'm supposed to believe that you tried to hook your own girlfriend up with another guy out of the goodness of your heart?" I roll my eyes. I knew Lucas was dim, but this is a stretch even for him.

He wrings his hands nervously, and then says, "Okay, so maybe it wasn't just for you. I had the hots for Angel and I didn't want to break up with you. You can be really scary," he finishes with wide eyes.

"What?" I shake my head in confusion.

"I never made you happy, but I knew Rand could." He smiles.

I hear the words that are coming out of Lucas's mouth but they don't make any sense. Was I the only person at Comfort High who couldn't look past Rand's D-list status to see the real person? I guess there was one other person, Angel. I shiver as I realize that I'm not so different from my evil nemesis after all.

"You're crazy about him, aren't you?" Lucas grins.

I start to cry as I nod my head yes.

"But he deserves someone better. Someone who doesn't base a person's worth on their social standing."

"You're that person now, Aspen." he says, putting his hands on my shoulders.

Who knew that Lucas actually had depth?

"Now, go get 'em, tiger," he says, raising the microphone to my mouth. I watch his still quarterback-perfect butt walk down the steps and off the stage.

This is it. I peek around the giant backdrop. Rand is headed directly toward me. The gym is packed to capacity with students dressed in their homecoming best. The DJ flips on the sound system bringing the microphone alive and crackling in my hand. I have to do this *now*!

I take a deep breath and then bring the microphone to my mouth. I'm still watching Rand out of the crack.

"Comfort High, can I please have your attention?" Rand jerks his head around searching for me. Most of the students stop their conversations and quiet down. I move to the center of the stage and push the button to retract the backdrop. Whispers turn to hooting and hollering as the backdrop rolls up exposing more and more of my hideous ensemble.

By the time I'm fully exposed everyone is practically screaming with laughter. For a moment I'm not quite sure I'm going to live through this. But Rand isn't laughing. He is standing frozen directly in front of me with a blank expression on his face. I have no idea what he's thinking. I swear, if I'm going through all of this for nothing, Mom is in big trouble.

I wait for the laughter to die down before speaking again. It doesn't die down so after about a minute I tap the top of the microphone with my palm. The loud boom reverberating through the gym finally silences everyone.

"I'm sure that all of you know who I am, but for anyone who has been in a coma for the last four years, my name is Aspen Brooks. I'm an A-lister here, at least I was," I say, glancing down at my dress, which gets some laughs.

"Does anyone want to know why I'm committing fashion suicide tonight?"

At least a hundred people scream "yes."

"I'm doing all of this"—I gesture from my head to my feet—"for a guy." More cheers erupt, but nothing from Rand.

"Not just any guy, but Comfort's king, Rand Bachrach." I get drowned out by the excited shouting. I bang on the microphone again to gain control of the crowd.

"Yes, ladies and gentleman, I've got it bad for Rand. The problem is he doesn't believe me. He doesn't believe that I just know in my heart we are supposed to be together. He's known it since first grade, but I'm just now catching up. I deserve this doubt, because until a few days ago I was more concerned with the frosting than the cake." I can tell by the confused faces that I need to elaborate.

"I was into how people looked on the outside. Clothes, shoes, purses, their frosting. I never really cared about the cake."

I thought I saw the tiniest smile form at the corners of Rand's mouth, but it disappeared so quick I'm not sure it was ever really there. I really thought the frosting/cake metaphor would get him. That's okay; I have plenty more to say.

"I tried to do things this week to show him that I'm trying to change. I don't want to lie. I'm never going to lose my love for frosting entirely. Even right now, as I try to convince Rand that we should be together, I'm screaming inside that it has been at least six weeks since Labor Day and Jill Johns is wearing a white skirt. Sorry, Jill. I just couldn't help myself."

Jill shrugs like it's no big deal.

"I know a lot of you including Rand probably think I just like him now that he's frosted. He is a total hottie now, but I guarantee you I'm all about his cake."

I think I've abused my frosting/cake metaphor too much because my audience is looking a little lost.

"What I mean is there are a lot of things that I like about Rand besides his looks."

Some guy way in the back yells, "Like what?"

I was hoping someone would ask because I finally have my list all ready. Rand is standing with his arms crossed in front of him waiting intently for my answer. I'm going to blow him away.

I look directly at him and say, "I like that you are the only male alive that looks sexy in a wife-beater." Cheers go up from the females. Rand doesn't look impressed. I guess that comment was a little "frosting" oriented.

"I like that when you kissed me in the hospital, I had never felt so safe in my whole life." He likes this one and gives me a tiny smirk. The crowd oohs and aahs.

"I love that your second toes are so long they curl over your third toes," I continue. He gives me a huge grin. The crowd is torn over this comment. I hear a few "aw, that's sweets" mixed in with some "freaking grosses" as well.

Mr. Lowe slips in the gym door with a confused look on his face. I wonder if he is confused because of that dorky outfit he's wearing. It's a blue-and-white seersucker suit complete with white pleather shoes. He's got a white rose boutonniere pinned to his lapel. Until his arrival there were no authority figures present. I have a feeling he is going to put a halt to my public display of humiliation. I need to seal this deal quick.

I move my eyes back to Rand. "I may not have pined over you for years, but I don't have to. Because after just a few days I already know that I just can't get enough of you. I don't know how this happened or why it happened. I just know that I'm in love with you." Wild cheers go up from the crowd.

I haven't even lowered the microphone when I see Rand leap onto the stage. He runs to me and lays one of those delicious kisses right on my tacky hot-pink lips. I lose myself in his arms. I'm not sure how long we make out in front of the whole school, but when we finally come up for air, everyone is dancing and socializing, and they've forgotten all about us.

"You really do love me, don't you?" Rand asks.

"Duh. Do you see what I'm wearing?"

"I kind of like it. Although . . . it would look better balled up on my bedroom floor." He winks at me.

"Rand Bachrach, do you really think I'm that easy? You've never even taken me on a real date."

"Would it change your mind if I said I had a present for you?"

"The old Aspen may have fallen for that, but not the new and improved Aspen."

He pulls a robin's egg–blue box with a white bow from his pocket.

"Holy shit, Tiffany?" I can't stop myself from swiping the box out of his hand. In my defense, I don't know a woman alive who is immune to those signature boxes. I loosen the ribbon and pop the lid. Lying on a cushion of white cotton batting is a sterling silver heart tag toggle bracelet. The heart is engraved with the initial A. I rub my finger over it, trying to catch my breath. I've wanted one of these ever since I saw Elle Woods wearing one. Elle is my hero. She is a brain, beauty, and fashion guru, and I aspire to be like her in every way. Some people would disagree, but I consider it perfectly acceptable to emulate a fictional character.

"Hey, wait a minute. This wasn't for Amy, was it?" I tease.

"Very funny," Rand replies, securing the bracelet around my wrist.

"It's beautiful, Rand. But I don't understand why you got this for me. I thought you didn't want to be with me."

"Aspen, I've always wanted to be with you. I was just afraid that you would get tired of me. I wasn't sure I could handle losing you. Then I realized that I would rather spend five minutes with you than a lifetime without you."

I am *so* in love with this guy! I want to get away from all of these people and be as close to him as humanly possible.

"Aspen, I'm so sorry I tried to push . . ."

I hold my hand to his mouth to shush him. "Do you wanna chitchat or hit that?"

His dazzling green eyes get huge and he starts to drag me off the stage and through the crowd. We are just pushing through the gym doors when we come face-to-face with Detective Malone.

"Well, if it isn't Detective Buzzkill." I just can't resist giving this guy shit.

"Aspen, I need to talk to you," he says, all business. He glances down at Rand and my intertwined hands.

"Okay, so talk."

"I think it would be better if you heard this alone." He glances at Rand.

"No. Anything you have to say to me you can say in front of Rand." Jeez! This guy is so dramatic.

He takes a deep breath, then says, "All right, your . . ."

"Wait, I'll tell her." My father comes racing around the corner out of breath.

My stomach drops instantly. I know immediately that this is bad. I tighten my grip on Rand's hand in anticipation of Dad's horrible news. I imagine that Mom has been arrested for shoplifting after realizing she couldn't use her credit card. This is all my fault!

"Aspen, Mom's missing. I've been trying to find her since I got home."

I feel like I've just entered some kind of parallel universe. This cannot be happening. Just a few seconds ago, the man of my dreams told me he didn't want to live without me and presented me with Tiffany jewelry. Now my whole world is turned upside down. How can Mom be missing? Have they checked Neiman Marcus? Maybe they are having a huge sale and she just lost track of time. Even I know this isn't possible. I should have been worried when she didn't make it home to help me get ready. I should have done something then.

"There's nothing you could have done, Aspen," Rand says, doing his mind-reading thing.

"He's right, sweetie," Dad agrees, putting a protective arm around my shoulder. I can feel his body trembling. He's trying to be strong for me, but he knows this is really bad.

"Why don't we head back to your house, Dan? I need to ask Aspen a few questions. I'll be there right after I talk to your principal."

We all agree that a hallway filled with hyper, sex-crazed teenagers isn't the place to discuss a missing persons case. Is Mom really a missing person? I wonder if we will have to make fliers to post around the neighborhood? I have no idea what to put down for her weight. Mom will be mortified if I overestimate. The pressure makes me crack. I bury my face into Rand's chest. I really hope this Mary Kay makeup doesn't run or Rand's new button-down is going to look like one of those old "I ran into Tammy Faye Bakker" T-shirts.

Rand leads me to the parking lot. His Jag is parked behind Mom's car.

"Why don't you ride with me and we'll come back and get your car later?"

"No, I'd rather just take it home now. It's only a few blocks," I reply, unlocking Mom's driver side door.

"Whatever you want." He kisses me on the cheek, then opens the door for me. I slide in and start the ignition. I'm about to put the car into drive when I notice something on the front windshield. I roll the window down and stick my hand out to grab it. It is a single long-stemmed white rose. Rand must have left it here. I think white means purity. Rand thinks I'm pure? I was about to show him serious evidence to the contrary before Detective Buzzkill's news. Poor Rand gets put on hold again until we find Mom. I glance in my rearview mirror; he smiles and waves to me. If anybody can help me get through this, Rand can.

A half hour later, I am au naturel after a long, hot shower and some serious help from my assortment of Clinique cleansing products. Mom's dress is hanging safely in her closet awaiting her return. I am much more comfy in jeans and a T-shirt, which makes me feel a little guilty. What if Mom isn't comfortable? I'm just walking down the stairs as Rand lets Detective Malone inside.

We all sit down at the dining-room table. I waste no time with small talk.

"What do you know?" I ask him.

Detective Malone lays a large plastic baggie down in front of me on our glass-topped table. There is a note inside that looks like a kindergartener's cut-and-paste project. Magazine letters of all colors and sizes are pasted to a blank white page. The message reads, "Some people don't deserve to be beautiful." Alongside the note is a chunk of ebony-colored hair.

"That's not my mom's hair. Her hair is chestnut," I say, feeling better now that this is obviously just a huge mistake.

"We know. We've confirmed that the hair sample belongs to Angel Ives. The hair and the note were found taped to your car this afternoon."

All this time I was convinced that Angel was faking her disappearance to get attention. How could I have been so wrong? She really has been missing, and possibly dead, for six days. The same maniac that took Angel has Mom. What if? No, I can't start thinking like that. I have to focus on trying to help Detective Malone figure out who did this.

"Aspen, do you know any possible connection between Angel and your mother?" Detective Malone removes his tiny spiral notebook from his shirt pocket. I wonder if he still has my little rant about not being a couple with Rand still in there. Jeez! What a jerk I've been. All I've been thinking about is myself. I have to make amends with Angel and, more important, find Mom.

"No. My mom doesn't even know Angel. Well, except for the things I've told her." I hang my head with guilt as I remember all the times I've ripped on Angel.

"Don't worry Aspen. We're going to find her." He touches my hand to comfort me. I don't even notice all the hair on his knuckles, I'm just grateful he's being so nice because I know I don't deserve it.

Detective Malone asks my father a few basic questions about Mom's normal schedule. Dad is seriously falling apart and can't even answer him when asked where Mom usually goes for lunch. Something inside me kicks the fear aside and takes over.

"Dad, why don't you go upstairs and lie down for a little while. I can handle the detective's questions."

Dad rises from his chair, kisses the top of my head, then makes his way slowly up the stairs. Detective Malone looks grateful. I don't think Dad has been much help in the investigation. He and Mom have been together almost every single second for eighteen years, and I don't think Dad has a clue how to function without her.

"I can't imagine anything that Angel and Mom would have in common except maybe the whole beautiful thing. They are both very beautiful." A few minutes ago I wouldn't have been caught dead saying Angel was beautiful, but she is.

"We know that they were both compulsive shoppers so we have someone questioning any strange behavior at some of the more popular boutiques and department stores."

My eyes widen at Harry's statement. "Did you tell Dad?" I ask.

He shakes his head no. "I figured your mom could do that when she gets back," he answers. I sigh with relief. Dad doesn't need to be worrying about money now, too.

A department store stakeout? That sounds weak. They've got nothing. The fear creeps back into my stomach as I picture Mom and Angel tied to a stake with flames curling at the ends of their feet. I run to the downstairs bathroom and hurl the Fruit Roll-Up I ate before the dance. Rand follows me to the bathroom and holds my hair out of the toilet. Now that's true love. He wipes my face with a cold washcloth and

I feel better immediately. I brush my teeth, then we rejoin Harry in the dining room.

"I'm really sorry about this, Aspen. I promise you I'm going to do everything I can to get your mom back safe and sound. Here's my card. If you think of anything, don't hesitate to call me, anytime." Before I can say anything he steps quietly out of the house. The house feels so empty without Mom's hyena-style laughing. I feel sick again. I start to sink down into a chair again when Rand folds me into his chest. I collapse into him, sobbing.

Rand lets me bawl my head off for a good fifteen minutes. My head is buried in his wonderful-smelling chest. I want to kiss him so bad, but now is definitely not the time. I have to focus on finding a connection between Angel and Mom so that hopefully I'll have something for Detective Malone to go on.

"There has to be some connection. Serial killers, or whatever this guy is, don't just do things randomly. They always have a detailed plan. I learned that in psych class."

"What does your Mom do for a living again?" Rand asks, while stroking my damp hair.

"She's a personal shopper for senior citizens. Why?" I respond, realizing that Mom may need to find a career less threatening to her addiction when she gets back home.

"I just thought maybe someone had a grudge against her for business reasons." He gently wipes away my last tears.

"I don't think Mrs. Winterbaum hit her on the head with her walker, then took off with her driving twenty miles an hour if that's what you were thinking." I start to laugh a little. I cut it off quickly feeling guilty for cracking a joke when Mom could be in pain. Or worse.

"I know my family gets death threats all the time, and we just make chocolate. There are a lot of angry overweight people out there just waiting to pounce on someone for making them so fat." He's trying hard to cheer me up. I give him a quick peck on the lips for the effort.

"I've got to find her, Rand. She's Dad's whole world."

"Then it's settled. We'll have to find her ourselves."

⊚

I wanted to start our investigation immediately, but Rand convinced me we couldn't do anything in the middle of the night. After tossing and turning for hours, I'm up at the butt crack of dawn ready to find Mom.

Our phone started ringing off the hook as soon as Harry released the news of Mom's disappearance to the media. Half a dozen news crews are already camped out on our front lawn. This kind of fame would normally dazzle me, but when I remember that Mom could be hurt or worse, I just want to go outside and scream at them to quit stepping on Mom's tulip beds. She is going to be super pissed if they don't bloom in the spring. Hopefully she's here in the spring. *No. No. No.* Of course she'll be here. She has to be here.

Harry is going to stop by and escort us to the police station to fill out some required paperwork. As I part my blinds I see him pull up in a black monster truck. Why does this not surprise me? I run downstairs and tell Dad he's here.

I grab Mom's keys and my Dooney. Dad is just coming down the stairs. He could easily get the lead role in *Night of the Living Dead* with the way he looks.

"Dad, I'm going to let you ride with Harry. I'm going to follow you guys so I can meet Rand later."

He nods his head even though I'm pretty sure he doesn't have a clue what I just said. I gently push him out the front door. Detective Malone is waiting to shield us from the reporters. As the three of us push through the crowd they shove cameras and microphones in our faces. They are all screaming questions at us. Is it true she had a Latin lover? Was she really a swinger? Did she really run off with a man twice her age from the senior center? Their questions are so hilarious I have to force myself not to laugh. We are almost to our cars when a short, slimy-looking reporter darts under Harry's arms and gets right in my face.

"So, Aspen. Who do you think will be the Beauty Bandit's next victim?" It seems the media has dubbed the kidnapper the Beauty Bandit. I guess it fits, but it's not very original.

Harry gives him a shove and he falls flat on his back. He is still screaming obscenities about police brutality when I jump into Mom's car.

I pull out of the driveway behind Harry's scary truck. He's got this thing loaded down with accessories. Fog lights, mud flaps, bumper guards, the works. Plastered across his back windshield is a bumper sticker proclaiming "Cops do it with their cuffs on." Huge red block letters on his tailgate spell out "WWDHD?" I'm drawing a blank on this one, but I'm pretty sure Jesus wouldn't mind his initial being replaced if he saw this truck. The pièce de résistance is the metal scrotum hanging from his trailer hitch. Aw, yes, nothing quite says "you're a manly man" like a pair of Truck Nutz. They are scarily realistic complete with veins. I'm a little surprised Harry didn't shave off some of his chest hair and superglue it to the Nutz to make his truck completely anatomically correct. I cannot believe the man responsible for bringing my mom home drives around voluntarily with metal balls hanging from his vehicle.

I need to call Rand and tell him to get started on our investigation without me. I'm not about to leave Mom's fate in Harry's hands. Once stopped at a red light, I grab my purse and start digging through it for my cell. Something sharp pricks my finger and when I pull my hand out my right index finger is bleeding. I look into my purse for the culprit. I see the withered white rose with a drop of blood on a thorn. I forgot all about it. I feel bad that I didn't put it into some water, but Rand will understand with everything I've been through.

The meeting at the police station yields no new clues. Harry is afraid for my safety since Mom was driving Cookie when she disappeared so he insisted that I go straight home. Which I did, and then I bolted as soon as Rand pulled his Jag into the driveway.

We cruise through Comfort in style. Rand pulls off on a side road I didn't even know existed. I've really got to start being more observant. The Jaguar glides effortlessly over the dusty dirt road. After several bends we arrive at a twelve-foot-tall black iron gate. Rand pulls up to what looks like a McDonald's drive-thru speaker. A small television screen comes on above the speaker and I see the face of a burly man dressed in security garb.

"Good afternoon, Mr. Bachrach," he says, then the gate magically slides open allowing the Jaguar access to a smooth concrete driveway. We drive for a full minute until we are in front of the biggest house I've ever seen in my entire life. I don't even think this monstrosity can be classified as a house. More like a stone-covered castle. It's fabulous. I can't believe anything like this even exists in boring Comfort. But then again, a week ago I wouldn't have thought Comfort would be home to a psychotic kidnapper either.

A Christmas tree stands directly in front of a huge picture window on the first level near the entrance. Rand catches me looking at it and says, "My mom likes to decorate the tree for every holiday. This month it has orange and black lights and ghost decorations for Halloween. She's a little eccentric."

"Thanks for the warning." I smile at him as he opens my car door. He leads me through the heavy wooden front door and removes his shoes in the foyer. I follow his lead as I notice the cream Berber carpeting throughout the first floor. For the first time in my life I feel a little bit intimidated. What if Rand's mom doesn't think I'm good enough for him? My parents do okay, but the Bachrach's are obviously banking. His mom probably had a blue-blood debutante from the country club all picked out for him. I'm not exactly on my game today either with Mom missing and all. My stomach lurches again as I picture Mom gagged and hogtied to a chair. I better get control of myself because purple Fruit Roll-Up vomit would not come out of this carpeting. Rand gently places his hand on my shoulder and guides me down a corridor into a great room with a thirty-foot vaulted ceiling.

"Mom, I have someone I want you to meet."

A petite woman of no more than five feet tall turns from the Halloween tree and shouts with joy.

"Aspen, I've heard so much about you." She rushes to-ward me as fast as her short legs will take her. She is dressed for the holiday in a black sweatshirt adorned with candy corn, blue jeans, and matching candy corn socks. Not exactly the Banana Republic/diamond tennis bracelet/perfectly ap-plied Elizabeth Arden makeup-wearing specimen that I was expecting. As she buries her head against my chest and gives me a bear hug I am so glad that I was wrong. She's the perfect mom and it makes my heart ache missing *my* perfect mom. For what seems like the hundredth time since the dance, I start bawling. My tear ducts have taken a serious beating the last two days.

Rand gives his mom the Cliff's Notes version of the kid-napping situation as she sits silently stroking my hair. I haven't met Rand's dad yet, but I'm thinking Rand is a carbon copy of his mom.

"So I was thinking we could get Steve on this and see if he can pick anything up," Rand says, confusing me.

"Who's Steve?" I ask, raising my head off Mrs. Bachrach's now tear-stained sweatshirt.

"He does a little private eye work for the family," Rand's mom answers. "And I'm going to make sure he is at your dis-posal. Rand, I don't want you leaving Aspen's side. If she goes anywhere outside her home, you go with her. Do you have protection?" she asks me.

I shake my head no and pray she's not talking about condoms. She walks into another room and returns holding a small black velvet bag. Ooh, gifts already; I really like this lady.

"This will protect you." She tugs on the drawstring of the velvet bag. She slips her tiny hand inside the bag and pulls out something silver. I can't tell exactly what it is until she flips her wrist and a two-and-a-half-inch serrated blade flies out. I jump back, bumping Rand.

"It's okay. Mom's a pro."

"Aspen, this is a Spyderco Harpy. This little knife will get you out of some big jams. Now just flip it like this," she says, folding it shut and flipping it out again. She's definitely had some practice. "To close it, just press down in the middle and fold it down. If you have to stab somebody, try to go for the leg, and after you stab them, twist the knife. That'll slow 'em down." I think she starts to notice the blood draining from my face. Either that or she's finally noticed Rand making the throat-slicing motion beside me that he didn't think I saw. "I just want you to be safe." She unzips my purse a little and drops the velvet bag in. Dad always said, "Dynamite comes in small packages." I never understood him until now.

I watch her as she walks over to the wall to press a button. A minute later a man with arms the size of tree trunks waltzes in. He is wearing a navy blazer whose seams are being pushed to the limit by his size. Any minute now those sleeves are going to split off. I stifle a laugh. Rand's family has some heavy hitters on the payroll. I feel safer just being here.

"Steve, this is my girlfriend, Aspen. Her mother is missing. We need you to find out anything you can." Rand starts listing all the times and places my mother was spotted before disappearing. Steve takes mental notes. Their conversation loses me as I'm stuck back on the "girlfriend" part. Why am I suddenly so giddy? I've been somebody's girlfriend lots of times so why the butterflies this time? As I look over at my new boyfriend talking animatedly with his hands, trying desperately to help me find my mother, it comes to me. I know what the butterflies are from. I thought I'd been in love before, but I never even got close until Rand came along.

Eleven

Rand and I are sitting at the local coffee shop when tree-trunk-arm Steve squeezes himself into the booth across from Rand and me. He slides a black folder toward us. He's been officially "on the job" for three hours. I'm about to freak out wondering what he's learned about Mom.

Rand removes the single piece of paper from the file. One piece of paper? This does not look good. My eyes scan the document that I can see now is a timeline. It starts at 11 A.M., which is when my mom left the house, and concludes at 5 P.M., which is when mom signed out of Cedarbrook Senior Center. The only thing Rand's private eye turned up that Detective Malone didn't have was that Mom stopped to fill up Cookie before going to the senior center. Somehow, I don't think this holds the clue to her disappearance.

I allow myself to lean against Rand and he puts an intoxicating-smelling arm around me and squeezes. I don't know how I would be functioning if he wasn't here with me. Dad just keeps crying and burying his face in Mom's pillow so he's not exactly a huge support system. This whole scene is like a really bad Lifetime movie.

"So this is it, huh?" Rand says, obviously disappointed.

"It's like she just dropped off the face of the earth, sir," Steve grunts, forgetting that he is talking about the person who gave birth to me, but at the same time remembering who his boss is. On a normal day it would be hilarious to think of someone calling Rand "sir." Today it just makes me sad. Tears form in the corners of my eyes and threaten to spill over onto my cheeks. I don't want a coffee shop full of caffeine junkies seeing me cry. I turn my head and wipe a few stray tears, then compose myself. I pretend that this is all a bad dream and Mom is actually back at the senior home making Mrs. Winterbaum try on a skintight T-shirt that says "porn star" on it. She actually did this once. I start to laugh, eliciting strange looks from Steve and Rand. They both obviously think I've taken that short leap to total insanity.

I try to focus on Rand's short list of suspects that he wants Steve to start surveillance on but my mind drifts.

Last night once it sunk in that Angel really had been kidnapped, I realized that she couldn't have been the one doing *all* the bad things that have been happening to me. There is no way that Angel could have taken the pictures that were printed by the school newspaper. Could the kidnapper be the one behind those pictures and some of the other strange things that have been going on?

I called Theresa Brown, editor of Comfort High's daily student newspaper. At first she wouldn't give up her "source" for the photo. Rand took the phone from me and threatened to cut off all funding for extracurricular activities including the newspaper (apparently Bachrach Chocolate has been infusing the budget of Comfort High for a few years); she admitted that someone had left the photos on her desk anonymously. No lead there, but the fact that the kidnapper may have been in my school doesn't exactly make me feel secure.

Rand and I are now on our way to the Cedarbrook Senior Center just to see if maybe Steve or Detective Malone may have missed something. Besides, half the people here have Alzheimer's so they might remember something now that they didn't earlier. I've felt a little like one of those people. Like something is catching in my brain, a nagging feeling, like I've forgotten something. Like when you "save" a really good memory to savor for a later time, then when you go back you can't remember it the way you want to. Only I feel like this "memory" could help Mom and it's driving me crazy.

"Hey, we're gonna find her." Rand takes one hand off the steering wheel and places it on my knee. I look around the car confused. I don't even remember leaving the café.

I turn to look at my gorgeous new boyfriend. Mom will be so overjoyed we got together. "I know we will," I say, not really believing my own words.

Rand pulls up to the retirement community that looks more like a row of frat houses and cuts the engine. He rushes over to my side to open the door and help me out. Together we walk past several elderly gentlemen playing a not-so-friendly game of poker. I heard "cheating bastard" before they saw us coming. A huge pile of money sits in the middle of a plastic table. These guys aren't messing around.

"Excuse me, gentlemen. I was wondering if we could ask you a few questions," Rand asks, interrupting their game. His request is met with a few scowls until I pipe up with, "It's about my mom, Judy Brooks." The scowls disappear and one of them rushes to scoot two more chairs to their table for us.

"We were so sorry to hear about Judy. She was a true lady, not many of them around anymore. No, sir. I am truly sorry, miss," says a scruffy-looking gentleman who is quite obviously the alpha male of this dilapidated pack. I know I should be grateful for his kind words but I'm not. I'm pissed.

"She's not dead, you know, just missing. They are going to find her. She's going to be fine!" I scream while pounding my fist on the plastic table, causing the bills in their pot to go flying everywhere.

"Of course, ma'am. I'm sorry to have implied anything different. Please forgive me," he says, lowering his head.

Great. Now I've gone off on some sweet old man who has about ten minutes left to live. I'm turning into a monster. Rand helps me out of my chair and escorts me inside while muttering an apology to the senile card sharks.

Inside the lobby he takes me in his arms. I know I'm wasting time having mini-breakdowns every five minutes. I need to be focusing on finding Mom, but I don't even know where to begin.

"Are you sure you don't want to just go back home?" he asks, burying his face into my hair.

"No, we need to be here. Let's go talk to Rosie." I lead the way to Condo 204.

Once there we knock gently on the door. No use giving an eighty-year-old woman a heart attack on top of all the other crappy things going on.

"Ned, get the hell outta here. I'm not putting out today," says a gruff voice behind the door.

Rand looks at me and we both start cracking up. To say that Rosie Winterbaum tells it like it is would be the ultimate understatement. She is almost an extension of our family since my mom met her two years ago. Mom bugs me to visit her more, but I've always had some lame excuse not to. I'm hit with a wall of guilt as I realize that Mrs. Winterbaum may have been the last person to see Mom alive.

I whisper something into Rand's ear and he repeats it word for word. "Aww, come on, Rosie, just rub my old fireworks a little bit." Fireworks are Rosie's favorite term for male genitalia. The door flies open and a tear-streaked Rosie looks ready to give Ned/Rand a piece of something, but it isn't what he wanted.

She sees me and grabs my shoulders, bringing me to her. "Aspen, honey, I'm so sorry. Get in here, you might be in danger." Surprisingly strong for an old lady, she pulls both Rand and I into her condo before we can disagree.

Rosie insists on making drinks. A few minutes later, at tenfifteen in the morning the three of us clink our salt-rimmed margarita glasses together, toasting my mom with virgin margaritas. Rosie's not your average cookie-baking grandma. She prefers mixed drinks and naked Twister. I guess that's why she and Mom get along so good. Not that my mom likes naked

Twister, just because she is so unique. My mom is the smartest person I know. If anybody can outsmart a kidnapper and escape, it's Mom, especially if they make the mistake of taking her to a department store.

"So what did you and Mom talk about yesterday?" I ask, anxious to hopefully find out some new information.

"Well, she said that her and your dad were planning a trip up north in a few weeks for some 'freaky-freaky' time."

"Rosie!" I shout, trying to pull her into the seriousness of the situation.

"Oops, sorry. It was nothing out of the ordinary. We talked about you and she was thrilled that Lucas was finally out of the picture. She said there was some new guy she hoped you realized could be 'the one.' I take it you're him?" She puts her hand on Rand's arm, making his face flush slightly.

"I hope so," he says shyly, making my heart skip a few beats.

We visited with Rosie for two hours and didn't learn one clue. We spent the rest of the afternoon driving around trying to figure out who the kidnapper was. We have nothing.

"I better get home," I tell Rand, looking at the clock. It's already four in the afternoon. "I don't want to leave my dad alone tonight."

Rand agrees and drives me home. A few of the reporters have returned. Lightbulbs flash as I kiss Rand good-bye. For a split second I feel like a fabulous celebrity being stalked by the paparazzi.

I rush through them doing a fantastic job of ignoring their questions. Then I hear a female reporter make a very uncalled-for comment.

"Hey, Aspen? Did the Beauty Bandit steal all your couture when he took your mom?" She asks, taking in my jeans and ratty sweatshirt.

This stops me cold in my tracks. I turn to face the offending journalist. Fear crosses her face as she realizes what she's done. I'm about to rip her last-season Prada pantsuit to shreds when I realize that it doesn't matter what she's wearing or what I'm wearing. It only matters that I get Mom back. I decide that holding a mini–press conference might be just the thing to rattle the kidnapper's chains.

"What's your name?" I politely ask her. A bright camera light points straight at my face.

"Lindsey Waters, Channel Seven News," she responds proudly, thrusting her cheesy business card at me.

I shove it in my purse without even looking at it, which elicits an evil look from Lindsey. "Well, Lindsey. I just want to thank you for your concern. I appreciate all of you getting the word out about my mom. My dad and I are devastated. I think all of us, myself included, tend to be a little too concerned about appearances. When you lose someone you love, the last thing on your mind is looking fashionable. I hope that none of you ever have to experience what my family is going through. If anyone has any information about Judy Brooks, please call Detective Malone at the Comfort Police Department. Thank you." I turn to walk inside, then get an idea. I turn back around, stare straight into the camera, and say, "Beauty Bandit, if you're watching, you better pray that

Detective Malone finds you first, because if I do, I'm going to rip your balls off." I hear cheering as I turn and enter the front door.

As I walk through the great room my stomach drops as I hear my mother's voice. It's coming from the living room. I drop my purse and run to her. When I get to the living room, it's just Dad watching home videos. It's from our family vacation to Florida last spring. Mom is building a sand castle. I drop to the floor in front of the TV and sob uncontrollably. I'm heaving so bad I barely feel Dad wrap his arms around me.

After taking turns crying, Dad and I try to pull ourselves together. We both know that we have to stay strong and take care of each other until Mom gets back. I follow him into the kitchen while he makes us a dinner of burgers and fries, which is pretty much the only meal he knows how to make since Mom does all of the cooking.

I hop onto the kitchen island and hang my legs over the counter. This is something I could never get away with if Mom were here. Maybe if I start doing bad things, she'll come screeching in threatening to ground me. I wish. Not like Mom could ever stick to a punishment anyway. The only time I ever got grounded she ended up getting so bored having to stay home and monitor me that we ended up going to St. Louis for a shopping spree. In hindsight I guess maybe she needed a fix.

"So, you and Rand, huh?" Dad asks, eyebrows raised, while flipping a burger.

I sigh as the butterflies coming rushing into my tummy at the mention of my new boyfriend's name. "Yeah, I'm in love."

"Sweetie, that's fantastic." He puts one arm around me while holding the spatula with the other. "He's a super guy, but I didn't think he would be your type."

"He's exactly my type. It just took me a while to quit being an idiot and figure that out."

"High school's hard. Everybody's trying to be popular and the people who are popular are trying to live up to the conformities that come along with popularity."

"Yeah, but it doesn't sound like you ever did. Mom said you ditched the homecoming queen for her. That was a pretty bold move."

"Oh, Aspen. Your mother just took my breath away. Something about her just had me mystified. I couldn't get enough. I still can't . . ." He trails off, huge tears forming in his eyes.

"It's okay, Dad. We're gonna get her back. I promise," I say, rubbing his back.

We both nibble at our dinner in silence. We are both too upset to eat.

Dad finally breaks the unbearable silence. "Aspen, I need to ask you a question and I want you to tell me the truth. Deal?"

He catches me off guard so I just nod my head yes. Please don't let him ask me if I've had sex!

"Is Mom having an affair?"

"What?" I scream.

Very calmly, he repeats the question. "Is your mother having an affair?"

"Stop saying that," I say, getting angry. "Those reporters are stupid. Don't listen to them. One of them just had the nerve to question my fashion sense."

"It's not them. Detective Malone said she had a secret post office box and they found a white rose in her purse."

"What?"

"She has a secret . . ."

"No, about the rose."

"They found a white rose in her purse."

I bolt from the table and grab the cordless. I speed dial Rand's cell. I don't bother greeting him when he picks up.

"Did you leave a white rose on my car last night?"

"No," he answers, cautiously.

"Okay, I've got to go. I'll call you later." I click off and turn to face Dad.

"Mom has the post office box so you don't see the credit card bills. She's a shopaholic. We need to get her some help when she gets back."

"Huh?" Dad replies, looking confused. "You don't have to cover up for her, Aspen."

"Dad, listen, she's not cheating on you. We'll talk about the other stuff later. I had a white rose on my car yesterday, too. I assumed it was from Rand, but it wasn't. It's a clue."

"I'll call Detective Malone," Dad says, reaching for the phone.

I hear Dad tell Harry about the white rose clues then he starts apologizing for some reason. After he hangs up, he turns to me, and says, "He isn't too happy about your impromptu news conference. He's been bombarded with kooks calling in false tips." Oops.

"I was just trying to help."

"I know, sweetie."

We switch on the Channel Seven News, and Dad thinks my speech is perfectly lovely. Until they show me saying, "I'm going to rip your *bleep* off."

⊚

I'm driving myself crazy trying to figure out who would have left the roses for Mom and me. I finally flip on the TV in hopes that if I stop thinking about it, it will just pop into my mind.

I find an old rerun of *Full House*. I love this show. The Olsen twins were adorable before their eating disorders. John Stamos is such a hottie even with a mullet.

Blue and white. Reeks of Lands' End. Something is coming to me. I don't want to focus on it or I might scare the rest away. Focus on *Full House*. This is the episode where Stephanie is stressing because she is being pressured by some older girls to smoke. I wish she could hear me because I'd tell her to go ahead and light up. In a few years, when she's an ice head, a few cigarettes won't be such a big deal.

Wrinkled. Seersucker. Mr. Lowe. Why in the world am I thinking about Mr. Lowe's tacky-ass suit at a time like this? My uncanny fashion sense can really be a disability sometimes.

Wait a minute. Now I remember. Mr. Lowe had a white rose boutonniere pinned to his lapel. *Mr. Lowe is the beauty bandit!* It makes perfect sense. He was at the bonfire and could easily have kidnapped Angel. He could have taken the pictures of me and Rand and Tobi and Pippi and easily sneaked them to Theresa's desk. Then he somehow wrote that despicable note saying I wanted to have sex with him. Maybe he was mad that

I screamed in horror and that's why he kidnapped Mom. I always thought he was a little strange. It's all coming together now. I should call Harry with my lead, but I can already hear his annoyingly nasal voice telling me that he needs more proof. So I dial Rand instead.

"Hey, come get me right away. Drive your most inconspicuous car," I tell him.

"Do I even want to know what this is about?"

"I think it's better if we don't discuss that on an unsecure line." I click off and head toward my closet. I pull down several Gucci, Jacobs, and Choo shoeboxes until I find the black leather case I'm looking for. I place the case into my Dooney bubble-gum-pink Heart mini gym bag.

I change into a black baby-doll tee and black cigarette pants. While fondling my pink UGG boots my better judgment takes over and I lace up my Nikes instead. I might not win any best-dressed awards tonight, but at least I'll be able to make a run for it if I have to.

Headlights shine through the cracks in my blinds. I run downstairs to tell Dad that I'm leaving. He's crashed out on the couch with the cordless phone resting on his belly. If Mom saw how pitiful he was without her, she would love it. Quietly, I slip out the front door. Rand is waiting in a nondescript gray Camry. He is such an exceptional listener.

"You look hot," he says as I slide in.

"I know who has Mom and Angel," I reply, ignoring his comment.

"What? Who?" He puts the car in park and stares expectantly at me.

"Mr. Lowe."

He scrunches his nose up and makes a funny face. "I don't think so, Aspen. He's a pretty good guy."

"Just drive," I command, proceeding to tell him about the white roses.

"Maybe it was just a strange coincidence."

"Maybe monkeys fly out of my ass, too."

"Really? Let me see," he jokes.

"I'm serious, Rand. I know it's him."

He searches my face, then nods. "If you feel that strongly about it, we'll check him out."

I dig through my backpack and pull out our school directory. This thing is really coming in handy this week. After I find Mr. Lowe's address Rand heads in that direction. Comfort is so small that we pull up to his house in less than two minutes. His house is a typical bi-level, nothing fancy. His red Chevy S-10 sits in the driveway. Rand pulls off to the side directly across the street from his house and turns the lights off. The downstairs of Mr. Lowe's house is dark, but I can see his outline against an upstairs bedroom window. He is sitting in front of a glowing computer screen.

"See? He's probably just grading some papers." Rand says, turning the head lights back on.

"Kill the lights, Rand," I demand, grabbing the leather case out of my backpack. He shakes his head, but turns the lights back off. I unzip the case and pull out my night-vision binoculars.

"I don't want to know why you have those, do I?" Rand asks.

"I used them last year when I was stalking this guy I was dating."

He looks horrified. I put my hand on his arm and squeeze. "Hey, you don't have anything to be jealous of. That guy was history the minute I found out his primary mode of transportation was the city bus."

Rand starts laughing hysterically.

"There's never going to be a dull moment with you, is there?"

"God, I hope not." I put the binoculars up to my eyes and aim them toward the upstairs bedroom. The only thing I can see is the back of Mr. Lowe's head. I wonder if he knows he's got a couple of bald spots back there?

"Can you see anything?" Rand asks impatiently.

"Nope, just the back of his desperately-in-need-of-Hair-Club-for-Men head."

"Seriously?"

"Oh, yeah. He's losing acreage as we speak." A few more minutes go by and I still can't see anything. I get an idea. I pull out the directory again.

"Rand, block your cell phone number, then call this phone number." I rattle off Mr. Lowe's digits.

"Woman, you are so freaking brilliant," he says, dialing Mr. Lowe's number.

"That's why you love me." I smile. I put the binoculars back up to my eyes and hope that this works.

"Is it ringing?"

"Yeah, first ring."

Mr. Lowe rises from his chair to answer the phone. When he does, my eyes feel like they are burning in their sockets.

"Oh. My. God," I yell, jerking away from the binoculars.

"Did you see them? Does he have Angel and your mom?" Rand asks frantically.

"I don't know yet, but he wears thong underwear."

Rand is laughing so hard he forgets to hang up the phone. We both hear Mr. Lowe yelling hello over and over. Rand clicks off and I hurry to see if his computer screen holds any clues.

Pay dirt. Mr. Lowe is surfing bondage websites. I knew that fucking freak was behind this. I meant what I said to Channel Seven News. If he hurts my mom, I'm going to rip his balls off and I can be pretty tough if I want to be.

"Can you see anything?" Rand asks anxiously.

"Yeah, he's into S and M." Mr. Lowe's hairy ass comes back into focus and I drop the binoculars. I glare at his house and notice a light coming from a basement window.

"I need to see what's down there," I say, pointing toward the window. I move to open my door and Rand grabs my arm.

"Hold on a sec, Dirty Harriet. Don't you think we should call Detective Malone?"

"I just want to peek in that window. Mom might be down there. I can't just leave."

"I'll go," he volunteers. "You just keep an eye on him, and if he moves honk the horn."

I don't argue with him because I know he's right. If something really bad is down there, it wouldn't benefit my mental health to see it.

"I just need to tell you something completely insensitive. Once we find your mom, I'm going to ravage your body in about a thousand different ways." He bolts into the darkness, leaving me speechless.

I watch him run across the street and disappear into the shadow of the trees. I aim the binoculars at the back of Mr. Lowe's head and concentrate on watching him. I refuse to think about why his head is bobbing back and forth or why he has a jumbo box of tissues next to his computer.

Rand jumps back in the car nearly giving me heart failure. He hits the lights and takes off flying down the street. He is visibly shaken.

"What did you see?" I ask, not really wanting to know.

"Nothing. We need to go talk to Detective Malone," he says, driving toward the police station.

"*Did you see my mom?*" I scream.

"No. But I saw enough."

I decide not to interrogate him since he's so upset. I'll hear it all when he tells Harry anyway.

A uniformed officer shows us into Harry's office. He tells us that he is on the way. Rand sits stoically in a beat-up leather chair. I pass the time checking out Harry's personal photos. He and the blonde were quite the world travelers before the mini-blondes came along. There is one of them on a cruise, at a Vegas show, snorkeling in Aruba. One of Harry crashed out on a couch with a sleeping baby on his chest. Another picture is of him with no shirt on (*Yikes!*) sitting in a kiddie pool with his three little girls. Maybe I've been too hard on him. He looks like he's a pretty good dad.

He stumbles in with a serious case of bed head.

My mute boyfriend suddenly develops a serious case of diarrhea of the mouth.

"He's got posters, rope, duct tape, chairs, whips . . ."

"Whoa there, big guy. Take it easy," Harry says, settling into his chair. "First of all. Who are you talking about?"

Rand is about to start babbling again when I touch his shoulder.

"We have reason to believe that Mr. Lowe is the Beauty Bandit," I announce.

"Your accounting teacher?" he asks, bewildered.

"Yes, and we have proof." I've got his full attention now. I explain about the roses, the sex note, the S and M website he was surfing, and his thong panties. Rand adds what he saw, which apparently included several disturbing dominatrix posters, a roll of duct tape, a chair with ropes wrapped around it, and a male mannequin wearing a complicated-looking leather ensemble complete with matching face mask and zippered mouth.

Shit! No wonder he didn't want to talk about it. To think the school board trusted Mr. Lowe to mold our impressionable young minds. Just wait until Miss Hott finds out about this. Leatherface is going to be so fired!

Once Rand finishes Harry calls someone and is talking about judges and emergency search warrants. I feel like I'm on an episode of *COPS*. It's kind of cool. I just hope we aren't too late to save Mom.

The detective hangs up the phone and says, "I want you two to head straight home. I'll let you know as soon as we find anything out."

As if! I'm the one who figured out who the Beauty Bandit is. This is my bust. I totally have the right to be there when they take him down.

Harry immediately senses my attitude and raises an eye-brow. I wasn't born yesterday. I'll just give him what he wants so that I don't end up with a police escort home.

I flash him my sweetest smile. "I feel so much better know-ing that you are handling everything. I can't wait to give Dad the good news," I pull a dazed Rand out of his chair.

"Okay, see ya." I wave and shut the door behind the shocked detective.

Twelve

Safely back in the car Rand starts toward my house.

"No! Go back to Mr. Lowe's!" I shout.

"Hell, no! I'm not going anywhere near that freaky house of leather again. I'm telling you, Aspen, I'm scarred for life."

I start to stroke the back of his neck, then run my fingers through his hair. "Please? For me? I just want to see them get him."

"Damn you, Aspen Brooks. You're like my kryptonite." He laughs, turning the car around toward Mr. Lowe's house.

⊙

We've been sitting down the street from Mr. Lowe's house for twenty minutes and not a single car has driven by.

"He freaking blew us off. He thinks we are just stupid kids who don't know what we're talking about!" I scream, my blood boiling.

"Sweetie, calm down. These things take time. They can't just go busting in there or they might never find your mom," Rand says, rubbing my arm.

I know Rand is just trying to make me feel better but I can't help thinking that things could be speeded up a little. And I think I know just what I can do to help. I grab my purse off the floorboard and start riffling through it like a maniac. My fingers finally find the small white square of paper they were frantically searching for. I dial the phone number listed on the card and Lindsey Waters's annoying voice comes on the line.

"This is Aspen Brooks. If you want an exclusive on the Beauty Bandit, get to Three-twelve Sycamore as fast as you can." I snap my phone shut before she can bore me with her undying gratitude.

"Oh, no," Rand groans. "Aspen, that was a really bad idea."

"I don't have bad ideas." I inform him.

He just keeps shaking his head, which is getting seriously annoying. We are just about to get into our first official fight as a couple when two unmarked cars with their headlights off roll past us. I recognize Harry in the passenger side of one of the cars.

They come to a silent stop in front of Mr. Lowe's house and six men in plain clothes jump out. Two immediately head for the backyard and two more split up and each take a side of the house. Harry and a very tall accomplice head to the front door. Harry raises his fist to knock on the door and I can see he's holding a white piece of paper. A few seconds later a light in the upstairs window goes on.

Just as Harry raises his fist to knock again the front door swings open. A groggy-looking Mr. Lowe with bed head and the shortest terry cloth robe imaginable stands staring at Harry confused. Harry thrusts the paper at him and babbles for a good two minutes. I roll down my window to try and hear but they are too far away. Mr. Lowe nods and then Harry starts to lead him to the unmarked police car.

This whole scene is such a letdown. Why didn't they bust his door in and give him some street justice? And where is the SWAT team? Comfort PD doesn't ever have to worry about *COPS* coming here to film. *Boring*!

But then a white van skids to a stop right in front of Mr. Lowe's house. Lindsey Waters jumps out with a cameraman blasting Harry and Mr. Lowe with a million watts. Now this is more like it!

Mr. Lowe tries to use the bottom of his robe to cover his face and accidentally flashes his thong at Lindsey and the cameraman. I think Lindsey is going to have to blur out part of that video to make it acceptable for her viewing public. Rand is laughing so hard he's practically snorting.

A huge vein in Harry's neck pops out as he screams, "Get out of here or I'll arrest you. You're disrupting a police investigation."

I see Lindsey shrug, then get back in the van and speed down the road.

Harry and his partner help Mr. Lowe into the backseat then disappear around the corner. The other four detectives disappear inside Mr. Lowe's house.

A huge weight has been lifted because I know it's just a matter of time before Mom is found. I just have to find something to take my mind off of her for a while.

"What was that you were saying earlier about my body?" I ask Rand, running my hand up his leg.

◎

It's six in the morning and I'm trying to sneak back into my house undetected. What kind of daughter stays out all night when her mother has been kidnapped? A horny one.

After seeing Mr. "Leatherface" Lowe do the walk of shame in his teeny terry cloth robe, we snuck into the guest cottage on the Bachrach estate. I'm not the kind of girl who goes into graphic detail about her sexual escapades because I think that's white trash. But, if someone forced me to rate my three sexual experiences, I do have my own special rating system. On my sexual rating system Bryce (the guy I stalked last year) would be a pair of two-dollar Target flip-flops. Lucas would be a semidecent pair of Steve Madden Mary Janes. Rand is a pair of impossible-to-find vintage Jimmy Choos. All girls like wearing flip-flops and Mary Janes *until* they have a pair of vintage Choos in their closet. But once they have a pair of Choos in their closet they can't ever go back to flip-flops. Translation: I won't ever need to have sex with anyone, but Rand, *ever again*!

Luckily, Dad is still crashed out on the couch. I suppose I should feel guilty about being out all night fornicating while Mom is still missing, but I know that my brilliant detective skills in bringing down Mr. Lowe will get her home soon.

I creep into my bedroom and shut the door. I slip into my Nick & Nora pj's and climb under the covers. I am so not going to school today. I'm exhausted from the excitement of Mr. Lowe's bust and the mind-blowing sex. My eyelids flutter shut only to fly open again when I hear someone banging on the front door. I pull back my blinds to see Harry's unmistakable truck. He's got news about Mom; maybe he even brought her home. I fly down the stairs and nearly tackle the detective.

"Did he talk? Did you find her?" I ask him, breathless.

"Aspen, what are you talking about?" Dad asks, confused.

"Come and sit down, you two," Harry says, wearily leading us to our dining-room table. I don't like the look on his face one bit and Mom definitely didn't come home with him.

All three of us take a seat. I notice poor Dad's hands trembling as he pulls his chair out. He knows it's bad news, too.

Harry takes a deep breath, and then finally speaks. "I'm sorry, but we don't know anything more than what we knew yesterday."

"What do you mean? What about Mr. Lowe?" I shout.

He holds his hand out for me to stop. Dad hangs his head in his hands.

"Aspen, I appreciate that you want to find your mom, but I can't have you and Mr. Bachrach meddling in our investigation. We arrested an innocent man last night. And now because of that ditzy news reporter you called his life is ruined."

"What about the rope and the duct tape and all the weird leather stuff?" I interrupt him.

Dad raises his head back up and asks, "What the hell are you two talking about?"

"I take it your dad knew nothing about your adventures last night?" Detective Malone asks.

I shake my head no, knowing that I'm in for it.

"Could someone please tell me what the hell is going on?" Dad asks again, his voice raising.

I decide to plead the fifth on this one. Let the hairy asshole bust me if he wants to. All I care about is finding Mom and it sounds like I'm going to have to start all over.

He starts explaining to Dad my white rose theory. Then he describes how Rand and I "Peeping Tom'd" on Mr. Lowe.

I can't stand it anymore and interrupt. "Last night you agreed with us. You even had guys searching through his house. So why are you trying to act like this is all *my* fault?"

Harry gives me a dirty look and I realize that I just outed myself about hanging around watching the bust go down last night.

"So does Mr. Lowe have something to do with my wife's disappearance or not?" Dad asks, angry and confused.

"It seems that Mr. Lowe has some questionable sexual habits, but he is not a kidnapper," he answers.

"What about the chair and the rope?" I interject.

"He paid a prostitute to tie him up and cover his mouth with duct tape while whipping him."

Eww . . . that is one mental snapshot I don't need.

"Jesus, this man is a teacher?" Dad asks, horrified.

"I'm getting ready to pay a visit to the principal about that right now. School has been cancelled this week due to the kidnappings also."

"What about the roses? Did you ask him about the roses?" I can't let this go.

"Aspen, it's not him. It was just a coincidence."

"Did you ask him?" I insist.

"I didn't need to. I've been doing this a long time, Aspen." He lowers his voice to a soothing tone. "I'm going to find her, but I can't have you running around starting fires for me. I have to focus on this investigation."

Dad pipes up with, "Don't worry, Harry. She's going to be under lock and key. She won't be causing trouble for anybody." He gives me an angry look, and I feel about two years old.

"I'll let you know the minute we find out anything," Harry says, rising from the table. He lets himself out the front door.

Dad and I just sit there staring at each other. When he finally speaks, he says, "Aspen, I'm so disappointed in you." Jeez! Think how disappointed he'd be if he knew about all the hot premarital sex I engaged in last night, too.

Hello! I was trying to save the freaking day while everyone else was sitting around feeling sorry for themselves. I want to scream at him, but I don't because I can hear Mom's voice in my head saying he doesn't really mean it. He's just messed up because he's so worried about her. When I don't bother to defend myself, he turns and walks back upstairs without another word.

⟳

"Hi."

"Hey, there. I was starting to wonder if maybe I was just a one-night stand." Rand answers, laughing.

"Puhlease! Your shit is like crack and I'm developing a twice-a-day habit." I tell him, meaning every bit of it.

"Don't tease me. When can I see you?"

"Like never. I'm totally on house arrest. Detective Gorilla Arms came over and blamed me for his bogus arrest."

"Yeah, he came over here, too. I don't know what was worse, him chewing me a new one, or explaining to my mom what a dominatrix is."

We both start cracking up.

"I'm sorry I drug you into this," I apologize.

"Aspen, I'd follow you anywhere. You know that. Besides, I thought you were right. Boy, Mr. Lowe's got some issues, huh?"

"Ya think?" I laugh. "Hey, totally off subject, but I want to ask you something that's been bugging me."

"Shoot."

"Who called you that night in the Ravioli's parking lot?"

"You mean right before I was about to attack you?"

"You were trying to play it all cool. I knew you wanted me. So, who was it?" I'd never tell Rand this, but it's been driving me crazy that he went and met Amy later that night.

"It was my mom. She wanted me to pick up a gallon of milk on the way home."

"You suck. I was totally jealous."

"It was all part of my master plan to make you fall in love with me."

"It worked."

We both agree to get some sleep and talk later. I switch my cell to vibrate and slip it under my pillow. I don't need

Dad confiscating it. I fall asleep the minute my head hits the pillow.

☺

Minutes later, I wake up screaming, drenched in sweat.

Dad storms into my room. "Sweetie, what's wrong?" He wraps his arms around me.

"I just had a bad dream." I feel better instantly with his arms around me.

I close my eyes and try to block out the image in my nightmare. I open them and glance over at the clock on my bedside table. I was asleep for six hours, but it only felt like a few minutes. I can't believe all the mental investigation time I've wasted. I don't care what Detective Chia Pet says I'm going to figure this out myself. He will so be kissing my ass when I bring down the Beauty Bandit. This time I'll definitely be doing my own reconnaissance before tipping him off.

"Are you still mad at me?" I ask Dad. He hugs me tighter and starts to cry.

"Aspen, I'm so sorry about earlier. I just feel so helpless. What if Mom is out there hurt somewhere?"

I pull back to look him in the eyes. "Don't think like that. She's going to be fine. I just know it." I really want to tell him that I'm going to find her myself, but he might lock me in a closet so I better not. Dad wanders back into his bedroom.

Once I make sure that Dad is fast asleep, I try calling Rand on his cell, but just get his voice mail. He must still be asleep.

I burrow back into the covers. The horrible image from my nightmare pops right into my thoughts. It's Mr. Lowe dressed in his cheesy seersucker suit. He's wearing the leather mask; it's black, with a candy-colored zipper like my Dooney. He unzips it and laughs maniacally. Then in a high-pitched voice he says, "Do you like my rose?" He just keeps repeating it over and over. It is beyond creepy.

I jump out of bed and decide to shower to distract myself. While curling my hair I try to think of any kind of connection between Angel and my mom. I'm still not buying that their disappearances are unrelated. I make a mental checklist about Mom and Angel to see if I can figure out any similarities.

Angel Ives:
Head cheerleader of CH Seagals
Borderline intelligence at best
Beautiful in a slutty, psycho kind of way
Family richer than Bill Gates
Dates Jimmy McAllister
Blows Lucas Riley (tramp)
Has icky tramp stamp
Extremely devoted to her younger sister (in an attempt to
    possibly clone herself)
Uses really cheap lipstick

Judy Brooks:
Perfect mom
Perfect wife

Beautiful

Smart

Former geek turned chic

Eliminates stress through several weekly retail therapy appointments (read: shopaholic)

Personal shopper for senior citizens

I've got it! Angel was having an affair with an old geezer at the senior home where Mom works. Geezer's wife found out and whacked Angel. Mom happened to find Angel's bloody cheerleading outfit in the trash and was about to call 911 when geezer's wife knocked her unconscious with her cane. Geezer's wife is holding Mom hostage until her Social Security check comes and she can skip town.

Okay, so it's not my best theory. I'm drawing a total blank. Maybe it was pure coincidence that Mom and Angel were both kidnapped. I can only hope that they are keeping each other company chatting about Choos, Spades, and Ferragamos when the kidnapper isn't torturing them.

Maybe if I can get my stomach to quit growling, I can figure something out. I bounce downstairs and pull the fixings for a cheese toastie from the frig. Somehow I manage to burn the outer edges of the sandwich, but the middle is soggy and uncooked. Mom's cheese toasties are always golden brown all over with the cheese melted to the perfect consistency. I try to choke mine down anyway since I'm starving. Leatherface pops back into my head causing me to nearly choke.

"Do you like my rose?" He keeps asking me in that majorly creepy voice.

"Fuck off, freak." I respond to an empty kitchen. Great, now I'm losing it. I pitch the rest of the offending sandwich in the trash and head back upstairs. I have to shove my door hard to get it to budge open just a little. My room is a complete disaster area. If Mom saw this, she would not be happy. I get to work sorting clothes into piles of dry clean only and normal wash. Mom is going to have a lot of laundry waiting for her when she gets back.

Mom's hot-pink pumps are thrown carelessly in a corner. I pick them up and tiptoe into Mom and Dad's closet. I replace them in their shoebox and slide them back on the shelf. I turn to leave and something really hard smacks me on the head. "Shit." I yell. I peek out to make sure I didn't wake Dad. He's still snoring. I reach down to pick up the nearly deadly weapon. It's Mom's yearbook. I take it back into my room and crawl into bed. I flip through pages of black-and-white photos until I get to Mom's senior picture.

I was so horrified when she showed this picture to me the other day. But when I look at the picture now, I just see my beautiful mother smiling back at me. I can't stop the flood of tears from spilling down my cheeks.

I miss my mommy! I sneak back into Dad's room. Very gently, I pull Mom's pillow from Dad's sleeping grip. Gripping it safely in my arms I go back to my own room. I hold the pillow in front of my face and take a deep breath of Mom's scent. The perfume she wears that I've always hated fills my nostrils. It's really not so bad after all. I read somewhere that scents evoke powerful memories. Memories of Mom fill my mind. Mom holding a bouquet of white roses.

Mom holding a pink picture frame. Mom performing cheers with just one turquoise pom-pom. I put the pillow down. That's weird. I don't remember any of those things actually happening, but how could I have memories of them if they didn't happen?

The yearbook has fallen open to the picture of Dad with the good-looking blonde. Suddenly I hear my mom's voice as clear as if she was in the room with me.

"He dumped the homecoming queen to be with me."

I get another whiff of Mom's perfume again, and I'm bombarded with a collage of images. I look down at the picture again. There isn't a doubt in my mind this time. I know who the Beauty Bandit is!

I jump off my bed and grab my backpack. I tip it over and dump everything out on my bed. I grab my cell from under my pillow and the student directory. In a panic I find Mr. Lowe's phone number and dial it.

"You people stop calling here. I'm not a kidnapper!" he screams into the phone.

"Mr. Lowe, it's Aspen. I need to know who gave you the white rose at the dance," I plead.

"Oh, hello, Aspen. I guess I have you to thank for being strip-searched and having all of my orifices checked for contraband last night. It really was a night to remember. Now I'm unemployed as well. So, just what is it that *you* need *me* to do for *you*?"

Yikes! Bitter much?

"Listen, Mr. Lowe. I am super sorry and I promise to help you get your job back. But right now I need to know who gave you that white rose."

He reaffirms what I already knew. I click off and rush to wake up Dad.

$$\odot$$

He's lying on his stomach, face turned to one side, snoring like a bear in hibernation. I gently shake him but he's not responding. I start to shake him harder, but he just keeps snoring. Then I notice a pill bottle and a half empty bottle of water on the bedside table. I pick the bottle up and read the label. Valium. Shit! He's OD'd because he can't face living without Mom. I dump the remaining pills in the palm of my hand and count nine. The label says the prescription was for ten pills. He only took one pill. Probably just to fall asleep. I'm getting a little paranoid. One thing's for sure, he's not going to be any help. I bend down and kiss his cheek.

I rush back to my bedroom and throw open my closet door. Which Dooney do you take to confront a kidnapper? Too bad they don't make one with mini skulls and crossbones, something like that would be perfect. I think maybe I'll e-mail that idea to the company when all this mess is over. I grab my black Doodle since it matches the outfit I had on last night that I just threw on again. I can't believe I'm wearing an outfit twice without washing it. A few more days of this intense stress and I'll be reduced to wearing something with an elastic waistband. The horror!

I know that I should call Rand and tell him my suspicions, but he'd never let me go alone, and I don't want to put him in danger. Harry wouldn't listen to me, and even if he did, he'd never let me use myself as bait. I'm that kick-ass action heroine again, only this time in real life. Right about now I'm really wishing I had stuck out a few more years of karate. I slip into my pink UGGs and slide my RAZR into the side of my left boot.

I'm about to leave the house when I realize I should probably leave a clue behind in case no one ever hears from me again. I grab the school directory from my Dooney along with a red Sharpie and circle a name and address, then prop it up on the table next to Dad's bed. I bend down and give him another kiss. Now I'm ready to save the day!

Cookie is still in police impound being processed for evidence according to Detective Folically Unchallenged. I think he's full of shit and just thinks if I don't have wheels that I'll stay out of his way. Wrong.

I slide into Mom's Acura and head toward Walgreens. I have a brilliant plan, but I need a few supplies. I fly into a handicapped parking space. I think getting ready to make yourself the equivalent of human chum and dangling yourself in front of a great white shark qualifies for a handicapped spot. If not, freaking bite me.

A very Goth-looking twenty-ish-something guy behind the counter looks up from his *National Enquirer* as I stomp on the rubber mat causing the glass door to slide open. We both nod an acknowledgment to each other's presence, then I go tearing down the aisles in search of supplies.

Three minutes later and my arms overflowing, I dump everything in front of the Marilyn Manson wannabe. I see a grin playing at the corners of his mouth. I look down at my purchases and can't blame him for laughing. My supplies consist of three bottles of eyedrops (the kind the stoner kids use to disguise their bloodshot eyes), a package of razor blades, one giant sampler box of Bachrach chocolates, and a very discounted pair of one-size-fits-all thong panties leftover from last Valentine's Day that say "yummy" on the cotton panel. Classy, I know. I was walking by the giant bin of thong panties wondering to myself, How desperate would you have to be to buy undergarments at Walgreen's? when I had another brilliant idea. So I snatched a pair up. Besides, Rand might think they are funny once all this is over with.

I peel two twenties off my roll of allowance cash. I wonder if Harry will be able to reimburse me for this stuff? I mean, this is supposed to be his investigation, so he should be footing the bill or at the very least, the tax-paying citizens of Comfort, not some allowance-challenged seventeen-year-old who has to scrape for every last penny. Marilyn hands me my change, scoops everything into a plastic bag, then tells me to, "take it easy on the wacky tobacky." If I weren't in such a huge hurry, I would challenge him on his stereotypes of people's purchases. Luckily for him, I've got two people to save.

I pull into Cedarbrook Senior Center at 3:30 P.M., otherwise known as dinnertime in these parts. The card sharks have a hella pot going. I'd buy in if I didn't have this mystery to solve. I stuff the Walgreens supplies into my purse then head toward Rosie's condo.

The gamblers are careful to offer greetings instead of consolations this visit. When I reach Rosie's door, I tap gently. It flies open and Rosie's dressed in the "porn star" T-shirt my mom bought for her. She's got jean capris and ballet flats on to complete the outfit. Rosie is like the Kate Moss of the retirement home. In the supermodel way, not the big cokehead way. She squeals and throws her bony arms around me. After a moment we retreat into her condo.

A really old looking guy is sitting on her couch watching *Dr. Phil*. He is chubby and has on gray sweatpants, a blue sweatshirt, and these funny-looking weaved plastic slippers. His head is bald except for a few sprouts of grayish-black hair. But when he smiles at me, his cheeks start glowing scarlet, and his tired eyes twinkle blue. He's adorable, in a grandpa kind of way. This must be Ned. I try really hard not to picture him and Rosie getting it on.

"Aspen, this is Ned," she says, making our introductions. Ned lifts his hand and gives me a small wave.

"Any news about your mom yet?" Rosie asks, cutting the small talk short. I can tell that Rosie is trying really hard to keep it together.

"No, I just came by to see if you remembered anything else from the last day you talked to her." This is total bullshit. But I know if I tell Rosie the real reason I came, she'd call the police and screw up my plan. I feel bad, but I just can't take that chance. My mom's life depends on this. Oh yeah, and Angel, I keep forgetting about her.

"It was a wonderful visit. The highlight of my week, just as usual," Rosie says, fighting back tears. I hate that I had to come here and get her all upset, but I didn't have a choice. She has something that I need.

"Rosie, can I use your restroom?"

"Why, of course, sweetheart. You go right ahead."

I grab my purse and head down the hall. Once I get there I quietly pop open the door on Rosie's medicine cabinet. On the second shelf I find exactly what I'm looking for and pop it into my purse. I pull the panties out, slip out of my jeans and Victoria's Secret panties, and slip into the Walgreens thong. My butt cheeks feel immediately chafed from the imitation cotton blend of the cheap panties. I am so going to need a full-body sugar scrub after this! I bet Harry has never made this kind of sacrifice to solve a case.

I dig through my purse for the velvet bag that Rand's mom gave me. Finding it, I slip the knife out of the bag. I slide the knife's clip over the string on the back of my thong. Having a knife placed pretty much in your ass crack isn't the greatest feeling, but I'm just hoping I can smuggle this thing in. I put my jeans back on and wash my hands.

I return to the living room and make forced small talk for a few minutes. I'm itching to get out of here and rescue Mom. Before bolting out the door I hug Rosie tight and make a mental note to visit more once this is all over with.

I pull up to the local park and line up all of my supplies on the dashboard. First, I take a razor blade and slice open the bottom of the plastic on the chocolate sampler. Gently, I lift the plastic lid I've cut and place it into the passenger seat. If the Beauty Bandit suspects the chocolate is tampered with, I'm screwed. I remove the cardboard Bachrach lid and set the chocolates in my lap. I remove the hypodermic needle I stole from Rosie (thank God she's still diabetic; well, not really, but you know what I mean) from my backpack. After removing the plastic wrapping from the eye drops I dip the needle into the hole in the bottle and fill the needle with the clear liquid.

One by one, I pick up the chocolates and inject the eye drops into the bottom of them. The mark the needle makes is so tiny you can't even tell they've been tampered with. After filling the last piece of candy I replace both lids and set the box down carefully in the passenger seat. I pick up my cell phone and dial Rand's number hoping I still get his voice mail. I do. I leave a message telling him how much I love him and that I always will. Just in case. I hang up, guzzle my twenty-ounce Jolt cola, and head toward Primrose Lane.

Thirteen

I pull into the driveway and am amazed at how immaculate the yard is. You'd never guess that a total lunatic resides here. I didn't inherit Mom's love of gardening, but even I can see that in the spring this yard bursts with blooms. How can the same person who kidnapped two people delicately tend to these blooms every spring? The blooms are dead now. The only remains are the brown corpse clippings sticking harshly out of the ground. *Dead.* Stop it. I can't start thinking like this. I have to be strong. Mom is depending on me. Oh, yeah, and Angel. She is so going to owe me.

It's amazing to think that just a week ago, I was nearly having a meltdown in Macy's because the slingbacks I wanted to go with my homecoming dress were sold out in my size. Damn that Amy! Now I'm about to face down a cold-blooded psychopath. I think I'd rather relive the slingback meltdown!

Anger twists and turns in my belly pushing the fear aside. It's now or never. I reach into the back of my jeans and feel the cold metal of the knife still residing in my butt crack. I grab the box of chocolates and slam the car door. My UGGs pad my steps down the brick sidewalk and up to the door. I take a huge cleansing breath and ring the doorbell. As I hear heavy steps coming toward the door I say a tiny prayer that my plan doesn't backfire.

The front door flies open with such force that the cheesy Halloween wreath is knocked off its peg and lands at my feet. Suddenly, I'm frozen with fear. The caffeine and adrenaline rush I've been on for the last few minutes has drained into my toes. This is real. I'm actually face-to-face with a cold-blooded kidnapper and possibly even a murderer.

"Why, Aspen! I was hoping you'd stop by. Won't you come in?" she asks, shuffling to the side to allow me access.

"Hello, Miss Hott," I say, sliding inside her front door.

It's funny. This doesn't look like a psycho's house. I mean, not like I've ever seen any shows about Ted Bundy's or Charles Manson's houses or anything. Although, that would be pretty cool. They could call it *Lifestyles of the Conscience Challenged*, or something like that. The parts of the house I can see are all decorated like a seaside cottage. She has all kinds of homemade picture frames with seashells glued to them. It's quite adorable. Aside from Miss Hott being so obviously insane, she does have good taste.

I trail a good foot behind her as she leads the way through the house. I'm still clutching the box of candy as if it were a coveted Kelly bag or something. Miss Hott is decked out in a muumuu adorned with large flowers. Her ass is the hugest hibiscus I've ever seen. She's got an awesome pair of stilettos on. I'm guessing Jimmy Choos. I bet she lives for shoes and purses since you don't have to have a great bod for those. Her blonde hair is swept up in the most fabulous updo. I can't help but admire her for staying as chic as is humanly possible in a stressful situation.

"Can I get you a cup of coffee?" she asks, leaning against a countertop where a bar separates the kitchen from the living room.

"No, thanks. I'm not a coffee drinker." Does she think I was born yesterday? God only knows what she would put into my drink. Puhlease! She has me totally underestimated.

"I'm really sorry about your mom. How are you holding up?" she asks, looking genuinely concerned.

"I miss her," I hear myself saying. I lay the box of chocolates down on the bar.

"Of course you do. They'll find her soon," she adds, matter-of-factly. She is so easy to talk to and for some reason I find myself opening up to her.

"I realized this week that I take a lot of people who love me for granted. I don't want to do that anymore." Tears stream down my cheeks.

"Your mother knows that you love her, Aspen." She slowly waddles toward me. I'm frozen in place quaking in my UGGs. This is it. This is the part of the movie where she drives a knife right through my chest. Instead, she throws her meaty arms around me and envelopes me in a bear hug. I wait for the knife to be plunged into my back. She just hugs me tighter. Maybe I was wrong. Maybe Miss Hott isn't the psycho.

"I know what would cheer you up." She takes my hand, pulling me down a hallway toward a bedroom. I take one last glimpse at the box of chocolates, then disappear around a corner.

Miss Hott takes me into the biggest walk-in closet I've ever seen. I've died and gone to heaven! She has custom-built shelves that are filled to capacity with hundreds of shoeboxes screaming names like Gucci, Choo, Blahnik, Jacobs, and Prada. Off to the side of the shoe shelves are large metal hooks holding a priceless purse collection. Kate Spade, Coach, Prada bags call to me from their hooks. She doesn't have any Dooneys, but it's still an awesome collection. I run my fingers along their smooth skins. I take a deep breath and fill my nose with the crisp leather smell. Just as I breathe in I feel Miss Hott's sausage fingers clamp down across my face. She's holding a monogrammed handkerchief across my mouth and nose. It smells funny. The initial L stares back at me as the closet begins to spin. So, I was right after all. Miss Hott is a few rhinestones short of a tiara. I can't believe she tricked me. Damn you, Jimmy Choo!

❀

My feet are freezing. I look down at them and see my Gold Toes staring back at me. The bitch stole my UGGs. If she has my UGGs, that means she has my pink RAZR. Now it's really on.

I'm tied to a chair, a freakishly small chair, like the wooden ones from elementary school. I can't believe Miss Hott is so cheap she had to yank chairs from the elementary school. If she's going to kidnap and murder people, you would think she could at least put a little bit of money into it and do it with style. My legs have nowhere to go except straight out in front of me. I try to move my arms, but Miss Hott duct taped them to the back of the chair. I wiggle as hard as I can, but I'm not going anywhere. I could tip myself over, but then I'd just be lying on the freezing-cold cement floor. Not a good plan.

I must be in her basement. The smell of rotten meat permeates the air. At least I hope its rotten meat. The only light comes from a few strands of clear lights wound around two fake palm trees. My eyes search every inch of the basement. I'm alone. The walls are padded with the mats we use in gym class. I'm guessing to make it more soundproof. Not a good thing. A long wooden bench with craft equipment sits along one of the walls. This must be where she makes all of her seashell crafts, in her free time, when she's not kidnapping people. Why didn't I just call Harry? Now I'm going to rot in crazy Miss Hott's basement. They probably won't find me for a couple of years, and by then everyone will have moved on with their lives and forgotten all about me. Except Rand, he'd never forget about me. At least he better not. A grieving period of anything less than ten years would just not be acceptable.

A giant deep freeze catches my eye. The smell. What if it's not rotting meat? That freezer is definitely big enough to fit a couple of people in. Miss Hott is probably on her way down to stuff me in the freezer with Mom and Angel right now. My breathing is starting to get heavy. I close my eyes and demand

control of my respiratory system. I am not going to allow myself to shut down, at least not until I find out for sure what
happened to Mom.

A door above me flies open and a burst of light fills the
room. I hear footsteps on a creaky staircase. As the footsteps get closer I start hearing muffled noises. I turn my head
toward the sounds. Mom comes into focus. Then Angel.
Then Amy? I'm back in a corner and none of them see me. I
want to yell for Mom, but I don't want to provoke Miss Hott.
The crazy bitch herself brings up the rear. And what a huge
rear it is!

"Get over there and sit down. Don't even think about
trying anything!" Miss Hott shouts at them.

All three of them have duct tape over their mouths and
their hands are tied behind their backs. Miss Hott leads them
to three wooden chairs identical to mine. She binds all of their
chairs together using two whole rolls of duct tape.

"I don't think they're going anywhere," I comment on her
overly excessive use of duct tape.

Mom hears my voice and immediately starts trying to yell
through her duct tape. Angel and Amy look less than impressed
to see me. How did I not know that Amy was missing?

"Don't start with me, Brooks, or you'll be the next one
getting tape over your mouth."

"Why are you doing this?" I demand.

She waddles over and gets right into my face. The caring,
fashion-savvy principal known for her fabulous up dos is long
gone. Taking her place is a seriously disturbed, muumuu-
wearing freak show that looks like she could use a serious
dose of lithium right about now.

"I don't know, smarty-pants. Why don't you tell me why I'm doing this?" she mimics me.

Amy and Angel look bored. I guess they aren't interested in knowing why a total lunatic has kidnapped them and is planning their demise. That's understandable. *If you're a nitwit!* I can already see that even if I manage to figure out a way out of this, those two are going to be absolutely no help. I make eye contact with Mom. I can tell she's warning me. Miss Hott must be a ticking time bomb.

I take a deep breath before answering, and pray my intro psych classes will pay off a little bit. "I would say that you have deep insecurities about your weight. I think you miss being beautiful so much that you hate anyone who is beautiful. I have a feeling you weren't too jazzed about being dumped for my mom either."

Miss Hott starts clapping her chunky hands together. "Bravo, Miss Freud. You've got me all figured out."

I shrug like it was nothing, but I actually feel pretty proud of myself for figuring it out before Harry. Not that it's going to do me a whole lot of good once she kills me, but at least when Harry finds me, he'll know that I knew before him. That should haunt him for a while.

"You did get one thing wrong though." She glares at me.

"What?" I ask, confused.

"I don't hate all beautiful people. Just you." Jeez, nothing like sugarcoating it a little.

"So why did you kidnap them?" I ask, nodding toward Mom, Angel, and Amy.

She laughs a sadistic little laugh. "You were the only one I was ever out to get. Perfect little Aspen Brooks. With your perfect blonde highlights and Elizabeth Taylor eyes, and all of your adorable size-six outfits. Every time I saw you I was reminded of your dad dumping me the day of the dance. Do you have any idea how humiliating it would have been to go to the dance alone?"

Elizabeth Who? Oh, wait. She's that chick who makes that stinky perfume Mom wears. Before I can answer she continues her tirade.

"That was supposed to be my night. But I wasn't about to show up alone. I would have been turned into a laughingstock. I was the queen. Queens don't go stag."

"Dad never meant to ruin your life. He just fell in love."

She screams at the top of her lungs, *"He was supposed to love me!"*

"If there is one thing I've learned this week, it's that you can't help who you love."

"Well, don't you sound like a freaking Hallmark card?"

Okay, this conversation isn't going very well. I think my psychology book would say that I need to empathize with the psychopath. I make eye contact with Mom and wink at her so that she will know everything that is about to come out of my mouth is total BS. She winks back; I'm good to go.

"Miss Hott, that was a terrible thing they did to you. No one should ever have to go through something like that. But you showed them. Look at you now. You're a respected school official. You own your own home. Which is beautiful, by the way. I really love your seashell art."

She smiles and glances toward her workbench looking proud. For a second I think I'm making serious progress, but then she whips her head back around and sets her Satan eyes on me.

"I see you actually paid attention in psychology class, Aspen. Too bad I'm not dumb enough to fall for it."

Damn. What now? Maybe I'll just try a direct approach.

"So are you going to kill us or what?" I ask. Muffled screams come from the duct tape trio. Miss Hott starts laughing.

"The only thing I ever wanted to do was scare your parents a little bit." She glances toward Mom. "To take something precious away from them the way they took it away from me."

"So why involve everybody else?"

"They have you to thank for that. All week I've been trying to get a hold of you and all week you slipped away."

I do remember several times that she tried to get me alone. Wow! To think how close I came to being abducted. Wait, I am abducted. Well, I guess I am, even though technically I came to her.

"I thought I had you the night of the bonfire. I saw Lucas getting oral pleasure in the industrial arts building by someone who I thought was you."

I turn to Angel and mouth, "slut". Her eyes smile. My hands are itching to get out of this duct tape and knock that smile right off her face.

"Imagine my surprise when I accost my victim in the dark parking lot, drag her into my car, and get her home only to find out that I accidentally kidnapped the dumbest member of the human race."

I can't help but laugh. Miss Hott's definition of Angel is so right on. I suppose I should feel bad that she got kidnapped instead of me, but I guess she shouldn't have been blowing my boyfriend.

"She had already seen my face so I couldn't throw her back. Besides, I figure the world isn't going to miss one idiot cheerleader. I got up my nerve to try again a few days later. I followed your car as you were leaving some old folks' home. I saw you pull into the mall parking lot, which just happened to be deserted. I crept up behind your car and when you came out I gave you a face full of chloroform. You didn't give up easily. You sprayed me in the eyes with some hideous smelling perfume. But I finally dragged you back to my car and threw you in the backseat. Only guess what?" she asks.

"Um, you need glasses?" I joke. Good for Mom getting in a shot of perfume to the eyes. No wonder Miss Hott reeked like White Diamonds at the dance and her eyes were all bloodshot.

"Keep right on joking, Aspen. How funny will it be when your mom is six feet under and it's all your fault?"

"You better not lay a finger on my mom," I warn.

She ignores me and continues. "That's when I got desperate. I had two victims and neither were the one I wanted. So I cornered you at the dance and tried to lure you to the teacher's conference room. But you decided to send that little bimbo instead," she says, pointing at Amy. Amy sends a wicked look my way.

I try not to laugh because it really isn't funny. I just wonder how Amy will feel when she finds out that no one has even reported her missing yet. She probably won't care since she still has her prized tiara on top of her greasy-haired head. I mouth, "sorry," to her because I really kind of am. I'm still glad it was her and not me because then I wouldn't have won Rand over, but I do feel a little bad about setting her up.

"Then just when I'm about to give up and sell these three to the Aruban sex-slave trade, you just show up at my doorstep. Like a gift from the depths of hell."

"Why do you hate me so much?" I'm done trying to empathize, but I really do want to know.

"Aspen, you have everything. You're beautiful and smart. People worship the ground you walk on. You just walk around living this charmed life never realizing how you crush people in your wake."

"Excuse me? Everything you just said could have described how you were twenty years ago. So what's the real problem? That you used to be beautiful and just let yourself go and now you want to blame everyone else." This would have been a whole lot easier if Miss Hott had just blamed Bachrach Chocolates for getting her fat and filed a lawsuit against them.

"You're a bitch!" she screams.

"Takes one to know one. What's the matter, Miss Hott? Did I hit a nerve?"

"I'm nothing like you. I've struggled my whole life. People judge me everyday because of my weight," she says looking sad.

"But it wasn't always like that. I've seen my parents' yearbook. You were the most popular girl in school. You could have had any guy. I bet you didn't even like my dad that much. You're just trying to blame him for what you let happen to your life."

I look over to see Mom's reaction. She raises her eyebrows and I can tell she's impressed that I dug so deep into Miss Hott's psyche. I look back to Miss Hott and she's softly crying. She's a complete maniac, but I really feel sorry for her. I can't believe how much I've grown as a person this week.

"No one has ever loved me," she whispers.

"What about your parents?"

"I just got in their way. I moved out when I graduated from high school and I've never talked to them again."

How sad. I can't imagine not ever talking to my parents again.

"Do you have any brothers or sisters?"

"No."

"Grandma and grandpa?" I ask, grasping for straws.

"They all died before I was even born."

Shit. How am I supposed to reassure her that someone loves her when it is pretty obvious that no one does? *Think, Aspen, think.* Before I can come up with some lame-ass speech about the importance of loving yourself, Miss Hott snaps out of her sad/mopey mode and jumps full force back into psycho mode.

"It doesn't matter. This is my life now. Making sure that you"—she points at Mom—"or you"—she points back at me—"don't ruin anyone else's life."

"We are going to start by calling your little boyfriend. Rand is too special to spend the rest of his life pining for *you*. I want you to call him and let him know what a little bitch you can really be. By the time he gets done talking to you I want him to be thanking you for breaking up with him."

Rand will never fall for that. He knows how much I love him. Especially after the message I just left him. But what if he just thinks I'm bipolar and doesn't want to deal with it? No! He knows I love him. Doesn't he?

Miss Hott pulls my pink RAZR from her muumuu pocket and looks up Rand's number in the directory.

She yanks my hair so hard that the back of my head smacks against the chair. "This better be an Academy Award–winning performance," she says, hitting send. She looks at Angel, Amy, and Mom and puts her finger to her lips. Just when I think she is going to be stupid enough to put the phone to my ear, she hits speakerphone. He answers on the first ring.

"It's about time. I was starting to get worried about you," says Rand's sexy voice.

I have been relatively calm until this point, but the sound of his voice makes my stomach turn. When I think that I may never see, touch, or kiss Rand again, I just can't handle it. I have to make this good because if I don't, Miss Hott might go after him next. If there was just some way I could say something in code to make him understand.

I take a deep breath and begin the hardest breakup of my entire life. "Hi, Rand. I'm fine. Listen, we need to talk."

"Is it about your mom? Did you find something out?"

"Mom's fine." This gets me a swift kick in the shin from Miss Hott's left Choo. Ow, shit. "I mean, no, we haven't heard anything yet. I want to talk about us."

"Why don't I come over there?"

"No, I don't want you coming over here ever again."

"Aspen, what the hell is going on?" he asks, his tone getting worried.

"I'm really sorry, Rand. I just don't think this thing with us is going to work out."

He is screaming now. *"Aspen, what the fuck are you talking about?"*

"I think you were right before. About you only being a challenge. Now that I have you I'm just not that into you anymore." Miss Hott is nodding her head yes, pleased with my choice of words.

Rand doesn't say anything for a few seconds, but I can still hear him breathing.

"Rand, I'm really sorry about this, but you deserve someone who loves you back. We just aren't right for each other."

"This doesn't make any sense. Last night we made love the entire night and you said you loved me. How can those feelings just disappear?" Great. Now my mom knows I was out fornicating all night while she was missing. How humiliating. I look over to her and she shrugs her shoulders like it's no big deal. Mom and I are tight, but her knowing the intimate details of my sex life is a little too tight.

"Rand, don't make this harder than it already is. I don't know why, I just don't love you. Don't make such an issue out of it. Just move on."

I hear him draw in a sharp breath. Like something just came to him. Is he finally catching all of the telepathic messages I've been sending his way.

"So what about the bracelet?" Okay, apparently not.

"I'll mail it back to you," I answer, already grieving over the loss of my only piece of Tiffany jewelry.

"Good, I want to give it to someone who deserves it," he snaps back. *Ouch!*

"Okay, I guess that's it then," I say, trying not to cry.

I can't believe how quickly Rand gave up on me. But at least I don't have to worry about Miss Hott getting to him. She's wearing a huge smile while making a grotesque slicing motion across her thick throat. This is obviously her subtle way of telling me to wrap it up.

"Yeah, Aspen. I guess that's about it. You don't love me. You never did," Rand says, heartbroken. "I want you to know I'm not mad though. You'll always be my little harpy." Then he clicks off.

He figured it out! My gorgeous, brilliant, sexually gifted, rich boyfriend figured it out! And he even reminded me about the knife. How I forgot I had a three-inch serrated blade between my ass cheeks I'm not sure, but now I can work on getting the four of us out of here or at least buy some time until Rand sends help.

"What a stupid nickname," Miss Hott comments on the knife's name. I want to tell her it won't be so stupid when I plunge it into her heart. But I've got to keep up the act of being upset. I start crying hysterically. Then I get another one of my brilliant ideas.

Fourteen

I start breathing in and out really heavy. Miss Hott is busy chugging out of a champagne bottle she brought downstairs with her. She isn't paying any attention to me. Mom's eyes go huge, but I wink at her so she knows it's all part of my master plan. I try to remember how scary I sounded the night of the bonfire. I start huffing and puffing like my life depends on it, which actually it kind of does. She finally takes a break from the bottle.

"Oh, hell, no. You aren't going out that easy." She takes off waddling up the stairs as fast as her chubby legs will take her. Which is just what I was hoping for. I wiggle around in my chair, trying to lodge the knife off my thong. It moves just enough that I can shove my duct-taped hands down the back of my pants and grab it. I can hear Miss Hott's heavy footfalls upstairs as she rushes around looking for the inhaler that I now know she stole.

I try to throw the knife across the floor, but it lands under my chair. I start to freak out. Then I realize that this whole time my legs weren't bound. This chair is so little I can just stand up. I hear her plodding down the first few steps. Quickly, I stand up and kick the knife over to Mom. It slides right into the middle of their duct-taped circle. I slam myself back down and break a leg off my chair. I remember to start huffing and puffing again just as Miss Hott makes her appearance with my missing inhaler. I should have known Angel didn't take it. She just isn't that diabolical.

The girls try to act normal and I can't tell if any of them were able to reach the knife or not. I balance myself precariously so that Miss Hott doesn't notice the broken chair leg. She comes over and shakes my inhaler. I open my mouth while she squirts a shot of albuterol in. I try not to inhale it because it makes me all shaky and crazy feeling if I'm not really having an attack. I need to be on my toes in case one of the girls gets loose, then we can gang up on her.

I make a big show of getting my normal breathing back. Miss Hott looks concerned. She offers me another shot, but I refuse.

"I'm fine, thank you."

"You gave me a little scare there." She pops something into her mouth. I see now that while she was busting her fat ass getting my inhaler she also had enough time to pick up the box of chocolates that I brought. Although this seriously pisses me off, it is also a very good thing. We might actually make it out of here alive. I had Miss Hott pegged for a stress eater, and by the way she is shoving those chocolates in, I know I was right. The girls are all watching her, drooling. I really hope she doesn't offer them any or they will be able to add explosive diarrhea to the list of reasons why they hate me.

"You didn't really want to hurt me when you stole my inhaler, did you?" I ask, trying to get some dialogue flowing again.

"I didn't want you to die of an asthma attack, if that's what you mean. I just thought you might need it then when you couldn't find it, you'd leave the bonfire, and that's when I could snatch you. You see how well it worked," she says, pointing to Angel with a chocolate-covered fingertip.

"So, if you would have succeeded in kidnapping me first, what were you going to do with me?"

"I just wanted to keep you down here for a few days and make you miss the dance. I knew you were going to be crowned homecoming queen, and I wanted you to miss the one thing you had been looking forward to your entire life. You never would have known it was me. A few days later I would have let you go. I just wanted to mess up that charmed life a little bit."

"I think you've gotten a little bit off track, don't you? Now you've kidnapped four people and we all know it was you."

I sneak a glance over at Mom. It doesn't look like anyone was able to get the knife. I'm just going to try and keep her talking until Rand finds us.

"Everything would have been fine if this one," she says, pointing toward Angel again, "wouldn't have rigged the queen contest. Things just went downhill after that. Then I had a brilliant plan to frame Bob Lowe for the whole thing, but you had to go and screw that up before I had time to smuggle these three into his house."

"Why would you want to frame Mr. Lowe?" I ask, even though I know exactly why.

"You've seen the way he looks at me. Like I'm the most disgusting thing that ever walked the planet. Besides, he's a freak. I know you saw his little 'collection.' A person like that doesn't belong in the school system."

I am about to point out that she isn't exactly the spokesperson for sanity and probably isn't the best person to be mentoring young students either, but I figure I better not screw up the mellow vibe we've got going. The chocolate has her endorphins kicking in like magic; now if the eyedrops would just kick in, I could run over and get the knife and get us all the hell out of here.

"You can still let us go, you know." All four of us nod our heads yes.

"Oh, sure. I'm sure that you would all testify that I was perfectly sane and should be set free. Right?"

"I'm not going to lie. I think you need help. You need someone to help you see that you are more than just a number on the scale."

"What do you know?" she asks, shoving another handful of chocolate in her mouth and following it up with a champagne chaser.

"You have a killer sense of style, and I've always admired your updos." I answer honestly.

She puts a meaty paw up to her hair and caresses it a bit with a smile on her face. I hear something coming from the girl's side of the room. It sounds like a knife cutting through duct tape.

"I was really serious about the seashell art. It is supercool, and I don't usually like that kind of thing either," I shout to mask the sound of the tape being cut.

"I'm not deaf, Aspen."

"What are you talking about?" I shout, hoping she'll just think she's losing it. She gets a puzzled look on her face then goes back to guzzling her champagne.

"Why did you take the picture of Rand and me?" I am honestly curious to know her answer.

She wipes her mouth on the back of her hand and says, "I thought the embarrassment would kill you, then I wouldn't have to worry about trying to kidnap you. How was I supposed to know that this would be the week you would choose to have a total personality transformation and actually become a person with a soul?"

Jeez! Harsh much?

"Rand has definitely made me a better person. You were right when you said that I don't deserve him."

I see one of my mom's shoulders suddenly jerk back. I think she is partly free. I just have to keep up the therapy session a little bit longer.

"You're not completely horrible," she says, surprising me. "After all, you turned down the tiara when I tried to give it to you." I hear a muffled "what?" come from behind Angel's duct-taped mouth as she learns this.

"But Amy nearly grabbed the damn thing out of my hot little hands." She laughs. Angel tries to kick at Amy, but can't reach her. I wish Angel would quit screwing around and worry about getting out of here alive instead of that damn tiara.

"You know what is really funny?" Miss Hott laughs.

"What?"

"Amy had the fewest votes. I only said she won because I figured you would be so jealous of her and Rand that you'd accept it after all. Pippi came in third and Tobi was fourth. Amy only had like thirty votes. Two less votes and Melinda Paxton would have been a princess instead of Amy."

I turn to give Amy the evil eye. Her mascara is already forming black streaks down her cheeks. All of this drama over a fake-ass rhinestone tiara! I'd love to rip it off Amy's head and throw it out the window.

Mom starts to cough uncontrollably through her duct tape. I have a feeling it is about to be on. I slip into my kick-ass heroine mode and get things started.

"Miss Hott, I think Mom is choking on her spit. Hurry, help her."

Miss Hott looks alarmed and rushes to Mom. She pulls her duct tape off and before she knows what hit her Mom rises up off the chair and gives her a roundhouse to the face. Damn! I guess those self-defense classes paid off after all. I struggle to my feet and run up behind a dazed Miss Hott. I kick her square in the hibiscus. This knocks her off her Choos and she ends up eating some cement. Mom jumps on her and pulls Miss Hott's arms around to her back. Mom holds her while I attempt to find my cell in her muumuu pockets. My RAZR is nowhere to be found. Her enormous gut probably swallowed it whole.

"I'll run upstairs and get her phone," I yell. I'm about to start climbing the basement stairs with the dinky chair still attached to my arms when Mom starts to lose control.

Miss Hott starts heaving her body up and down. Mom looks like she's riding the fake bull at the Steak Rodeo, and she's about to get bucked off. I run back over and try to find some kind of weapon. I spot a plugged in glue gun sitting on the craft table. I put my face down on the craft table and nudge the cool handle of the glue gun with my chin until it falls off the table. Mom grabs it and squeezes hot glue all over Miss Hott's face and fabulous updo.

"That's for calling in a bomb threat and me never getting to wear my prom dress. I know it was you, you crazy bitch!" Mom screams, squeezing more hot glue onto Miss Hott's face.

Miss Hott is screaming like a cat in heat. She reaches an elbow back and clocks Mom right in the face.

Mom falls back and slams her head on the craft table. She falls to the floor with a groan and then nothing. I want to run to her, but Miss Hott is trying to get up. I try to kick her in the face, but with no shoes on it hurts me more than it does her. After a few seconds of struggling like a turtle on its back, she gets to her feet. If I thought she looked crazy before, the hot-glued hair and traces of blood coming out of her nose really paint a Hannibal Lecter picture. She is crazy angry. I look to Angel and Amy for help, but Amy is still completely tied up and Angel only managed to get one arm free. She is using her free arm to try and grab the tiara off Amy's head. I am so going to kick her ass if we get out of this alive.

I take off running across the basement and get halfway up the stairs before I hear a loud cracking sound and everything goes black.

⊚

My head hurts. I'm not talking about some little PMS headache. I'm talking somebody took an ax handle and cracked me in the back of the head. I might have brain damage. I'm thinking pretty clearly though so I might be okay.

I'm sitting in my tiny chair again, but this time I'm duct taped to a beam so that I can't stand up. Mom is still unconscious on the floor and I can't tell if she is breathing or not. Amy and Angel are staring wide-eyed in my direction as if they have just realized the gravity of our situation. Miss Hott is nowhere to be found.

"Where's the knife?" I ask the girls.

They both shake their heads no. Great. I have no idea how much time passed since I talked to Rand, but I know that Miss Hott is going to blow like Mount St. Helens and soon. Please let him find us.

The basement door swings open and a blinding light hits my eyes. Miss Hott saunters down the stairs in a hideous red dress that could double for the circus big-top tent. She is carrying the box of chocolate, the bottle of champagne, and clipped to her ribbon belt is my knife. Crap. Our only hope now is that the eyedrops will kick in and Mom will wake up and free us. I really thought Miss Hott would have the Johnny Quicksteps by now, but I didn't take into consideration her girth when injecting the eyedrops. I probably should have used twice as much since she is twice as big as a normal person. If Rand doesn't find us soon, we're screwed.

Miss Hott struts right in front of me and does a little twirl. I'm treated to an eyeful of back fat. As if I hadn't already been punished enough! Amy and Angel both start crying when they spot the knife. They've been with Miss Hott much longer than I have so they must both think this is the end.

Come on, Rand. Find us. Please, find us.

"It's almost over now, Aspen." Miss Hott says, swigging her champagne.

"So that's it, you're just going to kill all of us? What the hell is that going to prove?"

She acts like she doesn't even hear me. She sets down her libations on the craft table, flips open the knife, and starts walking toward Angel. I hate Angel, but I certainly don't want to watch her get murdered. Angel starts screaming behind her duct tape and wiggling around. Miss Hott places the knife up to Angel's pale neck and pushes hard enough that I can see an indention.

"You're going to get blood on your Choos. Blood and leather don't mix, just ask O.J.," I yell, trying to think of anything that might distract her. She seems to reconsider and moves away from Angel. I decide to keep talking—maybe something I say will make her let us go.

"Eventually they are going to figure out who killed us. I left my student directory next to my dad's bed with your address circled. They will find you. And if they don't, they'll put you on *America's Most Wanted*. By Saturday night, John Walsh will be telling millions of people how much you weigh. Is that what you want? I don't think so."

"So I'm just supposed to let you all go? Then what happens to me, Aspen? Even if I got off, which we both know isn't going to happen, I'd just go back to living a nonlife like before. I'll never have a husband, or children. No one has ever loved me and no one ever will." She looks so sad as she says this. This woman is probably going to kill me, but I can't help it. I feel sorry for her. It would totally suck to go through your whole life and not have one single person ever love you. I've only lived half the time that Miss Hott has, and I already have several people who love me.

"Wait a minute," I blurt out.

"Give it up, Aspen," she says, putting a drop cloth down over her shoes and placing the knife back to Angel's throat. Angel is squirming around like a worm on a hook. I close my eyes because no matter how much I may have disliked Angel, I don't want her to die. If only I could have done something else.

"Harry," I blurt out. "Harry Malone loved you."

She drops the knife to her side and gives me a perplexed look. "How in the world do you know Harry Malone? I went to school with him."

"I know. He's friends with my parents. I heard him tell them that he was crazy about you in high school. He said he was too intimidated by you to ever do anything about it."

"That's bullshit. I would have known if someone was in love with me."

"Look at me and Rand. He was in love with me for years, and I never knew it. Sometimes we are blind to what is right in front of us. He did love you, Miss Hott. That means that someday someone else could love you, too."

She considers this for a moment and looks just about to drop the knife when I hear a creak on the steps and look up to see Harry with a gun in his hand.

"She's right, Lulu. I was in love with you. It took me years to move on. Drop the knife and we'll go talk about it."

Miss Hott, uh, Lulu, is stunned. I'm not sure if it is because she has a gun in her face or she just found out that the man holding the gun in her face used to be in love with her. I've never been so happy to see someone in my whole life. I don't even care that a huge patch of black hair is billowing out of the top of his bulletproof vest.

Harry repeats himself in a firmer tone this time. "Lulu, drop the knife so that we can talk." She makes a quick swiping motion and I hear a crackling noise. The next thing I see is Lulu falling motionless to the cement floor.

Fifteen

He didn't kill her. It wasn't even a real gun. He did hit her with 50,000 volts of electricity from a Taser. She collapsed like a rhinoceros shot with a tranquilizer gun. Harry ran over, confiscated the knife, and cuffed her before she could recover from her little jolt of electroshock therapy.

"Is she okay?" I ask, watching him bend over Mom to take her pulse. My heart is racing in my ears and I almost don't hear him.

"She's going to be fine, Aspen." He gets on a radio clipped to the top of his shoulder and starts firing off demands. Within seconds the tiny basement is filled with men in uniform. I'm cut free of the beam and chair by a particularly handsome officer of the law. Mom is carried up the stairs on a stretcher and rushed to Comfort Memorial.

I walk over to where Angel is sitting and kneel down beside her. In one quick motion I rip the duct tape from her mouth. She screams at the top of her lungs.

"That's for saying I wear knockoffs. But just think, now you won't have to get your upper lip waxed for a few more weeks." I unwrap the tape from her other arm and legs and help her stand.

"Very funny, Aspen." She rubs her Angelina Jolie–looking lips.

"Seriously though, Angel, are you all right?"

She smiles and nods. "She didn't feed me much so I probably dropped a whole dress size. It's all good." She pulls on the front of her cheerleading skirt to see how baggy it is. Good old dim Angel. She gets kidnapped and almost killed and she's excited about losing weight. If I didn't despise her so much, I might actually like her. She reaches over and swipes the tiara from Amy's head, pulling several strands of Amy's hair with it. She places it back on her own head.

The same officer who freed me wraps a blanket around Angel's shoulders and escorts her up the stairs. As she walks up the stairs she turns to look at me and raises her eyebrows. I immediately recognize it as her trademark, "damn, he's hot" look. I kind of admire Angel. Not her fashion sense, because she has none. Not her loyalty, because she has none of that either. I admire her resilience. She just spent almost a week in hell and she's already on the prowl. Maybe she's not so bad after all.

Amy stays seated, looking dejected, even after she is cut free. I guess the news about her not really qualifying for queen was just too much for her to handle. Just wait until she finds out that no one even realized she was missing. I'm thinking she is going to be standing in line behind Lulu for some intensive psychotherapy.

Lulu is lying on the floor motionless. Her eyes are glassed over and she looks more like a lost little girl than a serial kidnapper. It must be hard to know that you used to be beautiful. I think it would probably be easier being born ugly so you don't know what you're missing out on. I can't help but feel sorry for her, especially when I hear her stomach drop over all the other commotion in the basement. Her eyes go saucer-wide and she starts yelling. Her words aren't making any sense so nobody is paying any attention to her.

"If somebody doesn't get her to the bathroom, like pronto, you guys are going to have to call in a biohazard team," I tell the officer standing next to me. He and a few other officers stand Lulu up and lead her up the basement stairs. On her way up, she turns toward me, and mouths, "sorry." I think she might actually mean it. She never meant to hurt anyone. Things just got out of control. Too bad she's going to spend the rest of her life paying for it.

Harry walks up to me and I have the distinct feeling I'm about to get the lecture of my life when he grabs me up in a bear hug. Eww . . . can you catch hair? Okay, it's not really *that* bad. It feels safe in Harry's hairy arms.

He releases me and says, "Aspen, you should have come to me. You could have been killed." He hesitates, and then continues, "But I probably wouldn't have believed you. You did a brave thing today. You saved your mom and Angel. Who was that other girl?" he asks, confused.

We enjoy a good laugh when I explain who Amy is. Amy finally agrees to be escorted upstairs and most of the other officers have cleared out. Something on the craft table catches my eye and I walk toward it.

"Oh my gosh, look at these," I tell Harry, picking up one of Lulu's creations.

"Holy voodoo dolls, Batman." He laughs, picking up a miniature version of himself.

Lulu created miniature versions of all of us with painstaking detail. My doll is exquisite. Her hair is the exact same shade and texture of my own and her violet eyes match mine exactly. Mini-Aspen is dressed to the nines in a pink cashmere sweater edged with pink fur, a black wool pleated skirt and teeny black Prada stilettos. My eyes lock on the bag in mini-Aspen's hand. Lulu custom made a Dooney. It's a pale pink bucket bag adorned with tiaras. OMG! I've got my own personalized Dooney! Could it be more perfect? I have to have this doll. Mini-Aspen makes Evening Gown Barbie look like trailer trash. Lulu is a genius, well, you know, for a psychopath and all.

"Please tell me I'm not really this hairy," Harry says, holding a doll that could double as a gorilla. The only reason I know it's supposed to be Harry is because of the badge pinned to its chest.

I stifle a laugh; after all he did just save my life. "Let's just say that a trip to a professional waxer wouldn't kill you."

"After seeing this, I think I'll actually go." He shakes his head and sets the doll back down. He picks up the Angel doll that is wearing a tiny cheerleader outfit. He flips her over and sure enough she's got a miniature tramp stamp on her lower back. We both start cracking up.

"Lulu's so talented. How could she base her whole life's worth on one guy dumping her?" I ask, picking up the Rand doll. The red-haired Afro tells me this doll was made before his spectacular transformation. He's still adorable though. I make mini-Aspen and mini-Rand kiss.

Harry watches me and smiles. "I know somebody else who was pretty concerned with what other people thought up until just a few days ago." He winks at me.

He's right. I could have ended up exactly like Lulu. The thought of being an overweight serial kidnapper who never leaves high school is enough to make me shudder. I owe so much to Rand for making me realize what is really important in life. Hot sex with your soul mate!

"I'm lucky to have him," I say, staring at the Rand doll.

"He's lucky to have you, too," I hear Rand say from behind me. I spin around and jump into his arms, covering his face in kisses.

"How did you figure it out?" I ask him, in between kisses.

"I knew there was no way in hell you would ever return Tiffany jewelry." Rand and Harry share a belly laugh. All I can do is stare longingly at the gorgeous face I thought I might never see again.

Rand gets serious and gazes down at me. "I thought I was going to lose you, Aspen. I don't think I could go on if something happened to you." He nudges my face up with his chin, looks deep into my eyes, and then kisses me like I've never been kissed before.

Harry slipped soundlessly out of the basement while Rand and I were making out. We stopped making out when it started getting really hot. Doing it in Miss Hott's basement isn't high on my list of places for a quickie. We decide to chill out and sneak back to the guest cottage later for a proper reunion.

"Look at these dolls she made," I tell Rand, pulling him toward the craft table.

"Damn. Mini-Rand wants to see if mini-Aspen is anatomically correct," he says, trying to lift my doll's skirt.

"Excuse me," I say, pulling my doll away from him. "Mini-Aspen does not show her goodies on a first date." We both start laughing.

"Do you think Harry will let me keep them?" I ask Rand while scooping up the rest of the dolls. There are dolls in the likeness of Mom, Dad, Rand, Angel, Harry, me, and Mr. Lowe, whose doll is wearing a tiny black leather mask. That one is too freaky. I decide to leave it here.

"He'll probably need to keep them for evidence," he answers.

"These beauties don't belong in some smelly evidence bag. I'll just have to sweet-talk him." I laugh.

We head up the basement stairs to begin what is sure to be hours of questioning.

⊙

We are all sitting around on Lulu's plastic-covered furniture eating pizza. Harry wanted the interrogation to be as easy on everybody as possible so he turned it into a little party. He's really starting to grow on me.

Dad already called from the hospital and said Mom is going to be fine. Apparently, Lulu had to be rushed there also to get her stomach pumped. My little chemistry experiment worked better than I thought it would. She'll be fine and as soon as she is able to get off the toilet she'll be moved to a maximum-security prison.

I've already explained to Harry and the other officers what Lulu told me about mistakenly kidnapping Angel, Mom, and Amy, thinking that they were me.

"So how did you figure out it was her, Aspen?" Harry asks me, holding his pen over his little notebook.

"I kept having this image of Mr. Lowe with his freaky leather mask on. He kept asking me if I liked his rose. Then I smelled my mom's perfume and remembered smelling it on Lulu at the dance. It was weird. All of a sudden these memories started fitting together. A picture of a skinny Lulu look-alike in her office, a pom-pom in her car, all the times she tried to get me alone that week. Then I remembered seeing a picture in Mom's yearbook of the skinny blonde with my dad and heard Mom's voice saying that he dumped the homecoming queen for her. All of the pieces were there. Then I called Mr. Lowe and he told me that Lulu gave him the white rose. I knew she was trying to set him up to take the fall for her."

Harry sits staring at me in amazement. When he finally speaks he says, "Aspen, I know we haven't always seen eye to eye, but I'd be proud to have you for a partner any day."

I beam with pride. It is kind of amazing that I put it together before he did. But in his defense I think it worked in my favor that the perp was a female. A male wouldn't ever truly understand the horror at the thought of going to a formal dance without a date.

"Okay, so we've established that Angel wrote the lipstick mirror graffiti. Angel, did you put the pornography in Aspen's locker?" Harry asks.

Angel gets a guilty look on her face and I have a feeling it's not because the hottie officer has his arm around her shoulders.

"Yeah, I did it," she admits. I stick my tongue out at her.

"Where in the world did you get so much porn?" I ask.

"My dad brought back suitcases full of it the last time he went to Vegas. I guess they just hand it out on the Strip." She gets a sad look on her face. "He and my mom split up over it."

If the amount of porn in my locker was any indication of his addiction, I can understand why they split up. That does suck for Angel though. No wonder she is so close to her little sister. I have to admit that she's starting to grow on me a little bit, too. I can't believe what a softie I'm turning into.

"Why the hell did you want everyone to think I was gay?" I ask, curious.

"Um, hello, your best friend has a boy name and she's a total dyke. It really wasn't that much of a stretch. Besides, I wanted Lucas for myself. It wasn't fair you had two lovers," Angel answers.

I cannot believe even dim-ass Angel knew Tobi was gay. I'm so glad I've started working on my powers of observation. I couldn't handle being one-upped by Angel too many times.

"Angel, you slashed Aspen's tire, right?" Harry asks, trying to get us back on track. He knows that one false move and this whole night could end in one big catfight.

"*Excuse me?*" Angel asks, shocked.

"It's okay to admit it, Angel. You aren't going to get into trouble, we just have to get everything correct for the report," Harry adds.

"I did *not* slash your tire," Angel yells, glancing disgustedly over at me.

I roll my eyes. So much for her growing on me; why can't she just admit it and move on? She's so freaking immature.

"Angel didn't slash your tire. I did," Rand says from next to me.

Everyone gasps and turns to look at Rand, who is now turning crimson.

"I wanted to give you a ride home. I was tired of waiting for the right moment. I decided to make my own right moment."

Everyone ohs and aws. I'm stunned. All this time I thought that Rand was 100 percent good guy. Now it turns out he's got a little bit of bad boy in him after all. Just when I thought he couldn't turn me on any more.

"I'm going to assume you don't want to press any charges?" Harry asks me.

"Don't worry, I'll extract the damages somehow," I say, giving Rand some fuck-me eyes.

"Okay, so Lulu admitted she took your inhaler, right?" Harry asks, trying his best to ignore all the teenage hormones raging in the room right now.

"Yeah, I faked an attack and she brought my inhaler to me."

He shakes his head and jots something down.

"I guess that means that Lulu is responsible for taking the pictures of you, Rand, Tobi, and Pippi and writing that sex note about you and Mr. Lowe, too." He looks to me for confirmation.

I nod. "I think she thought she was going to humiliate me so much I'd go off the deep end."

"Instead, you showed up here with a knife stuck in your butt crack and a box of tainted chocolates hoping to save the day?" He laughs. I notice a strange-looking officer eyeing the evidence bag holding the knife. I have a feeling he's going to cop a sniff when the rest of us are gone. Gross!

"Well, I did, didn't I?"

"I think Angel's nine-one-one call helped a little bit," Harry answers.

"What are you talking about?" I ask, confused.

"Rand came to the station and was in a panic that you had been kidnapped. We were trying to canvas the entire town searching for your car when a nine-one-one call came in from Angel's cell phone. We could hear you and your mom fighting with Lulu. That's how we knew where to find you."

I look over at Angel for an explanation. She looks up from her cat-and-mouse routine she's got going with the hottie and says, "When your mom cut my arm free I was finally able to get my cell phone out of my cheerleading briefs. So I called nine-one-one. I totally saved the day," she says all cocky.

I'm shocked. Not that I have to share my glory of saving the day with Angel, but that she wears anything under her cheerleading skirt. I never would have guessed. But Angel won't be so cocky when she sees the big chunk of bangs that

Miss Hott cut off to put with the fake kidnapping note. Life is good!

I lean back against Rand and he squeezes my shoulder. I can't wait to get out of here and be alone with him. I wonder if he'll like my Yummy thong? The thought makes me giggle a little bit. Harry senses everyone's desire to be done with all of the kidnapping stuff for the night.

"Okay, I guess that about wraps it up," he says, standing to escort everyone out.

"Wait. What's going to happen to Lulu?" I ask, genuinely concerned.

"She's looking at four kidnapping charges, attempted murder for stealing your inhaler, and various other crimes. Let's put it this way. The only designer outfit she's going to be wearing for a while is an orange jumpsuit and flip-flops." I shudder at the thought. Poor Lulu. All she ever wanted was to be loved.

"Is there anything I can do to help her?" I ask.

Harry looks up with a surprised face. "I might be able to get her into an institution instead of jail. If . . . you would be willing to testify?" he asks, unsure. I nod my head yes. He looks very happy. I think he still has a soft spot for Lulu and wanted to help her, too, but he didn't want to make me feel like I had to do something I didn't want to. I think I'm actually going to miss having Harry around when life goes back to normal. Whatever that is anymore! I've just done him a big favor so now would be the perfect time to slip in my doll request.

"Can I keep these?" I ask, pulling the dolls from behind my back.

Harry looks them over and makes a quick judgment call. "All right, but I might need to see them sometime, so don't be doing anything nasty with them." He laughs. I toss Angel her doll and she squeals with delight upon seeing her doll's matching tattoo.

"Where's mine?" Amy asks, finally breaking her silence.

"She didn't make one for you. Sorry, Amy." I shrug.

Poor Amy. This was the final straw. She starts sobbing uncontrollably and Harry puts his arms around her.

"Come on, Amy. Let's get you home. I'm sure your parents are worried sick." He looks at me and makes a face like he hopes they are or Amy might end up sharing a room with Lulu at the loony bin. Before Harry gets to the front door, he pauses, then turns around and looks at me.

"Aspen, I'm sorry I failed your mom. I was so close. I made a huge mistake not asking Mr. Lowe who gave him the flower. I was already suspicious of your principal because every time I tried to meet with her she would ditch me. I was so close, but this could have ended really badly and part of that is my fault." He shakes his head miserably.

I run over and hug him. "But you did find me and you saved all of us without hurting Lulu. You're the reason this ended as good as it possibly could have. I'd be glad to have you for a partner any day," I tell him, repeating what he told me earlier. He smiles and leads Amy out to his monster truck. I just thought of something that I have to know. I run out the door yelling for him.

He lowers his window with a concerned look. "What's wrong, Aspen?"

"WWDHD?" I ask, breathless.

He smiles, then answers, "Come on, Aspen. I expected better from you." He takes off down the road, but not before yelling, "What would Dirty Harry do?" out the window. That hairy guy is a trip!

⊚

Rand and I stop by the hospital to check on Mom. When we get to her room, she and Dad are curled up together spooning each other in her dinky hospital bed. It's enough just to see her sleeping peacefully for tonight. We tiptoe away so we don't wake them.

The sexual energy pulsing between Rand and me is like nothing I've ever experienced before. We sneak back into the guest cottage and I show him my Yummy thong. He likes it. Actually, he likes it four times.

I have my head lying on Rand's chest, listening to him softly snore. I'm way too keyed up to sleep right now.

I can't believe all the drama that has unfolded in just one week. I lost the homecoming tiara, suffered countless humiliations, my ex cheated on me, I had a near-death experience, found out my best friend is gay, wore clothes that should have never been allowed to exist, and got kidnapped. I am so in need of a spa day. But, best of all, I fell in love.

Being with Rand is making me a better person. I'm trying hard not to put so much value on a person's outward appearance. I'll always love my designer labels, but I realize now that the love I've found with Rand and my friendship with Tobi are so much more important. I mean, I wouldn't turn down a Dooney, but tell me a girl who would? Besides, there is no twelve-step program for fashion addiction so I'm completely on my own. I might just fall off the wagon and fondle a Choo here and there. I'm only human.

Sixteen

Six months have passed since I saved the day. Lulu's trial was like so long and boring that I thought I would lose my mind. There was no *Law & Order* stuff at all. Just endless hours of boring testimony from pretty much every person who had ever met her. The jury was unanimous. Lulu Hott would spend the next seven years in Comfort Seaside Sanitarium. I'm not sure where the seaside comes in being that Comfort is located in the middle of a cornfield, but it makes it sound better, than say, Comfort Loony Bin. Besides, Lulu likes seaside décor.

I've had my fifteen minutes of fame and then some. I can't go anywhere without being recognized or asked for an autograph. An awesome picture of me was on the front page of the town newspaper with the caption of "Stylish supersleuth saves the day." It's been totally fun getting all of this attention.

Detective Malone tapped into some junior detective fund and gave Angel and me scholarships to State University. I can't believe I have to put up with her for another four years. We have formed a tiny bond since the kidnapping though. I'm not talking best friends or anything, just a bit of a truce on trying to completely destroy each other.

State University wouldn't be my first choice, but now that my parents don't have to pay tuition, I'll be able to rush a sorority. Heck, when they find out how famous I am, I won't even have to rush. They'll be begging me to join. I'm even thinking about going into law. I think I'd like to defend people like Lulu. I could be like a real-life Elle Woods.

Rand even turned down Harvard to follow me to State. He is absolutely smitten with me. I'm so glad we are going to be together because I don't think I could bear to be without him. I'm not talking marriage at eighteen or anything, because that's just setting yourself up for a midlife crisis. But we do have something special so who knows where it might lead someday.

I've even kept in touch with Lulu. I didn't think it was right to just dump her so she added me to her visitors list. I'm pretty much the only name on the list. I visit her at least once a week. She is so grateful that she gave me all her shoes and purses. Jackpot! Of course that isn't why I did it, but it was a total bonus.

I've tried to use my newfound fame to make her stay easier. The sanitarium requires that patients wear jumpsuits just like in prison. They are these hideous green rags that make everyone look totally washed out. I proposed a petition agreeing to let patients choose their own color jumpsuit. I mean, what the hell does it matter if they wear green or pink, if it makes them feel better about themselves? I circulated the petition around Comfort and collected 750 signatures. I hand-delivered it to the warden, who is going to take the issue under serious consideration.

Lulu is enrolled to get her cosmetology license through the local community college. Sometimes I even let her do my hair. She still does killer updos even with her hands being restrained. They had to cut off all her hair after the hot glue incident, but she's wearing it in a shaggy bob and it looks really stylish. I even talked to the cafeteria workers and they agreed to specially make her meals. I gave them a copy of *Enter the Zone*. Lulu is forever grateful. Between the eyedrop-diarrhea incident and her new diet, she's already lost thirty pounds. She's going to be fabulous by the time she gets out of here. She already told me that one of the guards has been flirting with her. I wasn't sure this was such good news, but she was so excited I didn't want to bust her bubble. The warden won't let her pass the time doing seashell art. I guess he's afraid she might file one of the seashells down into a shank and try to escape. They are letting her continue making dolls though. After seeing mini-Aspen, Mattel and Dooney & Bourke teamed up to create a line of Dooney-toting Barbies. They are even thinking about creating a line of purses with Lulu's tiara design. I better get the first bag since I was totally the inspiration for the design. Anyway, for the first time ever, Lulu is getting the positive reinforcement that she so desperately craves. Hopefully she can pull it together in the next seven years and come out a normal, functioning member of society. Not that you really have to be that normal in Comfort.

So right now I'm waiting in the backstage of the gymnasium. Tonight is our prom. Every year the school puts on a show called Grand March. The normal sweat-smelling, sneaker-streaked gymnasium is turned into a balloon-and-streamer-induced paradise for one night. One by one the couples parade across a stage and their names are announced. The entire town shows up to see how great they look together and reminisce about their own prom. This is kind of like Rand and my coming-out party. Everybody knows we're together, but we've never done an actual formal event until tonight.

I am looking fabulous in a custom-made Vera Wang (she couldn't resist once she heard what a hero I am) gown. It's the same petal-pink color as the first roses Rand ever gave me. It's a flowing satin and taffeta confection that cascades all the way to the floor. The fitted bodice is strapless and the entire dress is covered in the tiniest silver stars. This is the most glamorous piece of clothing I have ever owned. I feel like a princess. My feet are adorned with strappy silver heels that match the stars to perfection. My blonde hair is swept into a perfect updo (thanks, Lulu). My silver Tiffany heart tag charm bracelet dangles from my wrist. I don't think this night could get any better.

I'm still a teensy bit fashion obsessed, but I'm really working on it. I did buy my sandals at Payless. I figure if it's good enough for Star Jones Reynolds, it's good enough for Aspen Brooks. I wouldn't have been caught dead in Payless a few months ago. So this totally proves I've grown.

"Okay, this is it. Hopefully I won't trip," Tobi says, grabbing my hand for last-minute support. She's dressed in an adorable banana-colored form-fitting evening gown. She and Pippi decided to "come out" at the Grand March tonight. Her parents just think that she and Pippi really like having sleepovers. Tobi figured that her parent's wouldn't kill her if she comes out in front of so many people. I'm so nervous for her.

"Good luck. I love you," I tell her, settling for air kisses instead of the real thing so neither of us gets our faces messed up. I can't believe how stupid I was for ever thinking Tobi might hurt me. I'm so lucky to have such an awesome best friend. I'm so happy that she's going to State and will be at my beck and call for another four years.

She takes a deep breath and gathers her courage, then steps onto the stage. I peek around the corner to see Pippi coming from the guy's side dressed in an identical banana dress. Mr. Lowe announces the girl's names. A hush falls over the crowd. I spot Tobi's parents giving each other a glance that tells me they already knew their daughter's secret. Slowly her parents rise from the bleachers and start clapping. Soon the entire gymnasium is on their feet yelling in support of Tobi and Pippi. Tobi is beaming and looks fantastic. My best friend is getting her dream come true and I couldn't be happier.

It's almost my turn and I keep peeking to try to see Rand. The only person I can see is Lucas clowning around. He's waiting for Angel. They finally officially hooked up after the kidnapping incident. I think they might actually be good for each other. Lucas couldn't get into State so he's staying in Comfort to attend community college. I guess they'll have to see if their minuscule attention spans can survive a long-distance relationship.

"I think it would be safe to say that our next couple is the closest Comfort has to royalty," Mr. Lowe says. "Aspen Brooks and Rand Bachrach, come on out." Mr. Lowe has been really cool about not holding a grudge especially since Harry confiscated his entire porn collection. Hey, I wonder if Angel's dad has any he can spare? I gave a brilliant speech to the school board convincing them that while Mr. Lowe may be a total freak in his spare time, he is still a really great teacher. They decided to make him principal.

I take the steps to the stage carefully. I may look fabulous, but these heels and gown are not the easiest things to maneuver. Once I reach the stage I see Rand entering from the guy's side. Handsome. My caring, supportive, smart, rich boyfriend is *so* handsome. He's wearing a black Ralph Lauren tuxedo with a light pink tie and cumberbund. The tux is great, but it's not what makes him handsome. It's the way his evergreen eyes are taking me in. It's the way his perfect smile turns up at the edges just for me. It's the way he just mouthed, "I love you." I wouldn't even care if Rand completely reverted back to his old look because I love his insides way more than his outside.

As we get close enough to each other to touch he takes my hand and we turn to face the crowd. Everyone is whistling and yelling. But as I soak up every detail it's quiet in my mind. I've found someone who truly loves me. Oh, yeah, and I look totally fabulous. My life is perfect.

I can see my parents, who are both blowing us kisses. They haven't been apart for a second since the kidnapping. Mom confessed her shopping addiction to Dad and we are helping her work through it. Her therapist says her shopping addiction was a residual effect of her D-list high school social status. Even though she transformed herself into a total hottie with a fabulous life she still felt unfulfilled. She's totally getting it under control though. Just the other day she turned down an invitation to a jewelry party. I'm so proud of her! We even found a website called Bag Borrow or Steal. It's like Netflix for purses. We are saving so much money. Now if we could just find one for shoes. Eww . . . on second thought I don't really want to share somebody else's toe jam.

As much as I love the spotlight I figure we've hogged it for long enough. I step forward to climb down from the stage, but Rand gently pulls me back. I turn to look at him confused when Mr. Lowe starts to make another announcement.

"Well, folks, it looks like they really are a royal couple. After counting six hundred unanimous votes, I'm happy to say that this year's prom queen and king are Aspen Brooks and Rand Bachrach. Congratulations!" Cheers erupt throughout the gym.

I'm stunned. I was so absorbed in Rand that I completely forgot about the nominations. Someone places a tiara on my head, perfectly I might add, not a hair out of place, and hands me a silver wand with a star on the end of it. It matches my ensemble perfectly. Rand is fitted with his crown and then leans over and gives me one of those delicious kisses of his. It is so good to be me. Now, this is a movie moment.

Aspen Asks the Author

(**Author disclaimer: I was not given a list of questions before the interview. I apologize if this is a nightmare.**)

Aspen: So . . . how do we do this thing?
Stephanie: Well, you could start by thanking me for joining you, then just start asking me some questions.

Aspen: Whatever! I'm only doing this because you totally made me!
Stephanie: I did no such thing. I might have casually mentioned that it would be beneficial to your imaginary wardrobe if you cooperated.

Aspen: Like I said, I was *forced* to do this.
Stephanie: And your first question would be?

Aspen: Who are you wearing? (*stares author up and down, then rolls eyes dramatically*)

Stephanie: Um ... I was thinking more writing-related questions.

Aspen: Okay. What were you wearing when you thought me up?

Stephanie: (*sighs deeply*) I knew I should have given you a list of questions.

Aspen: But you didn't! *Ha! Ha!*

Stephanie: Fine. I was probably wearing an Eddie Bauer T-shirt, a pair of jeans from Target, and my Crocs because that's pretty much my standard uniform.

Aspen: I'm embarrassed to know you.

Stephanie: You better be nice to me or I'll write something really bad about you.

Aspen: Ooh, I'm so scared! *Not!* What are you going to write about me, fancy author lady?

Stephanie: Instead of going to college in your sequel you could just stay living with your parents and work the drive-thru of Comfort Cozee Dogs.

Aspen: You wouldn't!

Stephanie: I'm sorry, was that a question?

Aspen: How did you get the idea for *Revenge of the Homecoming Queen*?

Stephanie: That's much better. When I was a freshman in high school, the boys in our class thought it would be funny to vote one of the . . . ahem . . . less conventionally popular boys as the attendant.

Aspen: OMG, that's so horrible. So what about the girl who had to be his escort, did she go all psycho about it?

Stephanie: No. She was really sweet and charming about it. The guy looked like he had a great time and everybody really liked him so they weren't really doing it to be mean.

Aspen: Were you ever homecoming queen?

Stephanie: (*wipes tears*) No, my head is a tiara virgin.

Aspen: Eww, TMI! So were you a geek in high school or what?

Stephanie: No, I was not a geek! Our class usually voted for the same girl every time. She was so pretty, talented, and *nice* that you just couldn't help voting for her. Footnote: If you went to high school with me and I was a geek, don't feel the need to e-mail me this information!

Aspen: Did you always want to be a writer?

Stephanie: No. I wanted to be a fairy princess, zookeeper, lawyer, and then a writer, in that order. And for several years in between I just wanted to win the lottery.

Aspen: If you had to relieve high school over again what would you change?

Stephanie: Nothing. Everything I experienced led me to where I am today, which I wouldn't trade for the world.

Aspen: That's a lame answer. You have to have something you wish you could take back. How about that guy you dated? Hmm . . . what was his name again?

Stephanie: Okay, okay. I suppose my biggest regret was that I had a job at a hardware store during high school. I worked every weekend and missed lots of school activities. You have your whole life to work. I wish I would have been more involved in school activities.

Aspen: So what did you do for fun in high school without cell phones, MySpace, or reality TV?

Stephanie: Sometimes we would go cow tipping. I, of course, was only a bystander and not a tipper. One time a farmer came running after us and one of my favorite shoes got stuck in a cow patty. I had to leave it behind.

Aspen: That's the most disturbing thing I've ever heard. I'm truly embarrassed to know you.

Stephanie: You don't really mean that.

Aspen: If, for some crazy reason, this interview hasn't riveted people enough and they want even more information about you, where can they go?

Stephanie: www.stephaniehale.com—I'm always giving away cool prizes so come visit me! I also have a MySpace page at www.myspace.com/stephhale.

Aspen: One last question. Dooney or Coach?

Stephanie: Duh. Dooney!

Aspen: You just totally redeemed yourself.